EPITAPH

EPITAPH

BY

JAMES SIEGEL

Published by Warner Books

A Time Warner Company

ACKNOWLEDGMENTS

I'd like to thank Sara Ann Freed for her guidance and support, Arthur Pine for his enthusiasm and encouragement, Richard Pine for his ceaseless belief in me, and Catherine Drayton for all her hard work and kind words.

 Mysterious Press books are published by Warner Books, Inc., 1271 Avenue of the Americas, New York, NY 10020.

Visit our Web site at www.twbookmark.com

 A Time Warner Company

The Mysterious Press name and logo are registered trademarks of Warner Books, Inc.

Printed in the United States of America

First Printing: June 2001

10 9 8 7 6 5 4 3 2 1

Library of Congress Cataloging-in-Publication Data
Siegel, James.
    Epitaph / by James Siegel.
        p. cm.
    ISBN 0-89296-712-9
    1. Private investigators—New York (State)—New York—Fiction. 2. Queens (New York, N.Y.)—Fiction. 3. Miami (Fla.)—Fiction. 4. Physicians—Fiction. 5. Retirees—Fiction. 6. Nazis—Fiction. I. Title.

PS3569.I3747 E65 2001
813'.6—dc21   00-040116

For Mindy, Joelle, and Alexa, who believe in me as
I believe in them.

PROLOGUE

Mrs. Simpson finally noticed him on the third day. He'd been there before; standing in the amber shadows where the wooden overhang of a Cape Cod roof met the milkweed and thistle of the local lot. That it was milkweed and thistle she was sure of—gardening was her passion and it had taught her the virtues of careful observation. But her powers of observation had proved lacking—after all, she'd noticed him *now*, but he'd been there *before*. He smacked of familiarity, of something already seen, if not already noted.

She pointed him out to her husband, who peered at him through the kitchen window, then went back to the refrigerator with all deliberate speed.

"So?" was all he said, almost out of the corner of his mouth, a characteristic he'd inherited from his latest and most severe stroke, which had laid him up over half a year and left him sluggish, apathetic, and irritable.

Yes. *So?* It was a sound question, one she pondered on and off for the rest of the day and a good part into the night.

That he'd been there before? Well, maybe. After all, what was he *doing* there, hidden in the undergrowth like a greenhouse cat? Weed-watching? Or was he merely getting some air, getting it in a place that suited him—in a place with a view perhaps, though she couldn't imagine exactly what view that was.

It was when she noticed him the next day, back in the shadows like a reluctant suitor, and then again the day after that, that she slowly began to understand what it was that bothered her. Why it was that looking at him made her feel guilty as a voyeur—something she'd never felt with plants, or, for that matter, with sex—may it rest in peace—either.

What it was, was a mirror image. She was peeking on someone who was peeking on someone else—it was that simple. He was watching someone, someone or some-*thing*, and she'd stumbled onto it and compounded it all by committing the very same indiscretion. It was, in a sense, mortifying.

But mortifying as it was, she didn't stop.

She tried, *really* tried, puttering with this and that, busying herself with one thing or another, but the problem was she kept passing *that* window, and every time she passed it she had the overwhelming desire to look *through* it. So much for trying. Soon she found herself right back at the kitchen window. Watching the watcher.

And he was an artist at it, really—a professional, she might have said. For he didn't flinch, he didn't blink, he didn't seem to move a muscle. He just stood. And watched.

What or who he was watching was, however, a mystery. She couldn't tell—he was simply too far back into the shadows. He might've been looking left, or he might've been looking right; he might've, in fact, been looking at *her*. Yet even the possibility that this might be the case didn't deter her an iota. She was, in a way, too fond of him now.

For she'd begun to think of him as *hers*, the way bird-watchers tend to think of a returning cardinal or blue jay as *theirs*—their little bird. He was her little watcher, and the more she watched, the more cognizant she became of a certain feeling she had about him, a feeling she might have termed maternal. Though he was (even half obscured by weeds she was sure of this) quite as old as her, give or take a decade. Yet this only endeared him that much more to her.

She began to think of herself as his rear. His accomplice, if you will. And as this feeling intensified, she grew bolder, bold enough to actually consider going outside to talk to him. What she would say once she got there, she hadn't a clue—but it was her experience that these things tended to sort themselves out. A simple *hello* might do for starters—then, they'd see.

By this time, his visits had taken on the sameness of routine. He was always there when she woke; he always left for the better part of an hour just after noon (for lunch perhaps?); he always returned in time for the single bell struck at St. Catherine's across the road. By four he was gone. Give or take a minute, he stuck to that schedule as faithfully as a crossing guard.

It was well into the second week A.N.H. (After Noticing Him) that Mrs. Simpson decided to take the plunge. She waited till mid-morning, then, taking a deep breath the way her mother had taught her to when she was about to do something daringly out of character, she pushed open the kitchen latch and ventured outside.

If he'd noticed her, he didn't show it. He stood rigid as ever, still half obscured by shoots of milkweed and thistle, shoots grown thick and hoary in the early summer heat. She set her sights for his side of the street.

When she reached it, she turned right and began to walk straight toward him. She could see some details now: flat brown shoes with air holes in the tongue, the kind worn for comfort and nothing else; well-creased pants that fell just a bit long down the heel; a gray cotton shirt in need of ironing. A definite widower, was her off-the-cuff guess.

When she drew alongside him—and the ten or so yards needed to accomplish that feat seemed, at least to her, to take forever, she glanced, casually as she could, up to his face and said, "Nice morning, isn't it?"

But if he felt it was a nice morning too, he didn't say so. He didn't, in fact, do *anything*. He kept his face turned away—toward Mecca maybe?—and continued to act as if a woman had not decided (*foolishly* decided, she now believed) to pass him and reflect on the weather. One thing she wasn't, however, was a quitter. And she was about to try again, almost, in fact, had the words out, when something she saw made her stop, stop dead, as if someone had just clapped their hand around her mouth. She continued on down the block without looking back.

The next day he was there again, and he was there

again the day after that. But the next day, two and one half weeks After Noticing Him, he didn't show. And he didn't show the day after, or the day after that.

And she knew, in the way she knew most things, not with her head, but with her heart—that that was it. He was never coming back.

In the weeks that followed she found herself glancing out the window less and less, till she finally stopped looking out at all. She immersed herself in her plants again, and though she found them staid and rather lifeless after *him*, she was grateful for them, for they passed the time and left her pleasantly fatigued. Gardening, after all, was a *harmless* hobby, and she knew it was that, above all else, that gave her comfort.

Several weeks later, snuggled up in bed, her husband suddenly asked about him.

"That guy? Whatever happened to him?"

She didn't know, she said. Just gone, that's all.

But then, she suddenly felt the need to tell more, felt it as strong as she'd ever felt anything.

"He had a gun," she said. "I walked by him and he had a gun. I saw it."

And she began to tell her husband more, more of what she felt and what she thought and what she theorized. But halfway through, she gave up.

For he was fast asleep, turned to the wall like the class dunce, and certainly just as oblivious.

ONE

It was called a no-frills flight because that's exactly what you got—the flight. No more, no less.

Southeast Airlines Flight 201 out of a Long Island airport no one's ever heard of, departing Gate 13 at the ungodly hour of six A.M. Not that there was any shortage of takers—William had to queue up for a good half hour, stuck between Sophie from Mineola and Rose from Bellmore, who kept a running commentary going on the best buffets in Boca Raton. Sophie leaning toward General Tso's Szechuan Splendor with Rose touting a seafood buffet that sounded vaguely Lithuanian.

Once William actually made it on board, his initial feeling was immediately confirmed—the flight was packed solid. No matter.

You're a man on a mission, William. Remember that.

William had hoped for a senior citizen rate, but the *no-frills flight* was the best he could turn up, a name that kept proving itself right on the money. When he ordered a drink, he was told he'd have to pay for it, when he asked about food, he was given a price list. Earphones were five dollars, and then there were only two channels to choose from: mellow music and inspirational pep talks from America's most famous business leaders. There were only six or so magazines to go around, and no newspapers, and the magazines were of the kind found in dentist's offices—dog-eared, six months out of date, and completely uninteresting.

William didn't mind. For one thing, he hadn't been on a plane in years; he'd forgotten the way the ground looked, like one enormous patchwork quilt, the clouds soiled mattress fluff through which the plane kept punching holes. He found it . . . okay, exciting. Though he was just about certain he was in the minority there. Just look around. It was immediately evident why no senior citizen rates were offered on the no-frills flight. The airline could never afford it. Everyone on the plane—save for one little girl, the stewardesses (or flight attendants as they were apparently called now), and—hopefully—the pilots, was a senior citizen. *Everyone.* It was all Sophies and Roses and your good old uncle Leo.

They seemed to William like refugees, for they all wore a collective look of oppression. In *flight* all right, and in more ways than one. Running like mad from the crime, the cold, the heat, the noise, the annoying son-in-law— take your pick. Running from the loneliness too. What had Rodriguez said? *Just another old guy with nobody.* Sure. Refugees, on their way to the promised land.

And yet, he, William, senior citizen, wasn't one of them. *Technically*, he was one of them—his birth certificate said so. So did his body—that said so too. In fact, his shoulder wouldn't shut up about it. Okay, his prostate could be quite the blabbermouth too. But they were running; he was working. Yes he was. And he didn't *feel* like one of them either, didn't feel like one of the *herd*. He felt like devouring the herd. He had his appetite back, his hunger for all things human. What had those corny Charles Atlas ads said—*Be a new man.* Sure, why not. A new man.

Keep your eye on the ball, William. Stay focused.

The man next to him was called Oozo, and he owned a delicatessen in Fort Myers. Or his son did. Or they both did. William couldn't be sure because Oozo had an odd way of talking and William was too polite to actually interrupt him to ask.

Don't fall asleep on the job, William.

But at some point in Oozo's never-ending monologue, William, new man that he was, eyes open and vigilant, shoulder to the wheel, and man on a mission—did. Fall asleep. Soundly.

But maybe not too soundly—because he dreamt.

He was back in the funeral home. But this time with some old faces. Why, there was Santini, and look—Jean himself, and wasn't that Mr. Klein back there? What do you know? It was a reunion of sorts. Everyone getting to see everyone else and compare notes. Only, if he didn't know any better, he'd swear they were all staring at him.

I know, he said. *I got old.*

They didn't try to dispute him. They were just wondering, they said, if he could manage.

I'll manage fine. Man on a mission. Back in the saddle.

They reminded him about the girl. Five years old, wasn't she? About the white petticoat and the graffiti-scarred asphalt. And all that blood.

Hot on the trail, he assured them.

Sure, they said. Okay.

I'm sniffing the clues. I've got my nose to the ground.

But he was tap-dancing for time.

He knew it; they knew it. And now they were all starting to leave him, shaking their heads, and one at a time exiting stage left.

Man on a mission, he called after them.

But they were gone, each and every one of them, gone. And he was all alone with the coffin.

The coffin dull brown, open, and empty.

And his.

When he woke, catapulting himself out of dreamland like a man whose bed is on fire, the plane was halfway into its descent, the jet-black runway of Miami Airport rushing up to meet them.

His clothes stuck to him; there was a sour, acrid odor in the plane. He would've complained to the stewardess, whoops . . . flight attendant, about it, but he was just about sure it was coming from him. Besides, complaining might be extra on the no-frills flight; it might be listed as a *frill*.

This was good. Joking was good. He breathed in. He breathed out. Good.

He'd dreamt about death. He'd dreamt about dying and he'd been frightened by it. Imagine that. It seemed to him that this was very important, being frightened. That it might be the price you pay for being back in the real world. You decide to join the living, you get back your fear of death. Call it the price of admission.

When the plane landed, bumping twice along the runway before settling down, the passengers began clapping, all the old people whooping it up, as if they felt safe now. Safe at home. Safe at last.

Well, why not.

He bought two maps of Miami in the airport lobby. Then he went down the row of rent-a-car booths looking for the most disreputable one he could find. William had this minor problem. He hadn't driven a car in more than a decade; his license was older than that.

At the very end of the rent-a-car lane, two information booths removed from the rest, was Discount Rent-A-Car, a Cuban woman reading the *Star* behind the counter. "Who Broke Up My Marriage?" the banner headline, though William couldn't exactly see whose marriage it was. These days, probably everybody's.

"I'd like a car," William said.

The woman looked up at him and, without putting down the paper, slid a price list across the counter.

There was Luxury, Deluxe, and Comfortable.

"What's the difference?" William asked.

"Huh?" She peered at him quizzically.

"Between Luxury, Deluxe, and Comfortable?"

"Luxury and Deluxe have air-conditioning," she said. "Comfortable doesn't have air-conditioning."

"So Comfortable *isn't*."

"Huh?"

"Comfortable."

"Huh?"

"Never mind. I'll take Deluxe," he said, compromising.

She pulled out a form from under the desk.

"I need your license."

"Sure." William took out his wallet and after twenty seconds or so of leisurely rummaging, he pulled it out and slid it across the counter.

William A. Riskin—it said. Never Billy, Bill, or Willy, just William, thank you very much. *Date of issue*—never mind.

She barely looked at it. Instead, she started filling out the form, quickly and with no hesitation whatsoever. She had this rental thing down, William thought. As if her arms were moving on their own, her body set on automatic. Good, he thought, good; he was almost home.

But then he wasn't. Almost home.

"This license is expired," she said.

"Really?" William sounded surprised. "I could have sworn . . ."

"It expired *ten* years ago." She read him the expiration date. "That's ten years ago."

"Are you sure that's what it says?"

"That's what it says."

Silence. They'd reached a Mexican standoff. William made no move to retrieve his license; she made no move to give it back.

Then she said, "I've already filled out the form. You should have told me your license expired."

"Yes," William said.

"I've already filled out the form. See, it's all filled out."

Yes, he saw. It was all filled out all right.

"Shit," she said, "shit."

Then she said, "Don't run any red lights."
And William had his car.

He booked himself into the National Inn by the airport, and was given a room that faced directly onto the
runways.

"Don't worry," the bellboy said to him after he'd
dropped his borrowed suitcase onto the bed. "You turn
up the AC, you won't hear a thing."

Which turned out to be only half true. The air conditioner drowned out the planes, but its wheezing rotors
drowned out everything else too, including his thoughts,
which weren't much, but were, nevertheless, sorely needed.

Okay, William, get to work.

He turned off the AC, then spread both maps across
the bed, where he went at them with a blue Magic Marker
that he'd picked up in the hotel lobby.

*Follow the list, William. Samuels to Shankin to Timin-
sky. Follow the list.*

It took him over an hour to fix each of the names to
the maps, after which, sweating but good, he fit one into
his pocket and the other into his bag, *that* one for in
case. This sort of fastidiousness had been more Jean's way
than his, but that was the way he was going. He had
Jean's list, so he'd go the way Jean would have. *Copy the
habits*, he used to say. *When you're looking for someone,
copy the habits.* So okay, that's what he'd do.

Then he lay on the bed and stared at the ceiling, as if
it held the answers he desperately needed to hear.

TWO

It was already mid-afternoon when he finally eased himself into his car, an off-white Mustang which had seen better days, and took off. Of course the Mustang had also seen better drivers. Much better drivers. Compared to *him*—Indianapolis Speedway caliber drivers.

Ten years had made him rusty. Let's see: left turns, turn wheel left, right turns, turn wheel right. And the brake is the one on the . . . ? The problem, once he got the basics squared away, was that he overreacted. He turned too hard at corners and nearly ran into the curbs; he braked too hard at traffic lights and nearly propelled himself into the dashboard. The heat didn't help matters either; it didn't take him long to discover his air-conditioning was broken—the only thing coming through the vents was hot air. He opened both windows and loosened his shirt, which ten minutes of driving had turned dishrag limp.

Follow the list, William.

His first stop was 1320 Magnolia Drive—a Mr. Samuels—and to get there he had to ride through old Miami Beach. It had, William thought, the look of a tinsel town that had somehow lost its tinsel. Though, here and there, it was trying to get it back, scaffolded porticoes and plastic-covered bamboo roofs being restored to their original levels of tackiness.

Traffic had reached a standstill. It seemed a bus had somehow collided with a Porsche—at least that was the story being passed from car to car. The only people made happy by this turn of events wore *Stamp Out M.S.* T-shirts; they flitted from one passenger window to another like hungry pigeons in search of crumbs, which they collected in boxes that began to sound like maracas as they jiggled up and down across the avenue.

"Can you spare something for a worthwhile cause?" A girl in tight white shorts had placed her box directly at eye level; William could just about *smell* her youth. Ahhh.

He pushed a dollar bill into the box.

"God bless you," she said.

"I hope so," he answered, but she'd run off to the car behind him and didn't hear him.

The blocks groaned by. He'd reached a section where fast-food joints had weaseled in between the crumbling hotels. Texas Wacos, Wendys, and Big Jakes separated by red stucco, kneeling palms, and cracked neon. Limp white towels hung from serrated balconies like washed-out coats of arms. Cuban bellboys grabbed smokes outside empty lobbies.

The natives, mostly old, moved in time to the crippled traffic, clip-clopping along in white mules, their floppy hats casting huge shadows on the pavement. There was a purposefulness to their motion that seemed completely misplaced, as if, bent and beaten, they were merely following some timeworn route, some caravan track in the sand.

Fred's Fritos, the Crab Corner, the Dunes. The Beachcomber, Wiggles, and FleshDancers—featuring Wendy Whoppers and Ms. Nude Daytona. The traffic thinned out, his pace picked up a little. Soon Miami Beach itself was gone. Referring back to the map, he turned into a street darkened by huge grugru palms, a street saturated with the sickly sweet smell of plantain.

Now, evidently in the residential district, one block followed another with little change. They'd built their homes in the Spanish style here; only the color of the stucco varied—from red to brown to every combination of pastel. Each house had its small flat lawn, its thick spiraling palm, and filigreed iron gate. But it was the overall flatness he noted, as if the heavy Florida air, swollen with moisture from the sea, had pressed everything into a pancake.

It was quiet too. Except for the occasional bark of an unseen dog, silence permeated the very air, like the humidity, oppressive and inescapable. He flicked on the radio in an effort to pierce it, but the tinny country sounds that bled one into the other as he turned the dial this way and that seemed almost sacrilegious here—think laughter at a funeral—so he turned it back off.

Now the neighborhood began to change. There was no sharp demarcation, no single street separating the haves from the have-nots, but rather a gradual and insidious progression of ruination. The filigreed iron gates went first, then the grugru palms, as the lawns themselves turned scraggly and spotty. It was, William thought, like driving toward ground zero, bearing witness to the general and increasing denuding of the land, inching closer and closer to that terrible point of impact.

Which, in this case, was Magnolia Drive. No doubt about it. There was nothing further but swampland, acres of gold and green shaded by thick rippling swarms of badass insects. Magnolia Drive was several blocks long, was devoid of even a single magnolia tree, and looked very much like a repository for trash, of both the inanimate and animate kind. The houses were dilapidated things, slapped together like collages: design thrown out the window, crap piled up the walls. Old hubcaps, ragged pieces of knapsack, sheets of cardboard, all shape and manner of wood, chunks of scorched brick, and even what appeared to be swamp hay had been used in their construction. Their dirt yards were littered with the odds and ends of modern life: broken dolls, cracked china, yellowed newspapers, rusted rolls of chicken wire, crushed fenders, smashed TVs, ripped-open furniture, and half-eaten food. Nervous chickens ran amok from yard to yard pecking fiercely at the ground.

Mr. Samuels, William thought, had apparently fallen on hard times. His lack of a phone listing, then, was probably due to lack of a phone. In this neck of the woods, having a phone would be pretty far down on the list, right below, he guessed, room fresheners.

William pulled the car up to the first house, if you could call it that. He stopped too sharply—his head nearly hit the dashboard and he banged his knee on the steering wheel. He got out limping. It was worse than hot here; the air actually hurt. No kidding—it *scalded*. In addition, it was filled with all sorts of flying insects that got into his eyes and stung him. And the entire area had taken on the scent of the swamp, not to mention its purpose. Magnolia Drive was all about decay.

He saw his first inhabitant then. An old black man, white curls covering his cheeks like frost, hobbled out of the first house and stared at him.

"Excuse me," William said. "Could you tell me where 1320 Magnolia Drive is?"

The black man continued to do what he'd been doing; he stared. Then, almost imperceptibly, he shrugged—just that, and no more.

William's presence had brought others out—two barefoot black girls in dirty shifts, holding hands as if on a date. A white man with one leg, who scratched his head and looked down at the ground. A black woman who waddled out of the second house toting a baby in her arms.

"Anyone?" William asked. "Can anyone tell me where 1320 Magnolia Drive is?"

But Anyone couldn't.

It wasn't, as William first thought, because they didn't like him, and it wasn't, as he then thought, because they didn't understand him, and it wasn't even, as he finally thought, because they didn't want to.

It took him twenty minutes or so of skirting nervous chickens and nervous stares, of peeking through open doorways and broken windows, to understand that the reason they couldn't tell him where 1320 Magnolia Drive was, was because there wasn't a 1320 Magnolia Drive. It wasn't there. And, since the map clearly showed that there wasn't another Magnolia Drive in the greater Miami

area, that meant it didn't exist. And neither, at least according to what little he could get out of the local in-
habitants, did Mr. Samuels. They'd never heard of him.

So, William thought. What does *that* mean? He didn't
know. He didn't know, of course, a lot of things. What
he didn't know, in fact, far outweighed what he *did* know,
which was next to nothing.

*Follow the list—Samuels to Shankin to Timinsky—but
what if the list is bogus?*

He was stuck in a swamp, literally and figuratively
that's where he was stuck, the way out just as muddy as
the way in. Already, he was sinking.

Yet for all he didn't know, he did know one thing with
absolute certainty. For in walking back to the car, the
old black man had joined him, sidled up to him as if to
talk about the weather or the Dolphins or the price of
oil.

But he wanted to talk about something else.

"You know his bruddar?" the black man said.

"Brother? What brother?"

"Mista Samuels. Mista Samuels's brudda was here
lookin' for him too. You know him?"

"Yes," William said. "I think I do."

Okay, so he did know one thing then, didn't he?

That Jean had been there first.

THREE

FIVE DAYS BEFORE.

Ten A.M. the doors swung open and William sprang into action. Sprang being a very relative term for a man pushing eighty—*shuffled* into action was the way Jilly would put it. Four sweeps from right to left, four sweeps from left to right, the ripped-up OTB tickets eventually forming one big burial mound of yesterday's dreams. There were cruises to the islands in that pile, pool tables, second homes, pink Caddys, and golf trips to Myrtle Beach. No more though. Now they were just fodder, ready to be recycled into tomorrow's desperate fantasies. And William was just the man to do it.

"You missed a spot," Jilly said, already buried in *Gold's Sheet*. Jilly, who'd deigned to give William the benefit of his handicapping skills now and then—which, truth be told, bore a remarkable resemblance to Gold's handicapping skills—then deigned to give William a job. Sweeping up the losing tickets three times a week for some cold, off-the-books cash. William hadn't said no.

"Pamela's Prizes," Jilly said. "Tom's Term."

These were either horses Jilly liked or horses he called dogs, or horses he'd never heard of. This was the way Jilly communicated—in *horsese*, and William, who was used to people not exactly talking to him as much as around him, kept sweeping.

"Sammy's Sambo."

"Lucy Lu."

Besides, Jilly had once told him he should make like Mr. Ed.

"Mr. Ed?" William hadn't understood.

"Yeah. Mr. Ed never speaks unless he has something to say."

The implication being that William had nothing worth saying, William kept his trap shut and went about his business.

The first regular of the day—the first regular besides *him*—was a neat little Italian man named Augie, who was reputed to be connected, mainly because everyone he knew seemed to have *the* as their middle name. As in Nickie the Nose, or Roni the Horse, or Benny the Shark. Augie always coming to OTB with the morning paper tucked under his arm, which he'd dutifully hand to William, who'd retire to a quiet corner of the room to read. This morning he doffed his cap to Jilly, commented on the weather—*hot, isn't it*—and put the Queens edition of the *Daily News* into William's grateful hands.

And that's, more or less, how William found the obituary.

It had become a habit of his, reading the obits, a recent habit, like falling asleep in the middle of conversations and clipping toothpaste coupons. Sooner or later, after the race results and discount ads, he'd find himself buried somewhere in the back, where *beloved* fathers and *cherished* wives lay among the crematorium ads and latest dew count. And sometimes among the cherished and devoted, he'd find his friends, or at least people he knew.

Not that this was the reason he read them. He read them for the same reason people scan travelogues on countries they're about to visit, to get to know the territory, to become familiar with it. He was getting on, that's all, *beyond* getting on, and he wanted to see what the end of the road looked like.

And whose name should pop up among the newly expired this morning but *his*, stuck between a local alderman and a onetime exotic dancer. Ralph Ackerman and Tushy Galore, and sitting uncomfortably between them: *Jean Goldblum.*

Jean, he'd thought, *now there's Jean too*, and memories came traipsing into his tired old brain and put their feet up for a chat. One memory in particular, one memory in full vivid Technicolor, that he had no intention of sitting down with.

Out buster.

Of course the memories didn't listen to him—they never did. The truth was, these sneak attacks were becoming old hat. There he'd be preparing his dinner—okay, *preparing* usually meant folding the aluminum foil of his TV dinner left or right—but still, and suddenly he'd be staring into Jean's pinched little face, or bothering Santini for the sports section. His oven half open and

the frozen peas starting to give his thumb frostbite and
Jean sitting there asking him to do him a favor, just a
quick little snap-and-run at a local hump motel—if he
wouldn't mind of course.

I said scram.

Or sometimes it would happen smack in the middle
of a conversation with Mr. Brickman, who was always
barging through his door asking him to go somewhere.
A park, a diner, a lawn chair on the sidewalk—it didn't
much matter, all with a cheeriness William found frankly
irritating. After all, William had already signed his
armistice with life, signed it in blood, as with an enemy
who—let's face it—was sooner or later bound to win,
and here was Mr. Brickman just about bursting into a
chorus of "The Sunny Side of the Street." And William
would tell him that he didn't want to go to the park, no
thanks, not interested, only to find himself telling *Rachel*
something instead—to leave the light on because he'd be
coming home for dinner and please not to forget to walk
the dog.

This old age thing could be downright embarrassing.

For instance: Jilly was staring at him as if he had
Tourette's syndrome. Which meant William had either
said something horrifying or simply looked it. Maybe
he'd cried out *oh no* at the news, or worse yet, *oh yes.*
He didn't think he had, but it was entirely possible.

"Something wrong?" Jilly finally asked him, Augie turning around to stare at him too, William not used to all
this attention.

"Yes," William said. "I just remembered something I
have to do."

"Oh yeah?" Jilly again. "What's that?"

"Yeah," Augie echoed, "what's that?"

"A funeral," William said. "I have a funeral to go to."

The funeral home was stuck in Flushing, which William made it to by taking the number seven bus from Astoria, to the number five bus to Roosevelt Avenue, to the number eight bus to Kissena Boulevard, then hiking it through a kung fu town of Chinese takeouts and Korean fruit stands. No easy task when you're seventy-something, and wondering exactly why you'd bothered to make the trip in the first place.

The second he'd stepped off the number eight he'd been assaulted by a cacophony of alien sounds. Asians here, Asians there, Asians everywhere—all *speaking* Asian too. He might've been somewhere in China for all he knew—the most familiar thing he passed was a Chinese cleaners with a lone woman behind the counter, her head laid in her arms as if sobbing.

William was unaware he'd left *Chinatown* and entered *San Juan* until he almost walked into a bunch of Puerto Ricans in sneakers, ankle pants, and rolled-up T-shirts who were lolling against a couple of stripped cars, radios perched on their shoulders like parrots all screaming at once.

"Hey chief," one of them yelled when he walked by.

William kept walking.

"Hey chief, don't you hear me?"

Yeah, he heard him all right.

"Hey man, I'm talkin' to you."

So William turned, thinking—*okay, he's talking to you, answer him.*

"Yeah?"

"Hey, you got a problem or something? You *deaf?*"

"No, I'm not deaf."

"You sure about *that.* You should get your ears checked out, old man. I think you're one deaf motherfucker."

"I have to go." He *did* have to go. So *go.*

"You don't want to talk to me? You a busy mother-fucker, huh." He put down his radio, handed it over to a smirking girl who looked about fourteen but seemed more like thirty-five. "Maybe you want me to break your fuckin' head instead. You want me to do that?"

He wore a red headband; face-to-face now he barely reached William's chin.

"Hey man, I asked you a question. You want me to break your fuckin' head?"

William said, "No. I don't want that."

"You're damn right you don't want that, old man. I'll punch your fuckin' head in, motherfucker." The Puerto Rican spat at him. It landed on his left cheek, then dribbled down toward his chin.

"Hey, I spit on him," the Puerto Rican said. "I spit on this fuckin' *maricón.*"

William took a fresh handkerchief out of his pocket and slowly wiped it off, wiped it off with a hand he couldn't stop from trembling.

The Puerto Rican spat at him again, this time close to his eyes, where it burned like chlorine.

"I'm late," William said. "I'm late for a funeral . . ." leaving the spit where it was. He could hear the girl laughing, the girl and all the others. A *funeral*, a fuckin' *funeral* . . .

"You know man, you lucky this ain't your funeral." Laughter again.

William turned and quickly walked away, faster and faster, the laughter like a finger pointed at his back. It wasn't until he reached the curb that he finally wiped off the spit and threw the handkerchief into the gutter. It lay there like the white flag of a dishonored army. But then, he'd surrendered a long time ago; sure he had.

The Moses Greenberg Funeral Home was built of gray brick and decorated with donations from a few local artists. There were several lovely swastikas for instance, a Jewish star dripping blood, and a large misshapen heart that said *Julio and Maria 4-ever*. Trampled rhododendrons threw short brutal shadows on a ragged front lawn.

There was a schedule board covered in cracked glass: *Goldblum, J.*, it said, *One P.M.*

When William walked through the front door, still burning from the spit, the laughter, and the fear, *his* fear, he felt something familiar. Ahh—death again. Death was something he was getting particularly attuned to these days; it seemed to be everywhere he looked. In the obits, sure, but everywhere else too. All he had to do was glance at the passing traffic and sooner or later he'd spot a hearse followed by a long parade of headlights. Pick up a paper at the supermarket and nine times out of ten someone you'd heard of had killed someone else you'd heard of too. It wasn't his imagination. Death was in the air. Why, he could see it in people's faces, pick it out in the middle of a crowded street, all those shrunken cheeks and wasted bodies that suddenly seemed to have joined the daily human traffic. He was definitely developing a *nose* for death. No two ways about it. Sniffing it out the way others sense guilt. Of course, they were often entwined with each other—sure they were. In his old business, one had often led to the other. And that had been Jean's gift, one of them at least, to sense guilt like a priest. It's uncanny, they used to say, how Jean could tell just by looking.

William had asked him once how he did it. And Jean had said: "You find yourself in a terrible situation, a situation so terrible that you become like a madman, understand. A situation where you have to do everything imaginable. To survive, understand. You do *that*, and then you know. Understand?"

But William hadn't understood; Jean's a little crazy, *understand*—there were those who used to say that too. Though there were, they'd be quick to add, mitigating circumstances. Jean had suffered a bad experience during the war—that much was known—and though none of them were one hundred percent sure what that experience was, they knew enough. They had eyes. They could see the stark blue numbers on Jean's forearm, and the tattered picture of his wife and young children, one boy, one girl, that he'd drag out on special occasions and stare at, running his fingers over the wrinkled snapshot like a man reading braille.

Jean, it seemed, had been something of a hero during the German occupation—a Jewish weekly in Brooklyn once tried to write him up, an inspirational piece about this little French Hungarian who risked everything to help smuggle other Jews to safety, to Argentina or Brazil, somewhere, anyway, *south*. Jean had slammed the door on them. For whatever the whole story was, Jean wasn't going to talk about it. For him, it was a secret affliction. Like a venereal disease maybe, but with all those scars

right there under your nose. Mauthausen or Auschwitz
or Treblinka or whatever hell on earth Jean had been
thrown into had turned him inside out, distorted him
into something a little less human. Maybe it had to do
with that family that no longer *was*, with trying to do
something noble and being rewarded with a one-way
ticket to despair. So they didn't ask him about it, any
more than you'd stop to ask the terminally ill about the
progress of their funeral arrangements. And if Jean was
a little crazy, Jean was also more than a little good.

Now, however, he was neither. A man, older than
William—which these days was saying something—sat
on a bent bridge chair just inside the front door. He wore
a faded prayer shawl across his shoulders and an unmistakably sullen expression across his face. Well, why
not. William supposed he'd be just a little sullen too if
the only people he talked to all day were next of kin.
Off to the right a half-covered aluminum table supported
a lone bottle of Mogen David. Used cups, some crum-
pled, some half filled, surrounded the bottle like a still-
born litter. Maybe it was unavoidable—in the Moses
Greenberg Funeral Home, everything looked like death.
There were other men there—who, by the way, didn't
look so hot either; one against the far wall, another two
engaged in conversation, whispering to each other as if
plotting something dangerous.

William was late.

"Friend or family?" the old man by the door asked
him without really bothering to look up.

"Friend?" William replied, as if asking, thinking that
there really ought to be a third category for these kinds
of occasions, *old acquaintance* maybe.

"Well, you're late. The service is over."

"Sorry."

"You don't have to apologize to me. I just work here. And you don't have to apologize to the family, because there is none. Not here, anyway. You're it. Except for the landlord." He nodded at the man leaning against the wall. "Put a yarmulke on."

William reached into a wooden bin where yarmulkes of the kind Mr. Brickman wore on the High Holy Days lay in a soft multicolored heap. He picked a black one, black for death—*Jonathan Weinberg's Bar Mitzvah* it said in faded gold letters on the inside—then placed it on his head, just over his bald spot, okay, more of a *region* these days, and walked into the parlor.

A simple closed coffin lay at the front of the room.

I'm sorry, William thought when he'd walked past the empty seats to the end of the aisle. I'm sorry it ends like this, Jean. Like *this*. I'm sorry the seats aren't filled for you.

And then, touched by this feeling of pity, this notion that maybe Jean had meant more to him than he'd realized, he decided to open the coffin. To say his goodbye face-to-face.

He peeled back the top section; heavy and unoiled, it opened with a wrenching screech.

It was Jean. It wasn't Jean.

That was the only way to put it. And for a brief moment, he wasn't exactly sure why. After all, the features seemed just about the same: those thick eyebrows, the hollow cheeks, the drooped lip. Of course, he was *dead*. No doubt about that. But it was more than that, something else entirely. He tried to remember the last time he'd seen him, walking out of the office with a single box under his arm, *why hello there, Jean*, and then, like that, he understood. Jean had never been defined by his looks. He'd been defined by his, well . . . passion. For his work, for his regrettable parade of cases. Remember? Give him a new one and he'd get all lit up with a kind of perverse expectation, the way a house cat gets when its dinner lands by a half-open window. He'd just about lick his lips, Jean would. Then it would be days, weeks, of peek-a-boo, of coming and going, of in and out and *where's he gone to*, with the occasional glimpse of sly exultation as the case unfolded, as it turned to *red*, a euphemism Jean had coined due to his peculiar habit of changing files as a case progressed. The first file white, the last red, and the irony, William was convinced, firmly intended. For white was the color of innocence, something his clients could rarely claim, and red the color of penance, something they rarely did. But if his cases weren't exactly admirable, his *passion* was; at the very least it made him top-shelf at what he did. It made him *Jean*. Death had robbed him of the only thing that made him recognizable.

His hands, delicate hands for that body, were crossed over his chest like an Indian chief who'd died in battle, the kind that Randolph Scott was always running across and warning stupid white settler number *eight million and one* to leave alone. It was bad juju to touch a chief on his way to the underworld. Of course, no one ever listened to him, and before you knew it, half the Apache nation was out looking for their scalps. And now William wondered if he'd been just a little stupid himself.

He wasn't the only one. As he reached down and took Jean's left hand in his, shaking goodbye for the last time—

"Sir! Sir!"

William jumped; the sudden sound tore through the silence like a siren. It was the old man; he'd followed him in.

"Close the coffin, sir! Close it! We don't open coffins here without permission." His face was flushed; power had been usurped. "Closed coffin. Those were the directions."

Where was Randolph Scott when you needed him?

"You have to *ask* permission . . ."

Down went the lid.

"Closed," William said.

"You have to ask . . ." the old man muttered, shaking his head and walking back out through the entranceway.

William followed him; the old man back on his chair again, rigid and unforgiving.

The landlord came over to introduce himself. His name was Rodriguez. Only he wasn't the landlord after all— just the janitor.

"I just said I was the fuckin' landlord. The Jews don't respect you unless you own something, know what I mean."

Jean had asked him to take care of things if something happened to him.

"What exactly did happen to him?" William asked.

"Heart attack," Rodriguez said and slapped his chest. "The doctor came too late. He was already gone."

"Heart attack," William echoed.

Rodriguez hadn't known whom to invite to the funeral.

"He didn't have any family, did he?"

"No. He didn't have any family." William thought of that tattered picture; had Jean still kept it with him? held together with Scotch tape, taped and taped so that it became like a laminated ID, which, in a way, it was.

"Just another old guy with nobody," Rodriguez said. "No offense. There's a lot of them in my building—breaks my heart, right. So I put a notice in the paper, okay? I figured if anyone cares, if anyone knows him, maybe they'd come. Like you."

Rodriguez was wearing a yarmulke too, but inside out: *Sarah Levy's Bat Mitzvah* his head said. He asked how William knew the deceased.

"We used to work together," he said.

"Yeah—I thought it was you."

William must have looked puzzled.

"He's got this picture in his apartment. You, him, and some other guy," he said. "By a door—the Something, Something Detective Agency, right?"

"Three Eyes."

"Right. The Three Eyes Detective Agency. How long ago was *that*?"

"Long time ago."

"No shit. I bet you could tell some stories, huh?"

"Sure. Lots of stories."

He asked if William wanted it—the picture. There were other things in Jean's apartment too—he could take his pick.

William was going to say no, was going to say that he didn't want *anything* of Jean's, but then he thought the picture might be nice after all. "Okay," he said.

"Let's go."

"Now?"

"Yeah. *Now*."

"What about the burial?"

"Cremated," he said. "That's what he wanted."

Cremated. Off to some furnace to be burnt up. Like his wife and children went. If they weren't buried, he wouldn't be buried either. He would have wanted it like that, William guessed. Just like that.

"So," Rodriguez said. He'd gone back for the half-drained bottle of Mogen David. "What do you say?"

"I'll meet you there."

"You'll meet me there. Why's that?"

"I have something to do." He *did* have something to do; it had just come to him.

"Have it your way. Fifteen-twenty-two Beech Avenue."

William said fine. He'd be there in just a little while.

When he walked out, the schedule board said *Silverman, M.—4:30 P.M.* Out with the old, in with the new.

The Puerto Ricans were right where he left them, still leaning on wheel-less cars, their radios pouring out the same lyrics, more or less, that they were before. *Screw her booty . . .*

The boy with the red headband was sharing a tender moment with the smirking girl. He was shoving his hand down her pants, and humping her up and down in time to the music as she whispered into his ear.

William stood across the street, staring at them. *Do something*, he thought. You came back, now do something. *Anything*. But he didn't of course. Instead he suddenly felt like he did late at night when he'd wake to the sound of the TV he'd forgotten to turn off, something shrill and insistent on, *buy* this, *order* that, and him suddenly helpless and immobile, too weary to cross the carpet to turn it off. The TV was simply too far away to do battle with; and now, so were they. The street before him might as well have been a river; he was too old to swim it.

Then the boy saw him. He smiled, and ran his tongue across his girlfriend's ear. They both giggled. William, like something unimportant and ugly, had just been dismissed.

He turned and walked back up the street, his shadow just a stunted half-moon of gray, as if his sudden shame had just made him smaller.

FOUR

When Rodriguez turned on the light in Jean's apartment, bits of brown scattered in all directions as if a gust of air had just attacked the last leaves of autumn.

"Roaches," Rodriguez said, in a tone that somehow mingled disgust and admiration. "I hate them, but what can you do?"

William had found Rodriguez in his first-floor apartment at 15-22 Beech Avenue, slumped in front of his TV set with the empty bottle of Mogen David in his hand. There'd been no need for Rodriguez to buzz him through—the front door of the apartment building was permanently kicked in, the intercom suspended from the wall by one naked wire. When William knocked on his door, Rodriguez had screamed at him—*I'll fix the hot water when I'm good and ready, comprende?*

It's William, he'd said, *from the funeral,* and Rodriguez said *come on in.*

He was watching a program with the TV set on mute. Didn't matter. Someone had slept with someone's sister's husband; that's what it said right there for everyone to see, right next to this sad and angry-looking threesome. Something like that anyway—William's eyesight not being what it used to be, someone's sister's husband or sister's brother or sister's father. Anyway, someone was guilty of something. The man in the middle of this glum trio casting sullen glances this way and that, looking like he wanted out, wanted to be anywhere but there. William knew the feeling; it came with getting old, it was what getting old did to you, but the only place you could go was no place.

Not today though—today you could go here. To Jean's apartment.

It was a small one-bedroom situated on the third floor, actually a studio in the shape of a blunted L. In the real estate section it would be found under *charming,* but in the harsh light of day it looked like what it was—destitute, which is what's left when charm flies out the window.

Rodriguez asked him what it was like—being a detective.

"It was okay," William said.

He'd given him the picture—the three of them, Jean, Santini, and himself. Santini smiling, pointing to the freshly painted letters on the door—*Three Eyes*, the name had been his idea; beside him Jean, dark and dour, his cheeks pinched in like one of those faces from Buchenwald; then, of course, himself, looking frankly bewildered and completely unsure of everything.

"Sit down," Rodriguez said. "You want a Bud?"

"No. No thanks." But then he sat down anyway, not because he wanted a beer, although he didn't *not* want one either, but because he was tired, or because his knee was killing him, or because he'd simply been *asked*. Take your pick.

About that knee. Acute arthritis, the doctor said. It would, the doctor continued, get worse, striking him at any moment it cared to, in any number of joints, without any warning at all. One day it would come to stay. But then one day is always one day away. And that's how old people live.

Rodriguez asked him if he ever killed anybody. *"What?"* For a second William saw the little girl and all that blood again.

"On a case. You ever kill anyone on a job?"

"No," he said.

"You never killed anyone? Some detective you were. You ever shoot someone?"

"Shoot?" William said. "Sure."

"Yeah?" Rodriguez looking suddenly eager now. "What with? A Magnum?"

"A camera."

"Huh?"

"I took pictures."

"Pictures? What for?"

"For wives. For husbands."

"Oh."

"Sometimes they didn't trust each other. Sometimes they were right."

"I get it," Rodriguez said. "You caught them fucking around."

"Yes." *Them.* The ones who looked at the floor, at the

windows, at the desk, anywhere but at him, who talked about this, about that, but rarely about *it*, not at first, and sometimes not for longer so that he finally had to pull it out of their mouths like pieces of rotten tooth. He had cheaters and Santini had the missing in action. Jean? Jean was different. Jean had the kind of clients that paid the mortgage. He could not only spot guilt at fifty paces—he could embrace it like an old pal. Wiseguys, loan sharks, number runners, dope peddlers, and political goons tended to carry his card around in their wallets. Anyone who needed a bagman or a bogeyman or some queer stuff they could use to strong-arm someone else—they all came to Jean. It was his earlier career in reverse: instead of helping the innocent go free, he helped the guilty-as-charged instead. An avenging angel of sorts, but not the cherub kind—more like the one who'd skipped out on heaven and set up shop lower down. It was, maybe, a declaration on his part: If the world was intrinsically evil—and everything he'd seen in the camps had shown him it *was*—then wasn't it his job, his duty as a citizen of the world, to help it along? If the world was hell-bent on going to hell, he might as well hitch a ride, and as long as he was hitching a ride, he might as well take it all the way to the last stop. There was always, after all, plenty of evidence both ways. And as Jean was fond of saying, you find what you look for.

"You want that license?" Rodriguez asked him. A yellow license fastened to the wall: Jean Goldblum, Private Investigator, certified by the State of New York.

"No thanks."

"You got one too?"

"Somewhere."

"Okay. Now you got a matched set."

"I don't want it."

"Suit yourself. What about that?" Rodriguez asked him. He pointed to a brown cardboard box barely peeking out from beneath the bed.

"What's in it?"

"Junk."

"No thanks."

"Maybe it's not junk. It's junk to me. But to *you?*"

"No, Rodriguez. No thanks."

"Right. The drapes?"

"What?"

"The drapes. Maybe you could use them—you strike me as a guy who could use drapes. But I can't *give* them to you—I gotta charge you."

"I don't need drapes."

"You could always use drapes. How *old* are your drapes?—I bet you don't know."

Like TV, William thought. Rodriguez was like the TV he'd wake up to at night, like one of those shriller in-fomercials: buy this, order that, send away for this. *Click . . .*

"I don't *need* drapes. I don't need a box of junk. Throw it into the incinerator. I don't want it."

"Sure," Rodriguez said. "Why didn't you say so?"

But when William left, he took the box of junk with him.

Rodriguez carried the box down the hall for him. William heard the sounds of television, the mutter of a dog, the padding of slippers. When they passed the door closest to the elevator, it opened, slowly, cautiously, and a head crowned with the whitest hair William had ever seen peeked out to look at them. Rodriguez turned to say something, the head withdrew like a tortoise before a predator, and the door slammed shut.

"Mr. Weeks," Rodriguez said, and shrugged. "He's a little crazy, you know. Senile . . ."

"Sure."

Rodriguez carried the box all the way to the front door. Happy to be rid of it, he probably would've carried it all the way through Flushing and back to Astoria. But he stopped in the dilapidated lobby where a woman was vacantly rocking a baby carriage back and forth and two Indian children were kicking each other with silent glee.

Rodriguez said: "It's all yours," and handed him the box.

"Thank you," William said without really meaning it, as he nestled the box into the crook of his arm. He turned to the door where a blinding afternoon sun was streaming through the glass like oncoming high beams.

He shielded his eyes; bits of dust swirled past his face.

"Hey."

William turned back: Rodriguez had his hand out, palm up, waiting for one of those street shakes William didn't understand, the box beginning to feel all of a sudden very heavy, like a burden now, as Rodriguez grasped his hand and showed him how it's done, like the handing off of a baton in a relay race. Only he'd never catch up, not *now*.

"Take it easy," Rodriguez said. He turned back into the lobby.

And William, walking out into a heat that nearly slapped him, thought that he'd shaken hands twice today but that only one counted, only he couldn't figure out which one. Thinking that Jean's hand had already been like the hand of a ghost, so *white,* so *cold,* and wondering if such things actually existed, ghosts and such, if perhaps right this minute Jean was somehow near him, hovering, like smoke.

William suddenly realized he'd been thinking out loud; a young girl in shorts was staring up at him with a kind of disgust. He'd been speaking out loud and no one had been listening, an old man talking to himself. But then, that's what old men do.

FIVE

A dark yellow twilight was slanting in through the window, the kind of light a flashlight makes when its battery is about to die. All in all, perfect mood lighting for a serious drinking binge.

Shame to waste it, William thought. So he wasn't.

He wasn't just drinking, though—he was reconnoitering, searching his apartment for signs of life, seeking like radar any intrusions into the sedentary. There: a not insubstantial pile of mail shoved under his door, a dewy-eyed beauty staring back at him from a picture frame on the TV table, a child's drawing pinned to the door of his refrigerator. Of course, the mail—*Have you considered a retirement home in the Poconos? Think you're too old for insurance? Congratulations William Riskin, you've just won* . . . was written by computer. The dewy-eyed beauty was long gone. And the child's drawing was by Mr. Brickman's granddaughter. *I told Laurie to do one for you,* he said, *because you don't have any.*

Pictures? William had asked.

No, Mr. Brickman said, *grandchildren.*

But that, of course, wasn't altogether true. He might have some grandchildren or he might not; the truth is, he didn't know.

What he did know was that when you follow a trail of human accidents you're bound to join them. That when you tailgate them to dark and lonely places, sooner or later, you crash.

After all, he'd had cheaters. He had them Friday nights and Sunday mornings and sometimes anniversary nights and even July 4th weekends. He had them on the brain and on his conscience. He had their victims in his office every day throwing up all over the pictures he'd taken the night before. The pictures they insisted on looking at, even when he'd advised them against it. He understood; they just needed to see what their heart wouldn't acknowledge.

Once upon a time, William had wanted to be a priest. He made the mistake of telling that to Jean early on when he thought volunteering an intimacy might get him one in return. *I'll tell you mine if you tell me yours.* Jean, of course, had sneered and told him nothing. Instead he began to refer to William's office as the confessional— *Father William's in the confessional,* he'd announce. And he was right—it felt that way.

Because the people who entered it wanted him to do nothing less than restore faith. No, your wife's the perfect angel you married, she wouldn't dream of handing it out to the milkman, the postman, the local delivery

boy, or your neighbor Ed, who, rumor has it, likes to
borrow a little more than the sugar. God's in his heaven
and all's right with the world. But he couldn't restore
their faith—the pictures wouldn't let him. Because that
was the secretary in the backseat of the El Dorado taking the kind of dictation they didn't teach in secretarial
school, and Ed may have been coming for the sugar but
there he was in a nicely framed eight-by-ten leaving the
cream. If William was a priest, he was a bad one; all he
had to offer was a clean handkerchief and platitudes, and
if they entered his confessional with weakened faith, they
left it with none.

He never explained this to Rachel. He never did sit
her down and said this is what I do. This is what it feels
like. Maybe he wouldn't have been able to put it into
words, not then, maybe he was simply afraid she would
laugh at him. William had neglected her, and what's
worse, he'd neglected to tell her *why*. Perhaps it all
would've turned out differently if he had.

I'm throwing something your way, Jean told him one
night.

Yes Jean, okay.

*Piece of cake. Another horny wife. Another husband who's
never home. You know the story.*

Yes, Jean, I know the story.

*She tells him she's just playing pinochle. But I don't think
so. I think she's playing with something else.* Leering smile.
Here, he handed William a card with the name of a motel
on it. *It's pinochle night.*

Why are you doing cheaters? William said, something
like that. *Why you?*

A favor, he said. *For a friend.*

And if William had only thought about it that night, if he wasn't so tired, because he *was* tired and just wanted to go home, if he'd only sat down and lit a cigarette and *thought* about it, he would've realized that Jean didn't *do* favors for friends, because number one—he didn't do favors, and number two—he didn't have any friends. Acquaintances, clients, enemies sure, but no friends.

But he *was* tired this night, the kind of tired that makes you say *no, no thanks, I'm going home,* but also the kind that makes you wither in the face of insistence.

This case you take, William. This case is up your alley— it needs your knowledge.

So okay. He took it.

The Par Central Motel. Not very far from home anyway, home, where he wanted to be. A motel specializing in short rates, with the parking lot situated in the back. William had seen hundreds of them; they all looked alike.

Jean had done all the legwork. Nice of Jean to do all the legwork, William thought, getting the motel *and* the room number. Ground floor too, how convenient for everyone. All William having to do is snap a few pictures. *Awfully* nice of Jean, thinking this more than once, as he crept stealthily around the back.

The curtains were open too; nothing could be easier. Snap went the camera. Snap. Snap again. The eye of a camera a funny thing because it reduces everything. Everything becomes small. Rooms become small, beds become small, people become small. Even your wife. Your dewy-eyed wife, Rachel. She becomes small too. And Santini as well, locked together in the camera's eye like a dirty cameo. So he stopped taking pictures. He should've started walking then, walking *away,* or walking *in,* or maybe just walking in *circles*, but the very worst thing about that night is that he did nothing. Not exactly nothing. He *watched*. And cried. That too. He didn't stop watching until another couple came walking out of the motel to get into their car and saw him there, hunched against the window like a Peeping Tom. Only he was a Peeping *William,* which was an altogether different thing. They shouted at him, and he left, slid away like a snail who'd lost his shell, which, in a manner of speaking, he had.

He went back to the office and drank himself silly, and like the camera reduces the world, he reduced his marriage to a dirty joke. The cuckold's favorite private investigator cuckolded. Out sniffing after other people's wives while his own was busy opening the back latch. He reduced it to sniggering comedy because it was easier that way. Because he couldn't blame her, he blamed himself. And because he couldn't blame Santini, he blamed Jean. He understood now. *A favor,* he'd said, *for a friend.* Well maybe Jean *had* done him a favor. After all, a man should know all about his wife. Know her friends, her hobbies, her interests. Rachel's interests included sitting on top of Santini. He hadn't known that before, but he did *now.* Why, Jean had done him a real good turn, one friend to another. Okay . . . so maybe Jean wasn't being entirely friendly. So maybe he was trying to make a different point, to paint him a picture. And the point was? *Betrayal isn't reserved for clients, stupid.* Not just for do-gooding Jews in Nazi France either. It isn't reserved—*period.* It's available to everyone free of charge, it's an equal opportunity affliction. Blind faith is blind for a reason; if it wasn't blind, you'd see through it. So open your eyes.

Three months later, they separated—Rachel and him. And after they'd separated from each other they separated by three thousand miles; she sold the house and moved out to California. And sometime after that, he heard something about a baby, but he never found out if it was his. He tried writing letters, but he never tried mailing them. He was constrained by a kind of loathing that had no name; he was rendered speechless by codes and mores and a lot of male shit that isn't so fashionable now but was all the rage back then. The truth was, he wanted her back. The truth was, he couldn't ask her. And that was that.

Oddly enough, the Three Eyes Detective Agency accomplished what his marriage couldn't—it survived, at least for a while. Santini and himself were, of course, never again friends; they avoided each other as best they could in a hallway cluttered with file cabinets, and when they couldn't, they tended to talk about things like the National League baseball standings and yesterday's weather. They never mentioned that August night. Never.

Jean, however, was a different story. The very morning after William's discovery, after William's binge, after William's self-pitying rationalizations, Jean showed up with William's *file*. Red, clutched officiously under his arm.

Yours, he said, laying it down on William's desk.

Of course it wasn't *William's* file, not really, it was Rachel's, Rachel's and Santini's: where they met, how many blow jobs, their very favorite positions. A first-rate job. William threw it into the incinerator.

But first, he asked Jean, *why?* Okay, the most useless word there ever was, the number one stupid word in the English language. But still . . . ?

Why, Jean. Why?

I thought you'd be interested.

Nice of you to be so interested in what I'd be interested in. You enjoyed it.

That's right. I enjoy my work. Not like you, William— it's too sad for you.

But not for you. It's a fucking joke for you.

William, please. I try to do you a favor, huh. Am I laughing? I even give you the file, friend that I am.

You made me watch Santini screw my wife, friend that you are. You sent me there to watch it.

Maybe if I tell you, you wouldn't believe me. You think Jean is telling tales. Some things you have to see for yourself. You ought to know that. They always ask for the pictures—don't they?

Okay, maybe they did. And maybe he could've badgered Jean all day and all night too and still not have gotten what he wanted. Which was for Jean to take it back, to make it so that it hadn't happened, none of it. But Jean couldn't take it back, and even if he could, *William* couldn't, because even though he'd ripped the film right out of the camera, he couldn't rip the pictures out of his head. He gave up.

Look, Jean managed to add before he left the office, *don't let it break up the business, okay. Santini and you. I don't want it to break up the business.*

And so it didn't. Though the business didn't have all that long to go anyway. Their business, and the business as a whole. For times, of course, *were a-changin'*—wasn't

that what that kid with the whiny voice sang? One minute
a crew-cut hotshot called Maris was assaulting the major
league home run record and the next minute guys with
funny hair were assaulting his ears. People stopped getting haircuts and all of a sudden stopped wondering who
their wife was playing pinochle with too. Because *everyone* was playing pinochle. Laying their cards right there
on the table for anyone to see and saying so what? Suddenly divorce was the rage, *no fault* even, or more accu-
rately, everyone's fault, so no one's. Private investigators
becoming a casualty of something you could hardly pin
down, but something you could feel just the same.

Taboos weren't taboo anymore, dirt wasn't exactly dirt,
everything was relative to everything else, and suddenly
nobody needed detectives but TV. The new watchword?
"Security." Nobody had it, everybody wanted it. Clients
didn't need you to watch their wives anymore, just
their property—understand bub? Overnight, seemingly
overnight, private investigators became security experts.
Or sometimes security *guards,* which after a suitable
amount of downward mobility following the respectable
fifteen-year run of the Three Eyes Detective Agency, is
what happened to William. Five night shifts a week guard-
ing a tin shack filled with fan belts, radiator hoses, and
every kind of spark plug known to man. A lopsided bridge
chair, a discarded *Daily News*, and a very nice teal uniform, thank you very much—until that one particular day:
a long shift, a spring morning you could die for, and two
who did, one a small girl, dead. And the warehouse owner
who drove in from Long Island in a spanking-white Cadil-
lac and said, looking at William being carried off with a

bullet in his shoulder, *Old men, why do they send me old men?*

And so William, old man, was retired to a hospital bed and then to his room, and times became just a little lean . . .

"William . . . William . . . ?"

Someone was calling him; for just a moment William thought it sounded like, could *swear* it sounded like . . . but no, no . . . it was only Mr. Brickman, his good neighbor Brickman searching for a friend.

SIX

William?" He'd opened the door now; he stood half in and half out of the room, his shadow spread before him like a stain.

"Hello, Mr. Brickman," William said, raising his glass, toasting his entrance, except that Mr. Brickman hadn't entered, not exactly, and thinking that this wasn't like Mr. Brickman, standing half in and half out, that something had made him cautious.

"William. You drinking . . . ?"

"No." William took another swallow of bourbon; he'd already reached that point where his good friend Jack had stopped feeling like liquid fire and started feeling like solid fire. "What makes you think I'm drinking?" He was annoyed, annoyed at having company when he hadn't asked for it, annoyed too at the way Mr. Brickman was standing there, as if something was wrong, as if all of a sudden Mr. Brickman was going to begin making apologies and stop knocking on doors.

"What's the matter, Mr. Brickman?"

Mr. Brickman shuffled his feet, as if not quite sure where to put them.

"Eddie," he said. "Eddie was mugged today. There were two of them—they broke his ribs and punctured a lung. They don't think he's going to make it."

Eddie. Eddie Wilson—*Mr.* Wilson, who lived downstairs and was probably the oldest man in the apartment house, Mr. Wilson, who smoked a pipe and read Harlequin Romances, devoutly, as if trying to discover the secret of love. No more.

So, William thought. Mr. Wilson lies halfway gone and so does Mr. Brickman, half in and half out.

"Come in," William said, as solemnly as he could on three bourbons. *Four* . . . "Come in and sit down."

So he did. On the only other chair in the room, a bridge chair the landlord had given William when he'd first moved in, figuring even *he'd* have to have a visitor eventually, even if it was only Mr. Brickman.

"Drink?" William offered.

But Mr. Brickman declined.

"Where did it happen?"

"In the park. In the park, with me. You didn't want to go, so I took Eddie."

Had Mr. Brickman asked him to the park? Well maybe he had. William felt a stab of guilt at having refused him; that, and a palpable relief that he had. After all, Mr. Brickman would simply be in Eddie's room now, making Mr. Wilson put down *The Countess from Cordoba* so he could hear every word about William's bad luck, about the terrible beating, the punctured lung, and so on . . .

"We were almost ready to leave," Mr. Brickman continued, "when they came up to us, two of them, and asked us for money. Eddie said no. So they began to hit him . . ."

Eddie said no. Eddie said no because Eddie *had* no. Money. Maybe a silver dollar or two snuck away in a cardboard box. The Social Security checks he banked.

"What did *you* do, Mr. Brickman?"

"I went for help," saying it in a tone that suggested he hadn't found any. "I think something's happened, William, honest to God."

"Something . . . ?" not exactly understanding what Mr. Brickman was talking about, due to either the three bourbons, okay *four,* or the fact that Mr. Brickman himself didn't know what he was talking about, being, of course, not the old aggressive and gregarious Mr. Brickman, but the new cautious and possibly traumatized Mr. Brickman.

"Something's happened. I'm scared. They say it's a jungle out there, fine, only they don't tell you, they *do not tell you* you're the goddamn herd. You understand, that's who *we* are. The *herd.* You stay in the herd and maybe you're okay. Maybe. But you go off by yourself, you get caught alone, and then, they get you. Who? The *carnivores*—that's who. They wait for you and then they get you."

Okay, maybe Mr. Brickman did know what he was talking about, sort of. There was every possibility that he did. William was nodding his head at him on the chance that he was being entirely lucid, but it seemed to take a monumental effort to get it to move. He sensed that Mr.

Brickman was expecting him to say something; he sensed this because Mr. Brickman had stopped talking and was looking at him with an expression that could only be termed hopeful.

But William had nothing to offer him, nothing but the landlord's chair and a chorus of one.

"You have to stick together now, Will," Mr Brickman finally said. "There's safety in numbers . . ."

"Yes," William echoed, "safety in numbers," continuing to provide the refrain for a sermon he didn't quite grasp. But the truth was, he did. Even dead drunk, he did. Mr. Brickman, annoyingly gung ho, irritatingly life-affirming, was learning *old*: that when you dragged yourself to a scorched brown park in the middle of July someone else might have to drag you back. Mr. Brickman had become one of *them*, another terminal case, and it made William sad, sadder suddenly than he had any reason to feel.

"Maybe Mr. Wilson will make it," he said now, but he didn't sound very convincing, even to himself, on a scale of one to ten, somewhere south of two.

Mr. Brickman looked up then, as if he'd suddenly been reminded of something important.

"I'm sorry," he said.

So, William thought, *apologizing after all.*

"What for, Mr. Brickman?"

"You went to a funeral today, didn't you? You've had enough for one day."

"No." William finished his drink. "Not yet." A little drinking humor.

"Was it an old friend, Will?"

"Who?"

"The person who died?"

"He was old, but I don't think he was a friend."

"What does *that* mean?" Mr. Brickman sounded almost mad at him now, as if he found his tone disrespectful in respect to the dead, which, to be honest, was the very tone William was going for.

"That means I don't know if he was a friend or if he wasn't. I can't remember."

"You remembered," Mr. Brickman said, "enough to *go*."

"Right," William said. "I guess that's all you can hope for, isn't it?" pouring himself just one more, which is what he'd poured himself the last time and the time before that. "That people remember you enough to go." Interesting, he thought. Four drinks, *five,* and he became positively reflective. He was trying to remember Mr. Brickman's first name. He called him Mr. Brickman, all these years *that's* what he'd called him. Of course, that's the way he'd addressed his clients, always *Mr.* and *Mrs.*, never by their first names; perhaps Mr. Brickman was just one more client, another *parishioner,* another person in need of comfort, *carnivores* and things. But then, he had no clients anymore, he hadn't had any in a long time.

"What's *that*?" Mr. Brickman was pointing at the box, Jean's box, with a slightly quivering finger; or at least that's the way it looked to William's slightly quivering brain.

"Junk," William said. What had Rodriguez told him? *It's junk to me—but to you?* But Rodriguez was wrong. It was junk to both of them. He'd dumped the box by the front door on the way in, dumped it on its side, so that it looked now like a package the day after Christmas, almost like that, as if the wrapping had been ripped off and then the gift found wanting, so that now it was waiting to be returned to the store where it came from.

"Well," Mr. Brickman said after several moments of dead silence, *dead* seeming to be the theme of the day, "I will pray for Eddie."

"Yes, Mr. Brickman. That's a good idea."

And Mr. Brickman left, got up and left, peering into the hall first as if crossing a street in the middle of a block and searching for oncoming traffic.

Which left William alone again, savoring the last bit of glass number *five* before he embarked on glass number *six*. Only when he went to pour it, he committed the unpardonable. He knocked his good friend Jack right off the armrest.

Whoops.

Whiskey ran across his pitifully worn-down carpet like a flash flood, rolling out toward the door, and—*what's that?*—by way of innocent proximity—toward the box, Jean's box.

William sprang into action. Okay—crawled, stumbled, staggered, making it there just in the nick of time—lifting up the box before it was hit by a wave of eighty-six-proof alcohol.

The box seemed heavier than before; of course he was *drunker* than before. He dumped it onto the bed where it sank into the mattress with a slight groan.

What was *he* doing with it anyway? What would Rodriguez try to give him next—Jean's ashes? Ashes, drapes, and pictures.

William sat down beside it, looking it over, assessing

the damage. Everything more or less shipshape. He
opened the top flaps and peered inside.

Yeah, it was junk all right.

In Jean's box: a small retractable umbrella, a pair of
black rubbers, a library card, sunglasses—one lens
slightly cracked—a key chain—no keys—salt and pepper shakers with the words *Lake Tahoe* painted on the
bottom of each, a novelty pen which when held upside
down transformed a sweet demurely dressed girl into a
sweet undressed girl, three packets of dental floss, several utility bills from Con Edison, several threatening letters from Con Edison, a campaign flyer, a baseball
program. And a phone book. He dumped it all out onto
the bed.

Of course it was the phone book he was drawn to; old
habits die hard. A small black phone book, the kind bach-
elors in the fifties were supposed to carry around with
them, *little black books* filled with conquests. But this little black book was filled with empty pages, *mostly* empty
pages, and little proverbs that were printed at the top of
each page—one to a letter. A *rolling stone gathers no moss*
was one of them. *Don't judge a book by its cover* was another. Little pithy sayings, the kind of thing they started
putting in fortune cookies when they stopped putting in
fortunes. William wondered if Jean had read them, if they
had amused him maybe, even caused him to laugh out
loud. Probably not. Jean never laughed, certainly not out
loud. *Am I laughing, William?* William guessed that he'd
stopped laughing the day they turned his family into a
picture. And now, looking down at the contents of the
box spread helter-skelter like a rummage sale across his
bed, William wondered just where that picture was, be-

cause it wasn't here. Maybe all that Scotch tape had simply grown as brittle as the picture itself, finally splintering into a kind of dust, becoming, in a way, like Jean. Maybe one day Jean had simply looked at it and not known them anymore, the way a childhood picture becomes, after a while, just a picture of a child, any child or every child, but not you. William didn't think that likely, but then, it was hard to say. He suddenly wished he'd known Jean then, back when he was helping his Jews across the border, before they'd tattooed his arm and scarred his soul, back before the fall, because then maybe, just maybe, he'd feel sad that Jean had died. But that was crying over spilt *ash*, wasn't it. William put the pen, the bills, the shakers, the flyer, the baseball program, put it all back into the box; he left out only the phone book.

He barely made it back to his chair, not so much sitting down on it as flopping into it. The room was kind of spinning on him, a little like a carousel just before it comes to a halt, when nervous parents are already madly racing to grab their children who only want another go-round. William, of course, wanted off.

He began to leaf through the book again, to take a leisurely stroll through Proverb Land. Under P—*People in glass houses should not . . .* —was *Sam's Pizzeria* 872-3490. The page was worn, covered in thumbprints, pizza being a staple of sorts for solitary people who don't cook and don't go out, which in New York means half the people over the age of seventy. William had eaten his fair share of pizza. Under R, under *Rule your emotions and they won't rule you,* was Rodriguez: janitor, funeral director, and executor of the will. Under D, *Don't judge a*

book by its . . . were a few names, an Alain, a Marie, a
Michelle, but all without numbers, as if Jean had written them down to remind him of something, and under
I, *It's the bad wheel that does the most squeaking,* was a
number with no name: 873-5521.

If William hadn't been drunk, or at least *so* drunk, if
he'd had, say, two drinks instead of five, he would have
put the phone book back into the box then and drifted
into sleep, or at least collapsed into a stupor. In the morning he would have carted the box out to the garbage in
front and dumped it in. Then he would have gone to
OTB and laid a bet, laid several bets, starting with *Gold's
Sheet,* but quickly moving on to horses whose names
began with hard consonants. In this way, he would have
eventually lost all his money, *all* being a relative term,
since all his money wouldn't fill a regulation piggybank,
unless his luck turned, of course, which from time to
time it did, but with no regularity he could depend on.
Then, either so much richer or so much poorer, he would
have made his way back to his room. Just your average
day, in which he would've hurt no one and, with a little luck, no one would've hurt him. But okay, he'd had
five drinks, not four, and certainly not two. The room
wasn't spinning anymore, but it wasn't exactly standing
still either. And being five drinks stiff to the wind, being
just a little sorry for himself, grappling with this notion
that there'd been a serious omission in the matter of
Jean's death, because there'd been only two mourners
there when there should have been more, and both
mourners had mourned nothing, he stared at the lone
number for more than a minute, then called it.

A woman answered.

"Hello," she said. "Who's there?"

"A friend of a friend," William said.

"Uh huh," she said in a tone completely devoid of surprise. "A friend of *what* friend?"

"Jean. Jean Goldblum."

"Oh." Pause. So maybe she knew, had already scanned the obits and knew. "You'd like to see me I guess?"

Well yes, he would.

"Sure. Why not. I'd love to see you."

"Sure. Let me see . . . wait a minute . . . how about, oh, nine o clock? Is that okay with you?"

More than okay. Terrific actually. Couldn't be better.

"Tonight? Nine o'clock tonight?"

"Yes. Would you like to come *another* night?"

He'd have to consult his schedule on that one. Nope. Sorry, all booked up tomorrow night, it'd have to be tonight.

"Tonight's fine."

"Okay. Why don't you write down my address."

"Sure. Go ahead."

"Thirteen-eighty-one Yellowstone Boulevard. Apartment 9D. That's *Yellowstone.* A friend of Jean's, huh?"

"That's right. A friend."

"Yes. Well, we're all friends now, aren't we."

Absolutely. All of us, friends.

"I'll see you at nine," William said, then he put the phone back in its cradle, smacked it down hard, and wondered exactly what it is that he'd done.

SEVEN

He told himself on the way to see Jean's friend that he was just being friendly, that he was on a mission of mercy, a comforting angel here. After all, wasn't it right for the bereaved to seek out the bereaved? And if he wasn't all that broken up himself, perhaps *she* was, and if she wasn't, then perhaps he was merely tying up loose ends, paying his respects to Jean's memory. And then there were other reasons: that he was maybe just a smidgen lonely tonight, that is, lonelier even than he was on any other night, which was, when he allowed himself to think about it, *considerably* lonely. And then too she'd sounded sort of sweet on the phone, maybe even grateful for his call. Perhaps she *did* want to cry on his shoulder; perhaps he wanted to cry on hers. *We're all friends now, aren't we.* Well, sure.

But after he'd made his way to Forest Hills, a neighborhood of tall dark towers and rounded driveways, of metal jockeys and endless hedge, after he'd gotten past a rather rumpled doorman who sat stolidly behind a small bright monitor and waved him through, after he'd rung her button and she'd slowly opened her door and asked him in, after *that*, he'd immediately realized that, of course, they weren't all friends, that she really wasn't a friend of Jean's at all, and even if she was a friend of Jean's, she was unaware of something vital, of the very reason for his visit. She didn't, William was positive of this, know that Jean was dead.

For one thing, she was smiling, something that be-reaved people aren't generally known to do—crying, sob-bing, frowning, screaming, sure, but not *smiling*. Well maybe to acquaintances, but then, he wasn't. For another thing, she was dressed as if she was about to go out on the town, but, of course, she wasn't about to go out on the town. A silky black dress that plunged in front and plunged in back and was slit up the sides as high *as an elephant's eye*, all the way to a tattoo which said *Eat Your Heart Out*. That's what she wore. And then William re-membered the way the doorman had waved him through without first calling up, kind of like a ticket-taker. She was smiling for him, sure, but like this professionally decorated apartment, it was a professionally decorative smile. And she, of course, was a professional.

"Sit down," she said, very professionally too. "How about a drink?"

Drinks, of course, were the problem here. Five drinks had made him a little slow on the uptake, had made William a very dull boy.

"Sorry," William said.

"*Sorry?*" She twisted her eyebrows quizzically, perfect

eyebrows too, eyebrows she'd spent some time on. "What
for?"

"I'm not here for what you think I am."

"Okay," she said, still holding that smile, William thinking it must be hard holding a smile like that. "What are
you here *for?*"

"Well . . ." Not exactly sure how to answer that, but
willing to give it a shot. "Well . . ."

"Why don't you just relax and tell me."

He was already relaxed, his brain at least, which was
off somewhere sitting on a BarcaLounger.

"Sometimes it's hard to tell these things," she said, "but
you don't have to be embarrassed *here.*"

Well that was a matter of opinion, wasn't it? Her tone
very soothing now, like Muzak, William thought, amazing how she could switch it just like that, from genial
hostess to dental hygienist. *We'll just start the gas now
and then you'll feel a little prick . . .*

"You'd like me to guess, is that it? You don't like to
talk about it, that's okay. Have you been a bad boy? Have
you been a *very* bad boy? Would you like Mommy to
take you over her knee and spank you maybe, spank you
till you say you're sorry."

Actually, he felt like spanking himself. Yes he did.

"I think," William said, "I'm going to be sick." The
drinks had turned on him, just like that, they'd said
enough fun for you, old sod and turned on him. "Forgive
me . . . where's your bathroom?" But it was too late; everything he'd poured into him suddenly began to pour *out*
of him.

"*Shit!*" she said, finally and indisputably losing that
smile. "Get over there . . . over *there*"—pointing to the

hallway on the left—"shit . . . get to the *bathroom* . . . you're getting it all over the rug!"

So William ran, clutching his stomach, ran into the dark hallway, which ran into a dark bathroom, vomit dripping from him like sweat, got to the bathroom, then stood, hunched over the toilet, heaving.

In two dreadful minutes it was all over. White, trembling, he slowly straightened up, then flushed the toilet. She was somewhere behind him now, frantically laying towels over the carpet, trying to soak up his trail of vomit.

Wonderful, he thought. *Wonderful. A perfect end to a perfect day.*

He walked out of the bathroom.

"Please," he said, "forgive me. Drinks . . . five drinks . . . I couldn't handle . . . the funeral . . ."

"*What* funeral?" She was still down on her knees pressing the last towel against the carpet.

"Jean's. Jean's funeral. Your number was in his phone book. I didn't know . . ."

Okay. She didn't go teary-eyed on him, or gasp out loud, or even shake her head, but she did finally stop trying to soak up his vomit and look up at him with an expression that registered, well . . . *loss.* There was no other way to put it. *Okay,* William thought, *maybe she'd been a friend after all.*

"What did he die from?" she asked.

"Heart attack."

"Oh." She nodded, as if she'd expected as much. Perhaps she'd known a lot about Jean's heart; perhaps she'd been, in a way, an expert on it.

"Look," she said, finally getting up, "I made a mistake.

You made a mistake. Mistakes happen." She motioned toward the door, as in *the door's that way,* as in *nice seeing you, bye,* as in *leave.*

But he was staring at the carpet now, a deep shag, like something that had just been killed, or certainly, violated.

"What about the . . . ?" nodding at the tapestry of towels that had begun to take on the unmistakable color of Jack Daniel's.

"Forget it," she said. "I'll get it cleaned."

"Here." William reached for his wallet, only in reaching for it, lost his balance and nearly tipped over.

"You don't look so hot," she said. "Sit down."

He was going to say no, honest he was, but he was dizzy and disoriented and ashamed—not necessarily in that order. And just like with Rodriguez earlier today, he'd been *asked.*

He sat.

"How do you feel?" she said.

"Like death."

"I know the feeling," she said.

William was sure she did. He was precisely eye level now with her tattoo; *Eat Your Heart Out* in crimson letters on a bloodred heart, the bloodred heart like a bruise on her milky thigh. He tried to remember how many years ago it was that he was actually with a woman but they were like *light*-years, more explainable in the theoretical than the actual. He couldn't remember the last time he'd wanted one; he didn't know if he could.

"You and Jean," she said. "Were you close?"

"I hadn't seen him for years," William said. *Just another old guy with nobody,* Rodriguez said, *breaks my heart, right.* "We used to work together."

"Another detective, huh?"

So Jean hadn't just fucked her; he'd talked to her. About the *old* days, about feats of yore.

"Jean was a pain in the ass," she said now, as if reading his mind. "But he was *okay*."

William imagined she probably had a limited number of categories for men, possibly two: *scumbags* and *okay*. And Jean had been okay. *Okay, Jean* . . . good for you.

"He wasn't my usual, understand."

"Sure," William said, wondering why she'd asked him to sit, and why she was talking to him. About Jean, about anything. But then, that's what he'd come for, wasn't it, to eulogize the dead.

"We never really *did* it," she continued, as if it was important that he understand that. Maybe that was what made Jean *okay* in her book, her book otherwise being like the kind you buy at airports where they do it on every other page. Which led William to wonder what it was Jean and her *had* done, it being only natural to wonder a thing like that, because Jean had come to see her and he'd come more than once. Maybe, he'd *eaten his heart out,* maybe he'd *eaten to his heart's content,* which wouldn't be exactly doing it, but was close.

But no.

"He liked to take pictures. You know . . . playact." There she went again, reading his mind. Either that or stating the menu, because after all, it was still working hours and he was still here. And when you thought about it, William had taken pictures too, hadn't he, a whole lot of pictures, including his masterwork: Rachel and Santini at the Par Central Motel.

"What did he do with them?" William asked, because

he was kind of curious about this kind of thing, *pictures* and *playacting,* and if she was going to kiss and tell, he might as well sit and ask.

"*Them?*"

"The pictures?"

"How do *I* know? Kept them, I guess."

"I guess," thinking that's what he'd do, keep them, wondering now what *Eat Your Heart Out* looked like in the big picture that was her, like lipstick on a new handkerchief, *that* red.

"Hey look"—a kind of defensiveness crept into her voice now—"he didn't want me to beat him, okay. He didn't want me to piss on him, or dress him up like a sissy. He didn't want me to *fuck* him either. As far as I'm concerned, that made him a prince."

Okay, William thought, *Prince Jean.*

"I think it's time to go," he said. "I think I've done enough damage for one night," alluding to the patchwork quilt of towels, alluding also to himself, because he felt damaged too, though not exactly sure in which way.

"Nice seeing you," she said, but even with her smile back, *that* smile, it was devoid of conviction; it would be nice seeing him *leave.*

He lifted himself up off the couch, not an insubstantial feat given all the drinks, all the drinks taken and all the drinks given back, and given the pain too which was dancing the hokey-pokey in his shoulder and threatening to make him cry.

"Another retired detective you've been more than kind to." A nice closing line, a suitable amount of gentility and humble pie, a line just *right.*

"But he wasn't retired," she said, as if lightly correcting a guest's grammar.

William only half heard her. He was thinking if he shouldn't perhaps offer her money again for the carpet. He was thinking about the odds of making it home without falling down. He was definitely thinking that it had been a big mistake coming here like this, and that the only way to undo that mistake was to leave. Yet while half of him didn't hear her, half of him did, and so he echoed her, buying time while the part of his mind that was already out the door tiptoed back in.

". . . wasn't retired?"

"Right. He wasn't retired."

"What's that supposed to mean?" William said.

"It means he wasn't retired."

"Do you know how old he was?"

"Yeah. About as old as you."

William winced. "What makes you *think* he wasn't retired?"

"He told me," she said. "And *told* me."

"That he was still working?"

"Yeah. On a real case too. No more chasing runaways."

"Runaways?"

"Right. Runaways."

"Who hired him to do that?"

She laughed—okay, more like yuk-yukked. "He hired himself. He'd go down to the Port Authority and wait for them to get off the bus. Then he'd race the pimps to get there first. Sometimes he won. Sometimes he'd call up their daddies for the reward."

Jean wasn't retired and Jean had chased runaways. But

then he'd stopped chasing runaways—because he got a real case.

"This *real* case? What was it?" It was a little like old times, wasn't it—rattling off questions he didn't really want the answers to.

"The biggest case of his life," she said.

William didn't think he'd heard her right. Was sure he hadn't.

"*What?*"

"The biggest case of his life."

Now what was he supposed to make of that? *You* think about it and tell me you wouldn't want to double over with laughter.

"Okay," William said, "and what *was* the biggest case of his life?"

"Look." She was bored with this—with him. "He was an old man. He said he had a case. I said what case. The biggest case of my life. I said that's nice—what is it? I can't tell. You can't even tell me a little bit? No. I can't even tell you a little bit. But it's the biggest case—I know, I said, of your life. I'm glad for you. Then I changed the subject. Okay?"

She *was* bored with him—she walked over to the door.

"Thanks for dropping in," she said.

Outside in the hall, then later as he walked past the doorman, who seemed to admonish him with a dour shake of his head, and even later as he walked to the subway in the sticky summer heat, he tried to picture his day tomorrow. Breakfast at the luncheonette: two eggs over easy and some OJ. Then the paper: racing first, Yankees second, Mets who cares.

He tried to picture it, but his day seemed to pale before his eyes, a Polaroid in reverse.

The biggest case of his life.

He tried to remember if he had a token. Had he bought two on the way over—or just one?

The biggest case of his life.

He'd lied to her. A washed-up detective down to picking clients off milk cartons and so he'd lied to her.

The biggest lie of his life. Even she thought so.

And even if it wasn't a lie, who cares. What did it matter now?

But he had lied to her. He had.

Of course he had.

EIGHT

The Mustang's air-conditioning was still broken; the
Florida sun was still brutal. And so far, so was his day.

He'd managed to cover two more addresses. Two more
names on the list, and though he hadn't found *them*, he'd
continued to find someone else.

Hello Jean.

He was pulling *backup* again—that's what he was doing.
It was the old days all over again, and he was following
one of the other Three Eyes around in the dark because
they were going in blind and needed some protection.
Only this time he was the blind one and the Three Eye
he was following was *dead*.

The first stop of the day had been 1610 Beaumont
Street, a tenement only days away from demolition, its
only remaining tenants a pair of emaciated crack addicts
who shared a first-floor apartment—and who at first refused to answer the door, thinking, perhaps, that William

was a narc. Only a close-up view through the peephole, in this case, an actual hole big enough to put a fist through, was able to rid them of that particular notion. William, after all, was too old to be anything but what he said he was—someone looking for a friend.

However, they'd never heard of this friend, although one of them thought the name—Mr. Shankin—sounded suspiciously like his third-grade teacher.

"Thank you," William said.

The second address, *third* of the trip, belonged to a pet shelter.

"Are you here for a cat?" the fuzzy-haired girl asked him at the front desk.

"No," William replied. "I'm here for Mrs. Timinsky."

But Mrs. Timinsky, needless to say, wasn't there—and as far as the girl could ascertain, never had been.

Yet someone else, of course, *had*. Just as he'd been at Magnolia Drive and at Beaumont Street too.

Samuels to Shankin to Timinsky to . . .

"Someone else was here looking for that woman," the girl behind the counter said.

Yes, William thought, Mr. Samuel's brudda. And at Beaumont Street, one of the junkies had sung the same sad refrain.

"Sorry about not opening the door," he said, "but we get hassled. Someone came here about a month ago and nearly tore the place apart."

"What did he look like?" William asked, thinking that junkies were more polite than he'd remembered, or maybe just the ones down here in the Sunshine State.

"Like you," the other one said.

So pet lover Goldblum had been there too.

Later William found himself back at the National Inn, staring at plane after plane taking off into a nearly indigo sky, and wishing silently that he was on one.

He found something. Remember—he'd looked like he found something.

But what?

And even if he found what it was, would he know what it meant?

He had one hope, one admittedly, frail, feeble-assed hope: that Jean would somewhere, somehow, show him the way. *Okay, Jean, I'm waiting.*

And now, clinging to this hope the way people his age tend to cling to religion, reality intruded. His shoulder began to throb, to scream, to make a god-awful racket. Slowly, gingerly, he unbuttoned his shirt, then walked into the bathroom where he ran a towel under a warm tap.

The problem *was*, they'd left the bullet in, not all of it, but most of it, enough of it so that it hurt whenever the weather turned humid, or turned cold, or, in fact, *turned*. Sometimes it hurt in the morning, and sometimes it hurt at night, and though sometimes it didn't hurt for weeks at a time, sometimes it did. It was, he thought now, hard to predict.

There was a pink and wrinkled scar there, as if they'd gone and shot him a new asshole. He pressed the towel directly onto the pain with his right hand, then walked back out into the room.

He stood before the dresser mirror and stared at himself. He generally avoided mirrors the way he'd once avoided obituaries, but now that he'd looked at one he thought he might as well see the other. It wasn't, he thought now, a pretty sight. They say that age becomes a man, but the *they* who said it must have been guys as old as him, because while it might be true of *middle* age— this improving-with-years business—it definitely stopped there. It was kind of sad that at the very time in life when you stop thinking of yourself as a physical entity, your physical limitations force you to think of yourself as nothing else. One sad-ass poor physical entity at that. An entity that seemed to be caving in on itself, the top of his chest seemingly trying to touch the bottom, his skin starting to hang on his bones like wet laundry. Age doesn't become a man; it humiliates him.

Once, along with his Social Security check, they'd sent him a brochure on something called the Senior Citizen Workshop, a place, he supposed, where you learned to be a senior citizen. The brochure referred to something called *the prime of your life* and talked about being free from *work* and free from *raising a family* and free from *building a future*. And yet, as he was reading it, all William felt was free from hope. He'd thrown it into the trash out front—though later he'd seen it pressed between the pages of one of Mr. Wilson's Harlequin Romances. Mr. Wilson, free from raising a family, from work, and from building a future, and now free from getting beaten to death as well.

Outside, another plane was taking off, heading nearly straight up now, so that it looked for a moment like one of those visions you read about in the paper. You know the kind. Christ's face in a cornfield, or on a can of Campbell's soup, or on some billboard in Appalachia. This looked suspiciously like the cross itself, the red taillights like spots of blood on wrists and ankles. It looked that way at least until it flattened out over Biscayne Bay and disappeared into a bank of thunderclouds. And William, tired now as tired can be, fell asleep for the second time that day.

The first break came with his third stop of the day.
Follow the list, William, it's all you have.
His first two stops had been much like yesterday's—a candy store in the *let's kill whitey* part of town—*Mr. Who?*—the proprietor asked William, and a vacant lot, which according to a homeless person named Queen, had once been a *hooch house* for the rich. How long ago was that, William asked him. *Let's put it this way*, the man said, *longer than I can count*.

William, however, had no trouble counting. The vacant lot had made it five. Five addresses: no one home. He was slowly exhausting the list, playing connect-the-dots on his smudged and sweat-soaked map, but all he was getting was crayon scrawl.

Who are they, Jean?
Samuels—Shankin—Timinsky—Palumbo. Who are they?
His third stop of the day: 1021 Coral Avenue.

The first good omen he had was that it actually existed—a rather chichi-looking place guarded by a black brass jockey and tall hedge. The second good omen was that when the lady of the house heard who he was looking for, she didn't turn away, or scratch her head, or ask him to get lost.

"Funny," she said. "I think I've heard that name before. Mrs. Winters—is that who you said?"
Samuels—Shankin—Timinsky—Palumbo—Winters.
William nodded; that's who he'd said.

The woman before him had reached a sort of limbo between youth and middle age—it all depended on how the light hit her, and where. It reminded him of those Empress Nera rings he'd had as a kid, where the Empress changed position every time you moved the ring. Now smiling and confident, now in desperate peril.

"I'd ask you to come in," she said, "but I don't know you."

"Yeah."

"Who did you say you are? Her lawyer?"

"Not *her* lawyer. It concerns an inheritance. Mrs. Winters has some money coming to her. We heard she used to live here."

"I don't think so. I've been here, let's see . . . six, seven years. We got the house from an Italian family." She pronounced it *eyetalian.* "I can't remember their name, but trust me—it wasn't *Winters.*"

"You said something about having heard that name before," thinking now that she'd probably heard it from Jean, that in a minute she'd remember all about it and tell him about the *other* old man who'd come to her door asking for Mrs. Winters.

But no.

"A card," she said. "That's it."

"A *card?*"

"Yeah. Someone sent us a card. I *think* it was to a Mrs. Winters—you know, a Christmas card."

William felt the faintest hint of . . . what? Excitement? Maybe just relief.

"Did you send it back?"

"Uh uh. Who has the time?"

"You kept it then? You still have it?"

"I doubt it. But you never know. Look—why don't you come in . . . you look like you're about to keel over. I'll take a look."

Yes, why not. He probably *was* about to keel over. When he walked in he was slapped by a blast of central air-conditioning gone amok; it felt like the meat section at Pathmark.

She was gone about two minutes. Two minutes William spent slumped in a wicker chair suspended from the ceiling by long white chains. No kidding. He felt kind of precarious and completely silly. All that was missing was a playground buddy to push him back and forth.

"Here," she said, reentering the room. "The truth is, I never throw anything out—not if I can help it."

The truth was, William felt like thanking her for that. But he didn't, of course. Instead he took the off-white card from her hand and looked at it carefully.

Dear Mrs. Winters, it said inside. *Merry Christmas.* Signed *Raoul.* That was it, *all she wrote,* as if it was sent by someone used to paying by the word.

"The envelope?" William asked.

"Well, I don't keep *everything.*"

"Sure. But maybe you remember where it was posted *from?*"

"Absolutely. New York."

"And the address . . . ?"

"Are you kidding? I didn't get it yesterday."

"You're sure it was New York though?"

"Yeah. New York. Look," she said, "aren't you pretty *old* for a lawyer?"

It was as if she'd just looked at him maybe. Okay, Perry Mason he wasn't.

"Sure, but think of all my experience." He was still sitting in that stupid swinging chair; she was still standing over him like a concerned mother checking for boo-boos. *Where does it hurt . . . ?*

William got up, but it was like trying to disembark from a moving ship. He teetered, he tottered, he fell back down in the chair.

"Whoa," she said, taking him by the inside of his arm and pulling him up and out. "Take it easy, okay," leading him to the door as if he were Ray Charles maybe. "It's plenty hot out there."

Plenty.

"Oh," William said, "one thing. We sent a representative down here some time ago, but we never heard if he contacted you."

"Representative? Uh uh. *I* didn't see him. But then I've been in and out."

"Sure," William said. "Thanks anyway."

"Don't mention it. You can keep the card if you want."

But William was already ahead of her; he had it firmly tucked inside his pocket. He shook her hand, then walked back out into the furnace.

Okay, he wasn't ready to yell *eureka.* He was still running on fumes; he didn't have much of anything. But he had that card. You follow a list with names on it and none of them are where they're supposed to be. None of them exist. Up till now. Mrs. Winters was on the list, but Mrs. Winters was real. Because someone else had known her too. Someone in New York, someone who liked to send Christmas cards. He didn't have much, but he had that.

Merry Christmas, William.

NINE

Somehow William managed to make it back from the hooker's apartment in one piece.

Then he made the awful mistake of waking up.

First of all, there was the hangover: Someone had been using his head as a Chinese gong.

Second of all—there was the room: Someone had criminally assaulted someone else and not even bothered to cover up the evidence. Absolutely.

There was that overturned coffee table at the foot of the bed, and just *look* at his clothes—strewn all over the place as if they'd been ripped right off his body. Of course someone *had* assaulted someone else—only that someone was him—so was the someone he'd assaulted. He'd beaten *himself* up—with a little assistance from his good friend Jack. *Take a bow please.*

He surveyed the crime scene with sober dispassion—okay, almost sober, gazing at his twisted shirt stained with vomit, at his pants, each leg pointing in a different direction, at something caught just beneath the right leg, the tip of it barely peeking out. *What's this?*

He reached down and lifted it up.

The photograph. Santini, Jean, and himself. Three Eyes. It had fallen out of his pocket.

He stared at it through barely opened eyes. Still, this time he noticed things he hadn't seen before, little things: the very edge of a gun peeking out from the waistband of Santini's pants, a white streak on the toe of Jean's left shoe, and about himself—the way his jacket cuffs didn't match, one being clearly shorter than the other. He remembered now; Rachel was going to take it to the tailors, was just *about* to do that. But then Rachel had taken his heart to the cleaners instead, and so he'd continued to wear it that way until he'd worn it out.

Of the three of them, Santini looked every bit the detective. He was the only one who did. Jean, on the other hand, resembled a jailhouse snitch loaded with secrets, and *he* looked exactly like what he was. A fish out of water, someone who'd gone from investigating car accidents to investigating human ones with no particular talent for either.

William went into the shower and hung his head under a cold spray.

He felt like he'd been away—to a foreign country maybe, on some whirlwind tour like the kind Mr. Leonati went on—Mr. Leonati who lived across the hall and always left for these things looking calm and relaxed but always returned from them looking dazed and battered. The hotels had overbooked; the buses had broken down; someone had stolen his money. All those brochures filled cover to cover with pretty pictures of tranquil places had lied to him. It hadn't turned out the way they said it would. And now William, who'd never been on a whirl-wind tour, or any tour for that matter, thought that this is what it must feel like.

He'd gone on a journey too—and with similarly false expectations. He'd gone to bury Jean; instead he'd dug him up.

And now he remembered other things—his trip home for instance; she showing him to the door through his stench of vomit, spending most of the nauseating sub-way ride home replaying what she'd told him, all the while consumed by something. *What?* Envy, fear, hilar-ity? Okay envy—from someone who'd been put out to pasture to someone who was maybe still in the race. And just a *little* fear too—that all the things he thought were far behind him weren't, that the compromises he'd made, that that tidy little armistice he'd signed—were about to be challenged. *I know.* Silly of him perhaps, but age does that to you. *It's the biggest case of my life*—that's what Jean said. Between pictures probably.

Poor Jean, he thought, as he trudged out of the shower and spent five minutes over the toilet courtesy of his nagging prostate. Then back to the comfort of his chair where he downed three Bayer aspirin with a cup of stale orange juice.

Why had he said it? What did it matter? So Jean was down to chasing runaways. *Have you seen this child?* So Jean had maybe found a rich runaway, at least one with rich *parents* who'd been tremendously grateful when Jean collared them on the phone. So maybe he was going to get a big reward and retire to a big house where he could tell big stories to Miss *Eat Your Heart Out*—all about how he used to dig up big-time dirt on big-time people and dish it out to big-time lawyers, occasionally throwing the juicier tidbits to *Confidential* or certain columnists who'd print it blind. *What Park Avenue shyster is tiptoeing through the tulips in very light loafers? What very hot chanteuse is doing the rhumba with what very hot politico?* Remember? If not the biggest case of his life—maybe the biggest payoff, and these days maybe that made it the biggest case of his life.

He was an old man, she said. Sometimes that's what old men do. They lie—to themselves, to hookers with crimson tattoos on their thighs.

And even though, as he put forth this perfectly reasonable explanation, as he ridiculed the very notion of Jean back on a case—on *any* case—even as he knew that in large part it was a story created to appease the storyteller, knowing that didn't alter a thing. Not yet. After all, the storyteller *was* appeased. Just look at him.

Okay, *almost* appeased. Ninety-nine percent appeased— ready to stand up to anyone who'd dare suggest—*what if what he said is true*—and show them the door.

So now, his hangover dulled, it was his shoulder that began to act up. A sign, his shoulder was, a warning, a dear but annoying friend tap, tap, tapping him there to get him to look at himself and remember. Before he got too riled up and maybe started to believe things he shouldn't. And so he did remember. After all, he had the picture filed right under S for shooting, and right after R for Rachel. *There.*

There's William reading the *Daily News*. William sipping his coffee from Micky D's. William dozing off on

his suddenly comfortable bridge chair like old guys are
prone to do, guys who pull night shifts and dream about
their wife doing their business partner every way to Sunday on a motel vibromatic off Utopia Parkway. Guys like
that. Even as a Chevy Impala with one broken headlight
circles Weissman's Auto Parts like someone lost; once,
twice, three times around the block till it finally pulls
over and lets two black men out onto the pavement.
Three black men really—counting the one still sitting in
the car—seven empty cans of Colt 45, a stolen sawed-
off shotgun, and a spanking-new jigaboo special—.22 caliber to the uninitiated—check the police manifest for
further corroboration.

William still dozing, somewhere between Brooklyn and
Pimlico by now, although *what's this?* Clank, bink, boom.
Someone being rude enough to ruin his beauty sleep—
that's what it is. William opening his eyes and actually
hearing someone trying to jimmy open the front door.
Imagine that. They hired you as a *security guard,* didn't
they, and suddenly that's what you're being asked to do.
Guard. Not sleep, not sample the coffee and donuts from
every diner on Utica Avenue, not analyze the box scores
and handicap the ponies and do two words of the cross-
word puzzle. Guard. Used fan belts, four-horsepower
transmissions, and radiators of dubious lineage, but
they're all yours.

There's William with his hand already sneaking down
to his .45, trying to remember if he's ever really shot it,
even once, ever even taken it out and sighted it and *pre-
tended* to shoot it, and knowing that the answer is no—
not on your life, but taking it out anyway. Sidling up to
the door in a kind of bent three-quarter shuffle, then

stopping just in front of it—the door starting to quiver from the pressure of whatever they're using to jimmy it open or maybe just from the knocking of his knees.

I have a gun. That's what he says. Because it's true— he does, and who knows—maybe they don't, and the simple fact of him having one might make them reconsider their options here.

I have a gun he says again.

But they do too. They have a gun—or actually guns. A sawed-off shotgun, a spanking-new .22—check the manifest for corroboration.

Suddenly the door splinters open and there they are— the three of them, caught in an awkward moment Emily Post just can't help you with. William with his gun out, pointed in the general direction of black groin—though he can swear the safety's still on—and the two of *them,* one with the shotgun raised past William's shoulder.

No one says boo.

So the gun speaks for them. William's gun actually— the safety wasn't on after all—deciding to fire a shot into the black man's kneecap, the kick of the gun tending to lower aim by as much as a foot. The gun just deciding to do it—what William told the police later on his way into the ambulance. Because William has no recollection of pulling the trigger, none. There they were staring at each other and the gun didn't like what it saw. Bang.

There's one black man going down—Vernon M. Maxwell, by the way, five foot eight, one hundred eighty pounds, BedStuy by way of Rahway—two stints for breaking and entering and a dismissal on rape. And there's the other black man running back across the street and starting to fire as he goes.

William? He's wondering why his gun went off like that and considering if he should bring it up on charges. He's staring at Vernon M. Maxwell's right kneecap, which doesn't resemble a kneecap now as much as the ground beef in Pirelli's Italian Deli. He's *ducking* too—because the other man is firing at him and William can hear the bullets ricocheting off the tin walls of the warehouse.

Now the other man is back at the Impala where he's multiplying before William's shocked eyes. That is, he's becoming two men again—the driver has joined him of course, which means William is again outnumbered and possibly outgunned.

Now turn your attention to the left, ladies and gentlemen. It is a Sunday morning in spring. The kind of morning that makes Sunday mornings in winter bearable. The kind of morning that makes you think of possibilities instead of realities. The kind of morning a five-year-old girl puts on her Sunday best and decides to skip rope before church.

And there she is. Mom still in the apartment somewhere, but Deidre—yes, he knows her name—out there on the pavement with a jump rope. *A my name is Alice . . . B my name is Barbara . . . C my name is Carol . . . D my name is dead.*

Not yet though.

William crouching down behind an old fender just outside the door, with Vernon cradling his shattered kneecap and calling him every name in the book to his left. And now his two bros coming to get him. Both of them advancing across the street like gunfighters do—like Wyatt and Doc at the O.K. Corral maybe, only they were the good guys and these guys here are the desperadoes.

This is what William can see: A Chevy Impala still idling across the street. Two black men bearing guns—one of them for sure. The five-year-old girl skipping rope—yes, he's seen her by now. And one thing else.

He's seen this guy, *William*. You know him, don't you? This guy crying into his blanket, cowering behind an auto part, blubbering into the air. This pathetic security guard positively pleading with the deities not to take him yet. Can you believe this guy—I mean can you?

The two black men halfway across the street now, one of them with a small pistol aimed at the *chicken's* head.

So William raises his .45—the one with its own mind, only this time William taking charge. Even as he sees Deidre putting the rope down and walking curiously out into the street. Even as he sees—yes he does—a police cruiser rounding Utica Avenue just out of the corner of his eye. Still he raises the gun, still he pulls the trigger. Still he closes his eyes—that's right, ladies and gentlemen of the jury, you saw it right—he *closes* his eyes. Why? You'll have to ask him—maybe because he didn't wish to see. And bang. Bang, bang, bang. One of those bangs a bullet he takes in his left shoulder courtesy of one of the black men still walking. One of those bangs a bullet taking out the left front tire of the Chevy Impala. One of those bangs a bullet slamming into the front cranial cavity of a five-year-old jump-roper dreaming of summer.

Last snapshot.

There they are, strewn before the Brooklyn warehouse like the various pieces of a wreck, blood seeping like oil onto the cracked pavement, onto the willow leaves carried by the spring wind all the way from Van Cortlandt

Park, onto the white petticoat of the little girl right next
to him, because once he's opened his eyes and the sheer
awfulness of what's transpired here has begun to make
itself known, he's staggered, crawled, stumbled in her
general direction. The little girl in mid-moan, in terrible
gut-wrenching, bloodcurdling pain. He tries to tell her
to lie still, to keep quiet, that the doctor will be there
any minute, tries to tell that to her *and* her wailing mother
too, her mother and the police and the man in the moon,
all looking at him as if he's crazy, mad as a hatter, which,
of course, he is. For when he tells the little girl to lie
still, to be quiet, *shh . . . shh please . . . please . . .* the
whimpering *does* stop, but not because she's listened to
him. She can't listen to him   its technically and med-
ically impossible. Why? Because she has no *head*. One
of his bullets took it right off. The crying, of course, had
been his; he'd been comforting a corpse.

Old men, the warehouse owner said, *you send me old
men and this is what happens . . .*

TEN

It seemed to William, now very much back in the present and staring at that picture again, that it was from that moment on that he truly *became* old. You need guilt for that, it's an irreplaceable part of the equation. Suddenly it was as if they'd served him his birthday cake with all the candles on it after years of counting by decade. So many candles he'd never be able to blow them all out. So there'd be no wish for him that year, or any other year either; wishes were for people with futures. The ordinary courage it took to open your eyes and start the day was suddenly no longer there.

Not that the day held much in store for him. It's funny how easy it is to do nothing when you really put your mind to it. How easy it is to sponge off your disability and the various odd job, to pull up a chair and put your feet up and take a nap and never actually wake up. To bet the ponies and clip the coupons and kibitz with Mr.

Brickman and quietly settle into a kind of unofficial retirement. To take it day by day, then month by month,
then year by year, until you're suddenly sixty-five and
you can make it official.

William made his pact; he signed it in blood and he
kept it. He became an official lifer, the kind that takes
up basket weaving and finds religion; prison breaks were
for younger men.

But okay, yesterday had shown him there were definite chinks in the wall, rot in the bars. *Break them* the
day had shouted at him . . . *break them down.* Maybe that's
what yesterday had really been all about. His run-in with
the Puerto Rican—or rather the kid's run-in with him,
his ringing up that woman, his staggering journey home,
agonized and affronted by the specter of Jean. *Break them
down.* For what had really bothered him wasn't that Jean
died, let's face it. It was that he might have died *living*.

There.

So now his theory, his perfectly reasonable and entirely
logical accounting of Jean's last stand, all about rich runaways and big payoffs, could be seen for what it was. A
story, a bedtime story, the kind you tell yourself to help
you sleep. Why? Because even though he hadn't known
Jean well, he'd known Jean well enough.

Sure he had.

First off: A good payoff wouldn't have meant anything
to Jean. Jean had always been paid and paid well for
what he did, but that was never why he did it. With
Jean, it was strictly an affair of the heart; a wronged one,
a smashed-to-smithereens one. Santini had once said that
every case for Jean was the same case, and that the case
was his own. And Santini, for once, had been right; every

red file had as much to do with Jean as it did with his criminal of the week. If he was obsessed, and okay, maybe he was, it wasn't with money.

So maybe Jean was trying to impress her, to prick her interest a little so she'd maybe see beyond his eighty-year-old body, just another bit of *playacting*. Fine. Only impressing people had never been very important to Jean either, had always, you might say, been of zero importance to him. So why change now? And why start saying too much when he'd always said too little?

So okay. Maybe the only people who really knew Jean were the ones in that picture he carried around with him, but William knew this: If Jean said he'd been given the biggest case of his life, it'd be smart to believe him.

There. Almost eighty and almost dead, but some way, somehow, he may just have gotten hold of a live one.

While William had been weaving baskets, Jean was out there weaving cases, and had found one case bigger than anything that had ever come his way before.

And there, ladies and gentlemen, you have it.

And now that he *had* it, William could forget about it. After all, he had things to do. Sure he did. If he just gave himself a minute or two he could think of something he had to do today.

Of course.

All those horses just waiting to take his money. That huge pile of losing tickets just itching for a few additions from yours truly. If *he* didn't lose to OTB, who would? They absolutely depended on him. Of course they did.

*　　　*　　　*

Okay, this was the problem. It was the horses' names. That was one thing. There he was, giving the racing form the benefit of his practiced eye, and what do you think he saw there?

First race: Prince Jean. Swear to God, right there listed fourth—*Prince Jean.*

And in the second race: Moses. No, he wasn't kidding—there it was in black and white. Some Israeli owner named Yehudi. An Orthodox jockey maybe? *Moses*—son of *Esther,* who must have instilled a lot of guilt in her son about ever finishing second. After all, his track record was strictly first-rate. Moses—listed two-to-one in the second at Belmont.

So now he was really starting to get spooked. Starting to think that maybe there was a message there. Those horses' names—that was one thing.

And his fellow horse-*players*—that was the other.

Maybe it's the way they looked. Like him. As if they'd given some real thought to things they had to do today and all they'd managed to come up with was this. Like him. Even Jilly—he looked like him too—and Augie, back on his favorite stool with the racing form supporting his elbows like a place mat.

Funny how that had never bothered him before. Odd how it did now. There was this absolute lethargy in the middle of the OTB office that was positively draining. Okay, it was disrupted periodically by the actual races, when the crowd would suddenly and halfheartedly spring to life for about two minutes or so. Then right back to sleep. Think of an old married couple giving it the *once for old times' sake.* Not that he was an expert on old married couples—he'd had to get old all by his lonesome.

There'd never been a Rachel Two of course—that's a fact. There was very briefly a Catherine Anne, who hadn't lasted long enough to understand why he didn't care to talk about Rachel One. Catherine, a soon-to-be-divorcée, who'd hired him to find out if her husband was cheating on her—*yes, he was*—and if so, with whom—*a fellow schoolteacher at Public School 171, home room and Romance languages. Name of Harold.*

Nice girl, he supposed, but without a Chinaman's chance against *her*. He'd given Rachel the Ford Fairlane, half the profit from the sale of their Elmont home—not much, considering most of it was owed—and a more than generous piece of his still bleeding heart. The absence of *her* was simply greater than the presence of Catherine Anne. That's all.

Okay . . . maybe that wasn't all. Rachel had left him carless and homeless (throw in nearly penniless too), but worse yet, she'd left him with the kind of suspicious nature that finally and at last suited his life's work. William's new credo: a cuckold behind every vow, a cheater behind every shade—his included, *especially* his. This kind of outlook not particularly conducive to trusting long-term relationships. Catherine Anne—a good Irish Catholic who toiled somewhere in the bowels of the Garment Center and no stranger to betrayal herself, soon tired of being asked *five* times why she hadn't bothered to answer the phone the other night. Or where exactly she'd gone on her day off. Not because it was his right to know, or even really his *desire* to know (it wasn't like he was in love with her)—but simply because it was now his *nature* to know. What the scorpion said to the frog after fatally stinging him while being piggybacked across

the pond—*why* the frog asking, *why* both of them cat-
erwauling to the bottom. And the scorpion's response:
Because it's my nature bub, because it's my nature.

And then, he'd known Rachel forever and a day—the
kind of history that's pretty much impossible to sur-
mount, especially the *day* part. His first image of Rachel
being a thin blond girl throwing her head back in un-
abashed laughter on the corner at Martin Van Buren High
School. His last image of Rachel being the woman he
loved with her legs wrapped around someone else. And
in between, more or less, his life.

Catherine Anne, any woman who might be unlucky
enough to meet him, deserved better. He deserved worse.
William had had to grow old and defeated all alone.

Now, losing his money didn't seem like such a hoot
anymore. Now he started thinking again about other
things he had to do today. And the only thing he could
come up with, swear to God, was you know what.

So there he was again, ruminating about that old geriatric gumshoe Jean. About that tattoo. About the photo
of the three of them. Which suddenly, just like that, became a bunch of other photos.

Well, what do you know?

So now, what he had to do today was suddenly clear
as day. And while the pain in William's shoulder was still
there, still warning him back, the pain in his gut was
urging him forward. *Break them . . . break them . . .* whispering insidiously to him and getting him all riled up.

Look at it this way, he said to himself.

At least, it's somewhere to go.

ELEVEN

Rodriguez was on the roof.

A boy had answered Rodriguez's door and told William where he could find him.

On the roof. Catching some rays in a white beach chair, beer cooler to his right, radio to his left, oiled from top to bottom with Bain de Soleil; William saw the plastic bottle discarded on the rooftop. A pair of mirrored sunglasses reflected half sky and half tar. He was singing along to something catchy and sophisticated. *Do it doggie . . .*

"Rodriguez!" William called out to him.

No answer; Rodriguez hadn't heard him. William had to take a walk on tar beach, sinking a half inch into the roof with each step, then tap him on the shoulder before Rodriguez knew he had company.

Rodriguez stared at him. William's sweat-soaked face

stared back, *two* very tired, very old-looking sweat-soaked faces, one to a lens.

"Sorry," Rodriguez said. "I already sold them."

"*Them* . . . ?"

"The drapes. You said you didn't want them."

"That's okay. I don't."

"Fine." Rodriguez turned back toward the sun.

Doggie style makes me smile . . .

"Rodriguez," William said again.

"Yeah?"

"What *didn't* you give me."

"Huh . . . ?"

"Was there something you didn't give me?"

"Yeah. The license."

"Besides the license?"

"The drapes."

"Not the drapes. Something else?"

"I'm not following you, Cochise."

"Was there anything else? Anything you *didn't* give me?"

"Like *what?*"

"Like pictures maybe?"

"Huh?"

Doggie . . . doggie . . . doggie style . . .

"Pictures," William repeated.

"I *gave* you a picture."

"Sure. Maybe there were other pictures you *didn't* give me."

"Maybe I don't know what the fuck you're talking about. You want the *license?*"

"No."

"Right. You don't want the license."

"I was thinking about pictures."

"*Pictures?*" Rodriguez shook his head. "What kind of pictures?"

"Personal pictures."

"Personal pictures."

"Right."

"What the fuck you talking about? I *gave* you a picture."

"Yes, I remember. It's *other* pictures I'm thinking about."

"That's funny."

"Why?"

" 'Cause there ain't no other pictures. So that's funny. That you came back in this fuckin' heat to ask me for something I don't got."

Rodriguez was right about the heat. It might have been the hottest day of the year and if it wasn't, it might have been the most humid, and if it wasn't that, it was close. The sun was particularly brutal up on the roof; the top of William's head was starting to feel well-done, not funny at all. And the scent of Bain de Soleil was beginning to sicken him, the odor of fruit left too long in the sun.

"What's the matter," Rodriguez said, "something bothering you . . . ?"

Yes. The heat was bothering him. His shoulder was bothering him. Rodriguez was bothering him. Bothering to *come* here was bothering him.

"Okay," William said, "okay, so there were no other pictures lying around."

"What the fuck you think I've been trying to tell you?"

There comes a time when you either believe someone or you don't, and even if you don't, you have to walk away. So bye.

"Take it easy," he said.

"Uh huh." Rodriguez trained both mirrors on him; William looked like something basted now. "You know," Rodriguez said, "you're nuts. It's *hot* out, man."

"Yeah. I noticed."

Do it from behind . . . that's what's on my mind . . . the radio was wailing away; Rodriguez was turning away; William was walking away. Over to the stairway door which said *Chakalakaboo* on the top and *Fuck all Niggers* on the bottom, then through it and into the steaming elevator, when he suddenly realized that he needed something. Desperately and immediately. He needed water. If last night's drinking hadn't dehydrated him enough, buzzing around in ninety degree heat had. Now he had a choice: He could go back up to the roof and ask Rodriguez for a little something from his beer cooler. Or he could knock on someone's door and depend on the kindness of strangers. Or he could stay in the elevator and die of heat prostration—that too. Okay—door number two. He didn't think he could make it back up to tar land, and though dying had its attractive side—not having to negotiate his way back through kung fu city for instance, he thought two funerals in a week was a lot to ask of anyone—even Rodriguez.

He took the elevator down to the third floor. To Jean's floor, but not to Jean's apartment. No, another apartment just a bit further down.

Where Mr. Crazy lived. That old white-haired tortoise, Mr. Weeks. And why not. At least when he asked him for water he could ask him by name.

It took almost a minute of knocking before Weeks came to the door, but the second he opened it and looked out at William with an expression that was either one of fear or one of relief or maybe even one of both, William knew he may have come for water but that he'd be leaving with just a bit more.

"You're here about Jean," Weeks said. "Aren't you?"

"Yeah," William said. "I am."

Later, sitting in an armchair rough as sandpaper with a glass of water finally in hand, William thought that he could have knocked on any door, *any* one, but that he'd knocked on this one. Which made him think that maybe he should have stayed and played the horses after all. Fortune was definitely smiling on him today.

First William had knocked and Weeks had answered. Then William had asked for water and Weeks had given it to him. Then William had gone ahead and asked for something else.

"Jean's apartment," he'd asked, begging the same thing of Weeks that he'd asked of Rodriguez. "Did you take something from it—not steal, not at all—just borrow maybe—Jean being dead. Some *pictures* maybe?"

And though Weeks hemmed and hawed at first, he hadn't done it convincingly or done it for long. Maybe his heart wasn't in it, maybe he just had to resist a little before giving a lot. Maybe he'd only been waiting for someone to ask.

Pictures then. Lots of them—Weeks bringing them out in a large manila envelope. Pictures, because that's what the woman had said. *He kept them,* answering his curiosity, *he kept them, I guess.* I guess. But they hadn't been in Jean's apartment and they hadn't been in Jean's box and so someone had taken them. That's what had crossed his mind this morning smack in the middle of OTB, thinking of that picture of the three of them. One picture suddenly becoming many pictures.

And now he sat with the pictures on his lap, just a dutiful and polite neighbor leafing through the trip to Hoover Dam, the excursion to Mount Rushmore, the holiday to Disneyland. *That's me with Mickey . . . There I am with Old Abe . . .* Okay, maybe a bit more exotic than that. For instance no Abe here, and no Mickey, no Teddy or Goofy or Donald Duck. In fact no Jean either; just *her.*

Mr. Weeks's apartment suited this particular photographic retrospective too; dark, shuttered down, as if Mr. Weeks was trying to extricate himself from the outside world. Three fans were set up in a triangle around the room, streams of hot air converging on each other like separate rivers into a murderously hot delta, stirring up instead of silt and shells, fine dust and white lint.

Okay. The pictures. He'd gone for a certain look here, Jean had. A definite theme had been attempted, a common thread carefully sought. There was, for instance, the matter of her clothes. Black boots, black stockings, a brown cloth shirt. And on her arm a symbol most definitely *retro,* a symbol more commonly exhibited on rest room walls and in certain South American countries with large German populations. A swastika. Red, white, and absolutely true, your honor. A swastika. In every picture. The only thing, in fact, that changed from picture to picture was her position—now spread-eagled on a couch, now standing ramrod straight against the wall, now sitting defiantly on a small settee. And yet, William thought, perhaps he was wrong about that as well. Each picture had been shot from the floor up; to take such a picture, at that kind of angle, one would have to grovel belly down, no higher than shoe level. Each position was different but each position was exactly the same: superior. Okay, so maybe he *hadn't* enjoyed being beaten, remembering now what the woman had said, but what he *had* enjoyed was close.

"You shouldn't judge him," Mr. Weeks said now, softly, but with a certain undeniable firmness there. "Not by *that*. It's not fair."

And now William realized he'd been wrong about something. He'd been right about who'd taken the pictures, *give the gentleman a gold star,* but he'd been wrong about why. He'd assumed Mr. Weeks had taken them for the same reason he'd thought Rodriguez had. A little amateur pornography, *the Old Dick and the C,* the charming story of a retired detective trying to recapture those carefree days of Dachau. Something to look at on a rainy afternoon, something to hide beneath the bookshelf. But okay, he was willing to admit that's not why Mr. Weeks had taken them after all. It wasn't general horniness that sent him into Jean's apartment before Rodriguez got there; it was something more bizarre. A genuine regard for the deceased. Hard to believe considering the deceased was your old friend and mine, the utterly charming Jean Goldblum. But then there's no accounting for taste, is there. Instead of robbing the dead, Weeks had been protecting his memory. At least, he'd been giving it the old college try.

"Sure," William said, "I'm not judging him." But that, of course, wasn't entirely true. He wasn't judging him because he'd already condemned him. And while he was at it, he'd gone and sentenced him too. Death by general disgust. It was the swastika, of course. It was a swastika that had made Jean's wife and child disappear; it was the swastika that made William sick.

"You don't understand," Weeks said.

Fair enough. He didn't. Strange sex, after all, wasn't exactly his province these days. *Sex* was not exactly his province these days, though on occasion he could remember it quite vividly, especially the kind practiced in a certain ground-floor room at the Par Central Motel. But while that was worse, this was close, somewhere, at least, in the general ballpark.

"Sure I do," William said. "Jean was exercising his rights under the First Amendment. Jean was just having some fun."

"Jean didn't have *fun*."

"Oh, yeah. I forgot."

"Jean wasn't the kind of person who *could*."

"That's right. It slipped my mind."

"You didn't *know* him . . ."

"You can say that again," William said. "Hey, I don't *care* about the pictures. I don't want them. You can rip them up, burn them, sell them to Rodriguez, whatever you like. I'm not interested in them."

"Then why'd you ask for them?"

Yes. Why did he ask for them?

"It's a little hard to explain." Which was true, considering he hadn't exactly explained it to *himself* yet. "We used to work together," William said, a line he seemed to know by rote now.

"Uh huh." Mr. Weeks was still waiting; Mr. Weeks looked like he'd been waiting for a long time.

"Back when we worked together we sometimes had to

finish each other's cases. We didn't like each other all that much, but we'd *cover* for each other. Because it was professional courtesy. That's all."

"He's dead."

"Yeah. Right. You've got me there. But maybe what he was working on *isn't*. Dead. What do you say, Mr. Weeks? Is there something else you haven't given me? Just *one* thing else. Maybe something Jean really cared about, not like the pictures, something else?"

Okay, the cat was out of the bag. He *hadn't* come for the pictures. He'd just followed the pictures, the way you follow those signs on the highway that promise food fifteen, then ten, then five miles down the pike. He was hungry; after all, he hadn't eaten in twenty years, and he could just about taste the meal. The pictures? They were just the flyers that rummies hand out in the glow of topless bars. He'd come for the *show*. For if someone had taken the pictures, someone, for instance, like Mr. Weeks, it stood to reason he would have taken something *else,* the something he wanted, the something he'd come for.

And now Mr. Weeks was sitting stock-still, his shock of white hair rippling up and down from the fans, up and down like the hair of a cat caught between fear and hunger.

"Okay," Mr. Weeks said. "Okay . . ."

He stood up and walked to the back of the apartment where it was darker still, where Mr. Weeks disappeared into the gloom and all William could hear was the sound of someone rifling through drawers, through this, inside that, right down to the bottom.

Then he was back, and in his hand a file, which he

dropped ever so softly into William's lap, as if it were holy.

To William, it was. The file was thin, worn, and stained with thumbprints.

And it was red.

TWELVE

One of the fans had died, just like that, sputtering off like an aircraft engine hit by flak. Mr. Weeks had ministered to it for several minutes, but it was no go; machines were a mystery to him, he said. He readjusted the remaining fans as best he could but it made little difference—instead of three fans blasting hot air around the room, there were now two; it was nearly an improvement.

Yet the darkness in the room made it seem like the inside of a rain cloud: the heat, the moisture, and the sense that something was about to happen, that answers, like lightning, were about to light up the room.

But no such luck. The file was full, but full of what? William had spent several minutes flipping through it as if skimming a book for the dirty parts; but there were no dirty parts, nothing that juicy. Just a list of names: *Mr. Samuels . . . Mrs. Timinsky . . . Mr. Shankin . . . Mrs.*

Winters. Names and addresses—one to a page, and a check under each. And on another page some numbers— license plates perhaps, six to a group. That was it.

William looked up now at Mr. Weeks, who was back in his chair and staring back at him, warily, as if under house arrest. *Senile,* Rodriguez had said. Well, William thought now, *we'll see . . .*

He leaned forward, just enough to be friendly, like an old friend, like an old friend of an old friend.

"Did Jean ask you to *hide* this for him, Mr. Weeks?"

Mr. Weeks nodded.

"He said it was in case *something happened. Don't give it to anyone,* he said. *It's my last testament, it's what I bequeath, understand?* He made me promise."

What I bequeath.

"But you didn't keep your promise?"

"I know who you are. Jean showed me your picture once. When I saw you in the hall yesterday with Rodriguez, I *knew* you'd come back."

So, William thought, *so . . .* "Funny, isn't it."

"Funny?"

"Jean gets you to clean up for him—just in case. And Rodriguez to bury him—just in case. *Two* of you— just in case. And then Jean's *on* a case, that too."

"Yes . . . ?"

"It's just that Jean being Jean, we could say maybe something had him worried. Not just here, understand, but here*after.*"

Mr. Weeks blinked at him, at him, or at the wall, or just at the situation.

"So, Mr. Weeks, what *was* the case?"

"I don't know."

"You don't know, or you don't know if you should tell me?"

"I don't know."

"Not another something he made you promise, huh?"

"No." Mr. Weeks shook his head, a good shake, a no-doubt-about-it shake. "He never said a word to me. If you knew Jean, you knew that wasn't his way. I wasn't even supposed to look in the file. I *haven't*."

Okay, so he was right. That *wasn't* Jean's way. Even with that woman. *I can't tell you,* he'd said. *I can't . . .* Secrets, for Jean, were like insurance policies and he'd loaded up on so many of them that he'd long ago reached equity.

"Okay. Any guesses? Go ahead . . . it's free."

"I don't know anything," Mr. Weeks said, as if he were making a general statement of his intellectual worth, a totaling up of seventy-odd years' worth of acquired knowledge. Maybe the older you get, the less you *do* know. Maybe Weeks had gotten so old he was already into *negative* knowledge. On the other hand . . .

"Maybe you don't know what you know. Knowing things is like that." Like his clients, remember, who always knew, but didn't. "Why don't we see?"

"How?"

"Tell me about Jean's last few weeks. What he looked like, where he went, what he said. Walk me through them, okay, Mr. Weeks? We'll take a stroll, nice and easy, you and me. Okay?"

Somewhere outside, an ice cream truck was rolling up the street. There were these bells, this jingle, something insipid but kind of catchy . . . *Here comes Mr. Softee . . .*

over and over . . . *Here comes Mr. Softee* . . . but as far as
he could tell there were no takers. Not a one.

Now inside, it was different. *Here comes Mr. Weeks* . . .
and he had a customer too, a customer just about pant-
ing for something refreshing, for something tasty to chew
on.

Mr. Weeks had gone to the refrigerator for some juice,
had opened it, closed it, come back empty-handed, shuffled his feet, cleared his throat, made up his mind. He
would tell William about the last few weeks, but not *just*
about the last few weeks. He was one of those people
who have to start from the start, not from the end, not
even from the middle. To remember his lines he needed
the first cue, and the first cue here was Jean—not several weeks ago, but several years ago, more than that, a
Jean bored, broke, and nearly beaten.

He'd tried his hand at security years before, Mr. Weeks
began, but whether he'd resigned from it or whether he'd
been forced to, the experience hadn't been pleasant and
hadn't been long.

William picked *forced to*. Jean had always been a lot
happier breaking laws than trying to enforce them. Does
fox in the chicken coop ring a bell?

After *that,* Mr. Weeks continued, after a long while of
doing nothing at all, *really* nothing, because Jean didn't
read, or have a television, or even an *interest,* he tried to
start over again. Another agency, a one-man agency. He
found a storefront in Flushing, he fixed it up, he hung
up a shingle. No one came. One look at the man in the
one-man agency and would-be clients turned tail and ran.

"Christ, he should have been out on a golf course, they
thought, maybe shuffleboard, maybe not even that, the

exertion might have killed him, okay. He was seventy or so—and he looked ten years older," Mr. Weeks explained.

Anyway, the agency went bust. Quickly. The store turned into a Cantonese Buffet, Jean went back to his room.

"Then," Weeks sighed, "Jean maybe got a little desperate. A little seedy. That's what happens when no one wants you anymore and when you still think they should, when you think there's still a place for you."

Yes, William thought. The secret, of course, is realizing there *isn't.* A place for you. That tends to ease your desperation just a little, or at least, keep it quiet.

"Jean went *looking* for business, sort of," Mr. Weeks said.

"Sort of, how?"

"Well, he went looking for *children*"—Weeks winced here—"for runaways. He'd go down to the Port Authority, to the tunnel. Sometimes, he'd find them . . ."

"And when he found them?"

"He'd notify the parents," Weeks said.

"Is that so? He'd *notify* them. How responsible of him. What a good citizen. That's all then . . . ?"

"He'd ask for the reward."

"Sure. The reward. That's fair, isn't it, seeing as how he went to all that trouble. Just tell me one thing. Just asking, but what if there *wasn't* a reward?"

"Well . . ." There was that wince again. "He'd name a figure I guess, a figure he thought was fair . . ."

"Sure, Jean was always *fair*, wasn't he? But, just asking again, what if the parents, the ones he *notified,* didn't think the figure was fair? What if they maybe didn't have it, what if they were a little strapped for cash. What then?"

"*Then?*" Mr. Weeks wasn't happy now; William wasn't being friendly anymore, he wasn't being a friend of their old friend, laughing at his silly foibles, chuckling over those endearing eccentricities that made Jean such a card.

"Yes, *then*," William said. "The parents didn't have the money, let's just say they didn't, so our Jean would say, don't worry, if you don't, you don't, here's where your son is, your thirteen-year-old daughter, the one all the pimps are after, the one who's broken your heart. Here she is. Right, Mr. Weeks? That's what he'd do."

"Not exactly," Weeks said.

"Then *what* exactly?"

"If they didn't pay him the money, he'd hang up."

"Yeah," William said, "of course. I sort of thought that's what he'd do."

"You're just like Jean said you were," Weeks said.

So Jean hadn't just shown Weeks his picture; he'd provided commentary. *Did I ever tell you about Father William, Father William and his confessional down the hall, Father William, whose wife was caught playing nooky with the Monsignor?*

"What did he say?"

"He said you were a Boy Scout."

Okay, there was a definite change in tone emanating from Mr. Weeks's side of the room. No doubt about it. Mr. Weeks, who'd picked Jean's apartment clean of incriminating evidence, wasn't going to give up his friend without a fight. Maybe reliving the old days wasn't going to be such a hoot after all.

"Maybe just compared to him," William said. "Maybe compared to him, we *all* were."

"Look," Weeks said, "Jean thought if parents wouldn't pay the money, then they didn't really care."

"No," William said. "That might be what he said but that wasn't what he thought. What he thought was different. What he said was for us Boy Scouts. There's finding runaway kids and then there's *selling* them. Jean didn't distinguish. Jean wasn't a Boy Scout."

Mr. Weeks sighed, a sigh that seemed to say a lot, a sigh that said that maybe the jig was up.

"I told him I thought it was a little . . . *sleazy*. I *told* him that," he said.

"Sure. And I bet he cared too. By the way, why did he even bother telling you?"

"He said, *you're my conscience, Weeks.* That's what he said."

"Not a very big job, was it." Or maybe *too big* of a job, William thought. After all, there'd be so much to keep track of. You'd need to hire an assistant conscience too, then an assistant to the assistant and so on.

"Do you want me to go on?" Weeks said.

"Sure. I haven't heard how it ends yet. Jean's busy selling runaway kids, that's where we were up to. Sometimes they made it home, sometimes they ended up with the pimps. And then . . . ?"

"Well . . . *this*."

"Yeah." William was all ears now. This. *What I bequeath to you . . .*

"Well," Weeks said, "to begin with, he was scared."

"Scared? *How* scared?"

"Very. Because, you see, I'd never seen it before, not

from him. Jean wasn't exactly the emotional type. A little cool, if you know what I mean."

Sure. William knew what he meant. And maybe it wasn't coolness so much as coldness, which could be mistaken for coolness if you weren't careful, or if you happened to be a crazy neighbor who happened to like him.

"And then," Weeks said, "he comes in here one night looking like a ghost. Just like a ghost. Sits down in the chair—the one you're sitting on, and just sits. Sits and sits. Doesn't say anything. I think . . . I think, well . . ."

"Yeah? You think *what?*"

"I think maybe he wanted to be near someone, just that, just *near* them. And then after, oh, I don't know, an hour or so, he says, *I've got a case, Weeks. Not some runaway*—yes, I remember he says it just that way. *Not some runaway.*"

"So . . . ?"

"So I said, well, what is it, Jean? You look a little . . . sick. What is this case . . . ?"

"And?"

"*Big*. That's what he says. *Big. The biggest case of my life.* That's what he says and that's *all* he says."

So, William thought. The biggest case of his life. Again. The woman hadn't gotten it wrong. Two people, his neighbor and his neighborhood hooker, and he told it the same way to both of them. I'm not in runaways anymore, he says, I'm back in the big time.

"And nothing more?" William asked.

"Nothing. Nothing *said,* anyway. But after that, I saw a lot less of him . . ."

"Nothing about who *gave* him the case? Who hired him? Nothing?"

"No. Just walked in here and said he had the biggest case of his life. That's all. That's it."

"Okay," William said, wanting to get him back on track now, this track which had seemed to be going somewhere promising but now seemed to be going nowhere fast. "You saw a lot less of him . . ."

"Yes. Once, when he came in to borrow some medicine . . ."

"Medicine?"

"Yes. He burnt himself cooking."

"And then?"

"Then, not for a while. More than a couple of weeks. Then he just showed up again. He came in here and told me about the file, told me where he kept it, behind the radiator. And he told me if anything happens to him, in case he ever gets hit by a car, or has a safe fall on his head, to go in and get it. *Keep it,* he says. *Show it to no one. Promise me. It's my last testament, what I bequeath to you. Promise me.* So I did promise. And soon after that, it happened, his heart attack. And he died."

And you went in and took the file, William thought. The file *and* the pictures, a friend to the end.

It was nearly time to go. Sure it was. All the signs said so; the suffocating heat, the sobering quiet, the evident weariness of the storyteller. Time to shove off.

But William thought he'd take one more look at the file, one more shot at seeing if anything struck a bell with Mr. Weeks, the storyteller himself.

But Mr. Weeks didn't know even *one* of the names in

the file—*Samuels . . . Timinsky . . . Shankin . . . Winters*—
all strangers. He didn't know what the numbers meant
either—all of them mere mumbo jumbo. But when
William leafed backward and looked closely at the addresses, so carefully lettered in beneath each name and
above each red check, he suddenly realized that they
weren't *local* addresses. This one here was Miami. And
so was the next. And the next. And so on. All *Miami* addresses.

"All these people live in Miami," William said.

"Oh yeah," Mr. Weeks said.

"Oh yeah, *what?*"

"I think he went there."

"To *Miami?*" He had a sudden image of Jean at Sea
World maybe, of Jean munching bananas in the Keys.

"I'm not sure."

"What makes you think he went to *Miami* Mr. Weeks?"

"Well, he went *somewhere*. He said he'd been away. And
that last time he came to see me, he was *tan*. Not *just*
tan. It was the way he acted too. Like he'd been on the
best vacation of his life, rejuvenated kind of. Like he'd
found something."

"In Miami."

"I'm not sure," he said again.

Something wasn't right here.

"But why did you think it was *Miami?* I said all these
people live in Miami and you said *oh yeah*."

"I don't understand . . ."

"That's okay, Mr. Weeks. I *do*. You thought it was Miami
because you'd looked at the file and seen it there. You
said you didn't, but you did. You *peeked*."

Weeks looked just a little sheepish now, maybe even kind of embarrassed. Anyway, he didn't look too well.

"You know what, Mr. Weeks?" It was starting to come together for him now, not perfectly together, not beyond a doubt and *eureka* together, but at least he had this theory now, a theory he was starting to like, was starting to become even a little fond of. "I think you did what Jean wanted you to do. He bequeathed it to you, didn't he? I think he wanted you to look. I think, in a way, he was counting on it. That's why he gave it to you. I think he was counting on something else too."

"*What?*" His eyes, his whole tired white face seemed to be asking him, pleading with him, in dire need of an answer. And quick. For William could suddenly see that this, *all* this, had been a great strain on him. Think about it. He'd been appointed keeper of the flame, but he'd never been told why or for how long.

"Maybe," William said, speaking slowly, laying it out now, not just for Weeks but for him, "he was hoping one day someone *else* would come knocking on your door, not just anyone, but someone you knew, maybe someone whose picture you'd seen. Maybe even an old Boy Scout asking for donations."

There it was. As theories went, it wasn't half bad. It even made a little sense. Anyway, it'd *do*. And now, it *was* time to go, he was absolutely sure of it. But he had one more question, just one.

"Mr. Weeks, why didn't you go to the funeral? You, his conscience, why didn't you go?"

"Oh," Mr. Weeks said, as if he'd just been asked something inexplicably stupid, because he *had,* "but I don't go out anymore. I haven't gone out in years. Not in years."

And William, looking at the heavily draped windows, so carefully battened down against the light, thought yes, he's telling the truth, isn't he. He'd been sitting in a kind of zombie land, a land of the living dead, without a single spring or a single daybreak, a world stuck in time. And now he thought that maybe he'd been sitting there for longer than he'd realized. Outside was the real world, all they really had, where things were born every minute, and where they died only with a struggle, and sometimes not even then. He could be mistaken, but he actually thought he had a smile plastered across his face. No kidding. All because he was leaving the darkness for blue skies, his red file clutched firmly under his arm. Okay, put it this way. He was, in a matter of speaking, coming home.

THIRTEEN

Rise and shine.
Up and at 'em.
Charge.
Ringggg.
It was, he supposed, the first time in a long time that he'd picked up a phone in anger.

"Directory Assistance—for what city?" the voice said. And all William could think of, other than the fact that the woman who eventually came on the line seemed pissed off for no discernible reason, was that the bill would be pretty steep, or, at least, more than he could afford.

Funny thing—the phone. For some time now, it had sort of been reduced to just another aid for the elderly— like those buzzers they put at the bedside of an invalid. Call it a symbol of his own increasingly feeble existence. All his calls: to Social Security, to Con Ed, to the VA, a late check, a high bill, were, of course, all cries for help.

Last night's call to that woman hadn't been different, just more alcoholic perhaps.

"Miami Directory Assistance," the woman intoned, slightly more pissed off than before.

So, okay, this was a cry for help too. But this was offense instead of defense, action instead of reaction; this felt different. Though there was always the chance, William thought now, that he was kidding himself. Back as he was in the real world, there was always that chance, and given his track record, that likelihood.

Back in the real world, you can fail. Absolutely.

He'd fed the operator the first name in the file, and she'd answered "No such listing."

Okay, the fifth word in the Boy Scout Pledge: I promise to be faithful, loyal, thrifty (that one wasn't hard), courteous, and *diligent*.

Diligently, he fed her two more names. Which turned out to be the limit for one call. So he called back. And guess who came back on the line? You guessed it. But interestingly enough, it seemed that her level of courtesy began to increase in direct proportion to his level of futility. He could swear it did. As each name came back empty, her responses to him became more sympathetic, as if she sensed his frustration and was trying to soothe it.

"I'm sorry, sir, there isn't any listing under Joseph Waldron," she said in answer to his ninth, *tenth?* . . . inquiry.

Several names turned up several numbers, but those names lived at addresses different from the ones listed in Jean's file. What the hell—he took them anyway.

Finally though, the list was exhausted. And so was he.

It was past ten. The boarding house had long ago settled in for the night. He could just make out the buzz of Mr. Leonati's TV; it sounded like June bugs flying kamikaze-like into a zapper. Outside, someone was bouncing a basketball; someone else was giggling; two cats were screwing each other in the alley.

They were the same sounds he heard every night, more or less. But they didn't *sound* the same. Think about it. They were like the commotion of a neighborhood parade— July 4th maybe, the kind that used to make his pulse pound with excitement till he grew old and it made his head pound instead. From wanting to join up to wanting to tune out in the blink of an eye. But *now?* He'd say he was definitely in the wanting-to-join-up camp again. Yes, now there was a parade down there that he wouldn't mind joining, or at least tagging along with for a while. Nope, he wouldn't mind that at all. Then again, he wasn't exactly *Toby Tyler* anymore and this running-after-parades stuff took a bunch of things he'd thought he was fresh out of. Like *hope* for instance. Yeah, he was running a little low on hope these days. Still . . .

He dialed the first number: a Mrs. Ross.

"Hello," a woman answered.

"Am I speaking to Mrs. Ross—to Mrs. Alma Ross?"

"That's right. Alma Ross. What can I do for you?"

"You've got it backward," William said. "I'm about to do something for you. For if you're the Alma Ross, lately of 1629 Collins Drive, you're due for some money. An inheritance actually."

"I don't live at 1629 Collins Drive."

"No, of course not. But you did, didn't you, at one time?"

"I don't live at Collins Drive," she said again. "What inheritance?"

"Oh," he said, sounding very disappointed, which, actually, he was. "Perhaps there's been a mistake. You weren't contacted by our representative—a Mr. Jean Goldblum?"

"Never heard of him."

"And you never lived at 1629 Collins Drive?"

"No."

"Then there *has* been a mistake. I'm sorry for bothering you."

"What inheritance was that—"

He hung up, then put a line through her name. Different addresses, different people. Well, he thought, what had he expected?

He tried the other three as well. Two of them were home, one wasn't, but the two that were home weren't the two he wanted. One of them wanted to know if this was his cousin *Bob*, prankster *Bob*, the other one sounded nearly catatonic and wouldn't have cared if he'd just been told he'd won the lottery. Both had never lived where the file indicated they did, both had never heard from representative Goldblum.

A blank. Yet Jean had gone to Florida and Jean had found something there. *Rejuvenated*, Weeks had said. And there they were, a check under each name, a red check too, red to match the file, to indicate he was coming into the home stretch. But where exactly was he coming *from*?

It seemed like irony itself, as if irony had said ho hum *let's go pay a visit on old William*, when later that night, sitting before his rather shaky rabbit-eared TV which tended to sputter and reduce its picture to a single line across the screen, a commercial for Florida came on.

This time the picture held, this time the only sputtering was *his*. A dreary-looking man on a dreary-looking street on a dreary-looking summer day. A crowded subway ride, a sweltering walk through human traffic, followed by him slinking into the house as if he'd just been raped, or as if he'd committed one. Then, sparkling blue waters, oiled-up girls on pastel lounges, on water skis, on *view*, and the man, no longer dreary-looking, but looking pretty good indeed, looking like someone who's just screwed the Playmate of the Month and doesn't care who knows it. *When you need it bad,* someone sang, *we've got it good.*

Yes, William thought. You could say I need it bad. You could say that.

And now, suddenly, it seemed to him that he'd reached the moment of truth. In the old days, Julie—or Sandra or Lillian or Miss Whoever (whichever underpaid, overworked minion happened to have the bad fortune to be employed as their Three Eyes secretary at that particular time)—would always buzz them exactly five minutes after a client walked in. It took five minutes to know if a client was legitimate or just crazy, to know if he or she could pay you or couldn't (craziness and poverty both being sins, though not equal ones, poverty taking precedence). In five minutes they'd answer Julie or Lillian or whoever's call, and either tell the client that they'd have to get back to them—urgent business and such—or tell their secretary to get lost—*how many times do I have to tell you not to bother me when I'm with a client.* Three Eyes secretaries took a lot of abuse then. This five-minute system had been Santini's idea—William had gone along with it only reluctantly, because being less perceptive than Jean, and less brutal than Santini—who opened every interview by stating his fee—he found he often needed more than five minutes to tell whether a client was legitimate or not, and even then he often lacked the heart to refuse them.

But sometimes, that's what he did.

And now, he felt as if the five minutes were up and Julie was waiting on the line. The client was sitting across from him, but the client was dead, so it wouldn't matter if he told him that he'd have to get back to him, would it? He could show *this* client the door and not feel a thing.

But that, of course, wasn't exactly true, or at least, not true anymore. This client really needed him, sure, but while Jean might be the client, Jean might not be. What needed him was him. *He* was the client. Okay, he knew it sounded silly. He knew after years of playing the wall-flower, he had no business trying to get back out on the dance floor. It's not like they were still doing the rhumba out there either. Or even the boogaloo. He knew he was liable to trip over his two left feet. On the other hand he knew if he said goodbye to this client, if he said sorry, have to get back to you, if he showed *this* client out, he'd be slamming the door on you know who. Again. And for good.

We didn't much like each other, he'd said to Weeks, *but we covered for each other.*

So maybe now he had to cover for himself, do *himself* a professional courtesy.

Which meant, crazy as it seemed, that he just might have to take a trip. Either that, or take a sedative. Or at the very least, take a night to sleep on it.

That's what he'd do—he'd sleep on it.

The only problem was, he couldn't. He tried counting sheep. Then he tried counting glasses of Jim Beam. Then he tried *drinking* glasses of Jim Beam. No dice. Now that he had the old heart pumping, it was proving difficult to shut down. He'd forgotten how annoying the old heart could be, how it wanted what it wanted and *fongul* to everything else.

Now what. The first ghostly light of morning was already wafting through his venetian blinds. The first traffic horns were already crowing. When he opened his refrigerator he stared point-blank at an absolutely empty container of OJ.

Now if that wasn't a sign, what was? Oh well—he supposed he'd just have to go down to Florida to get another one.

Okay. He had several thousand dollars put away in the bank. Burial money, he'd thought. He had a life insurance policy, and his monthly Social Security, and a little stock that sometimes paid dividends and sometimes didn't.

He had a theory that wasn't half bad.

He had a file red as blood.

He had a reason. He had a cause.

He had a screwed-up shoulder.

He had a recently addled brain.

All things being equal though, he had a *chance*.

He didn't know what planes to Florida cost these days, he didn't know what planes to anywhere cost these days, but he could find out. Sure he could—he had a phone, didn't he? Perhaps there were midweek specials, perhaps there were senior citizen rates. Maybe he'd just hitch a ride there.

We've got it good.
Okay. Let's hope so.

He wrote a note for Mr. Brickman asking him not to
worry when he knocked on his door and received no answer, that he shouldn't break it down or call the police
or summon the firemen, that it wouldn't be because he'd
dropped dead but because he'd stepped out. Visiting relatives in Florida, he wrote. Only Mr. Brickman wasn't at
the park feeding pigeons, when he slid the note under
his door. He was on the other side of the door, and he
read the note with William standing there. *What relatives?*
he asked, but didn't wait for William to answer. Instead
he asked him if he wouldn't mind stopping by Boca Raton
and looking in on his friend Lizzie, who seemed to be
doing fine down there but had proved difficult to get hold
of. *I'm going to Miami,* William told him, *not Boca Raton,*
and Mr. Brickman said *thanks for telling me* and closed
the door. From Mr. Leonati he borrowed a suitcase, brown,
with stickers from nearly everywhere under the sun plastered across its worn surface like unusually colorful mask-
ing tape. *Florida,* William answered when Mr. Leonati
asked him where he was going. *To visit relatives.*

*Coral Gardens, Disney World, Universal Studios, and Sea
World,* Mr. Leonati told him, then wrote them down on
a piece of paper. *The must-sees.*

William said he didn't know if he'd have the time, but
if he did, he'd be sure to look them over.

Watch your wallet, Mr. Leonati admonished him as he
lugged the suitcase out the door. *Watch your wallet.*

FOURTEEN

Miami blues.

His next and very last break came later in the day, and when he most needed it. For the list was finally exhausted, done, completed, finito; so was he. The remaining addresses had been as barren as the first, and like a mailman on an unfamiliar route he was learning the terror of ignorance. Neither rain, nor sleet, nor hail—*maybe,* but ignorance, that was the kicker.

Someone was moving houses on him, turning *hooch houses* into vacant lots, sweet-sounding streets into slums. No one was where they were supposed to be, everyone was somewhere else. It was entirely possible someone was laughing at him. He could just about hear it every time he got in and out of the car, a process, by the way, that seemed to take longer and longer as the day went on, so that by the end of the day he wasn't so much getting out of the car as falling out of it.

He felt like giving up and going back to sleep. The fact was, Florida just wasn't working out the way he'd hoped. For if he'd come to find what Jean had, he'd found nothing, and if that was what Jean had found too—then he clearly lacked the knowledge to know what that meant.

It's what I bequeath to you, Jean had told Mr. Weeks. *My last testament.* But the testament was in code; the list was like the Book of the Dead, and not a Rosetta stone in sight.

I'm not in runaways anymore, Jean had said. No, just in missing persons. For that's what the biggest case of his life was turning out to be. A missing persons case. For there wasn't anyone on the list who *wasn't* missing— and come to think of it, everything else was too. For instance: a client. No one had come forward to claim Jean as their own. Whoever Jean was working for either didn't know he was dead, or didn't much care. Okay, maybe they *didn't* know—it hadn't been long. Maybe soon enough they'd come forward to offer their condolences— or at the very least, to ask for their money back. And yet, William didn't think so. There was, as Santini used to say, only because his favorite tough-guy actors in the movies used to say it, something *fishy* here. It had nothing to do with proximity to the water.

It had to do with a file that Jean had passed on like you pass on an heirloom in a bankrupt estate—one step before the tax collectors arrive. And it had to do with a crisscrossed map that was like one blind alley, and someone who came walking out of it with his eyes open. *Rejuvenated,* Weeks said.

Okay.

You find what you look for, Jean used to say. So be sure

you look for the right thing. Which isn't what he said, but is what he meant.

Okay. I'm looking.

But whether it was his failing eyesight, or just his general *failing,* he saw only questions. And like a test he hadn't studied for—Missing Persons 101, say—the questions mocked him, absolutely stuck their tongues out at him. And not a crib sheet around.

And yet it couldn't have been more than a few minutes later when he remembered the number with no response; he'd tried *four* numbers in New York where the same name had a different address. Two had been home— three, including Alma Ross—but one *hadn't.*

He dug into his wallet looking for the right slip of paper, hoping he hadn't thrown it out or left it home or simply lost it.

There—stuck between two wrinkled fives. Mr. Alfred Koppleman: 791-8350. There.

He picked up the phone and dialed.

Good things come to those who wait: page G of Jean's little black book.

He'd finished dialing Mr. Koppleman's number, but it was a woman who picked up the phone. So when he asked her if an Alfred Koppleman, lately of 1620 Fuller Drive, resided there, he fully expected her to say no.

But she didn't.

Instead she said, "Not anymore. He used to," she added, "but not anymore."

And did she know perhaps where Mr. Koppleman *did* reside now?

"Sure," she said. "He's in a home."

A home?

"That's right. An old age home."

And did she know where this old age home *was*?

"Yes," she said. She did. Then she put down the phone for half a minute or so, came back on the line, and told him.

"Thank you," William said. "Thank you, thank you, thank you." Thanking her, thanking Alfred, thanking a suddenly benevolent universe.

"Sure," she said. "But who is this—?"

But William had already hung up to dial his old friends at Miami Directory Assistance.

FIFTEEN

Golden Meadows. That's what it was called. And true to everything else in misnomerville these days—thinking, for example, of *Magnolia* Drive and *Peachtree* Lane, there wasn't a meadow in sight. Instead, there were liquor stores sealed with black metal bars as if waiting to be carted away to another location; there were grocery stores with taped-up windows; a completely gutted Dunkin' Donuts; and what appeared to be half a 7-Eleven—more like a 3-Five then. The most dignified-looking building in Golden Meadows land was a pawnshop whose front window was filled floor to ceiling with seven different kinds of crap.

And excepting for the yellowed strips of paint that were peeling off its walls in bunches, there was nothing golden about Golden Meadows either. It looked, then, just like an old age home should look—like a place to wither and die, in the kind of neighborhood where death of any kind wouldn't even slow traffic.

William arrived there at twelve sharp. The first thing he noticed was the look. Yes, absolutely; when he walked through the door—the very *second* he walked through the door—he was met by the look. What *kind* of look was it? This kind. The kind of look used car salesmen give to rubes. Think of it this way. He was a visitor, sure, but to them he was something else. Another customer, a future resident. Why, they probably had a nicely soiled cot all ready and waiting for him.

It was over ninety outside, and not all that much better inside, but he shivered as if doused in ice water.

He walked over to the front desk where folded wheel-chairs sat like shopping carts all in a row. A woman was waiting there, the woman who'd stared at him with preda-tory sweetness, and for just a moment William was ren-dered speechless. Words were told to report front and center, but they insisted on playing hide-and-seek with him. Okay, he was scared.

Once everyone's greatest fear was to die alone, uncared for, with no one there to hold your hand. But things had changed. Sure they had. Now there was something worse than dying alone, much worse. Dying *here*. In a place like this. Golden Meadows.

There were a whole bunch of things they talked about back home in the Astoria boarding house. The generally shitty state of the city, the generally shitty state of the Mets, the truly crappy state of their prostates. Among other things. But there were some things they never talked about. Things like old age homes. Things like that. The word had taken on the taboo aura of cancer; if you spoke

it, it might *happen* to you. Old age homes were like concentration camps—they knew they were there, sure, but
no one admitted it.

And now, standing there in the dimly lit lobby filled
with wheelchairs, black orderlies, and two residents
who'd drifted in with walkers and were mumbling, both
of them, at the floor, William felt the panic, the sheer
dread, of someone who's been shown his final resting
place.

"Yes?" the woman said to him, in a voice cool as ice.
"What can we do for you?"

"I called," William said, his voice suddenly back, and
with it, his mission, piss-poor as it was. "I called about
Mr. Koppleman. Alfred Koppleman. I'm here to say hi."

"Oh, yes. I'm sure our Mr. Koppleman will be very
happy to have a visitor."

William was sure *their* Mr. Koppleman would too; who
wouldn't?

She picked up a phone. "Trudy . . . we have a visitor
here for Mr. Koppleman."

She put the phone down softly as if afraid of scaring
someone, then said, "There's a visiting room through the
swinging doors. Why don't you make yourself comfortable and we'll send Mr. Koppleman out to you. Oh," she
said just as William turned away, "have you bought anything for Mr. Koppleman?"

"Bought? No," William said, "I haven't. Why?"

"We like to see everything our visitors bring here."

"Why's that?"

"There's a good reason for it, Mr. . . . ?"

"Jones."

"There's a good reason for it, Mr. Jones. Some people

bring boxes of cookies or candy, and they want it to go to the person they brought it for."

"Doesn't it?"

"Perhaps you've never been to a retirement home before," she said, a little too sweetly. "Our residents fight over things like that. You bring a box of cookies in there and five minutes later it's eaten. *And* someone's hurt. They are," she said, "a little like children."

And soon enough, her eyes seemed to be saying to him, *you'll be like that too.*

"Trust me," she continued. "We ask people who bring things to leave them here at the desk. We make sure it goes to the person it was brought for."

"Fine. But I don't have anything for Mr. Koppleman," William said, repeating himself, eager to end the conversation.

"No, Mr. Jones, you don't."

He turned then, and walked through the white swinging doors and into the visiting room. *It's a nice place to visit,* he remembered Mr. Leonati saying about Florida, *but you wouldn't want to live there.* You wouldn't want to live in the Golden Meadows Retirement Home, but you wouldn't want to *visit* it either; you wouldn't even want to visit the *visiting* room, *especially* the visiting room. Once upon a time, someone had tried to spruce it up with warmer colors, yellow and peach and pink, but that had been once upon a time, and the colors had faded to mere ghosts of their former selves, a little like the residents of Golden Meadows. Four or five of whom were scattered around the visiting room like props, waiting only for the arrival of an audience. Two of them were watching the lone TV without expression. *Which is it,* the toothy MC was saying, *the door on the left or the door on the right?* The two watchers had reached the age where they'd grown wise to this sort of con game; they knew that both doors eventually led to the same place—to here.

Another man sat by the window, staring down at his shoes, his right arm hooked to an IV. He, at least, had a visitor, the only visitor in the visiting room besides him— a young girl, his granddaughter, William guessed, who was trying to make conversation. She *was* making conversation, only it was just a bit one-sided. The only voice he heard was hers.

"So we took Sam to the veterinarian," she was saying, "and the veterinarian said he had worms or something, you know the way Sam scratches himself, you remember, don't you . . ."

But if her grandfather remembered, he didn't say so.

William sat down on the metal bridge chair furthest from everyone.

"Jack!" Someone, William suddenly realized, was calling out to him.

It was one of the men by the television.

"Jack," he repeated, staring at William with a rabid expression. "Jack, you old . . . you old . . . Jack . . ."

"Sorry," William said, feeling the old dread again, pulling at him like something drowning. "I'm not Jack."

"Yes you are . . . yes you are . . . yes you are . . . you're Jack . . ."

"Okay," William said. "I'm Jack."

"You don't say . . . you don't say . . . where's my candy, Jack . . . where's my candy . . . ?"

"I don't have it."

"Where . . . where . . . where . . . where's my candy . . . ?"

A black orderly wandered in.

"Now, Mr. Bertram, you *know* that's not Jack. Now when does Jack visit you?"

"Saturday . . . Saturday . . . Saturday . . ."

"That's right. You know what day it is today?"

"Saturday . . . Saturday . . . . Saturday . . ."

"No. Today is *Thursday,* Mr. Bertram. That's right. Jack will be here Saturday. You'll get your candy then."

Mr. Bertram seemed satisfied with that; he turned back to the TV.

A minute or so later, they wheeled in Mr. Koppleman.

William's first impression was that Mr. Koppleman didn't belong there. His eyes seemed much too alert, and his body, chairbound though it was, seemed much too sprightly. He actually wheeled himself in—two orderlies trailing him like Muslim wives, his arms, too long for his blue pajama sleeves, working the wheels like nobody's business.

He was looking right *at* William, another sign that senility hadn't claimed him just yet, that he knew, at least, a stranger when he saw one.

"You here for Mr. Koppleman?" one of the orderlies asked him.

"That's right."

"He's all yours, man." The orderly had a *Hustler* magazine tucked into his coat pocket. William could make out one large nipple and a pair of *fuck me* glossy lips. The orderly pulled it out of his pocket and flopped himself down in a chair at the end of the room. The other orderly went over to the man sitting with his granddaughter and without a word to either one of them grabbed the back of the wheelchair and began to roll it toward the door.

"I wasn't done talking to him," the girl said. "I didn't say goodbye."

"What's the difference," the orderly said without looking back at her, "he ain't gonna hear you anyway."

"He *does* hear me . . ." the girl said. "He does . . ."

But the orderly had already pushed him through the door and didn't bother answering her. He *too* wasn't hearing her anymore.

Mr. Koppleman chuckled.

"He *doesn't* hear her," he said. "He's not . . . aware anymore."

"No," William said, his attention back where it belonged. "But *you're* aware, Mr. Koppleman, aren't you?"

"Of everything," Mr. Koppleman said. His skin was the most unearthly white, William noticed, white as milk. "I'm aware, for instance, that I don't know you. I don't think I've forgotten you—pretty sure I haven't forgotten you—so it must be I never met you."

"My name's William," and he stopped here, not exactly sure what to say, quickly roaming through his grab bag of friendly lawyers, representatives, and old acquaintances. "I'm here about a friend. Someone, I think, you *did* meet."

"Well, I've met a lot of people, you know. More than a dozen. More than two dozen. Could even be as high as a hundred. How's that?"

Okay, William realized now, so maybe he wasn't *that* alert. Maybe he was slipping just a little. Maybe it wasn't exactly brightness he'd seen in Koppleman's eyes then, but the kind of glow a bulb gets just before it burns out for good. And now he wondered if Jean had seen it too.

"The person I'm talking about, you would've met real recently. No more than a month ago. His name was Jean. Jean Goldblum. What do you say. Does that ring a bell . . . ?"

"What sort of bell?"

"Your memory, Mr. Koppleman. I need to know what you remember. Now take *me*. Sometimes I forget what I did this morning. But when I meet an interesting person, that's different. Then I don't forget a thing. Are you like that?"

"There are church bells. Doorbells. Bicycle bells. Jingle bells. And wedding bells . . . those too."

"Yeah, Mr. Koppleman," William said, feeling the exasperation of someone who's passed countless *Food Just Ahead* signs down the pike only to find the place burnt to the ground when he gets there. It was the sort of hunger that could ruin your day.

"Alpine bells. Bluebells. Cowbells. Wedding bells—did I mention those . . . ?"

"Uh huh."

"My wife," Mr. Koppleman said, "was a lovely woman. My greatest pleasure was watching her before a mirror. I don't remember her face now, but I remember the way she put her hair up every morning before the mirror. With tortoiseshell clips. So elegant. There's a mystery there in women, that has to do with the way they put themselves together."

It was a little like listening to a faulty radio, William thought as Koppleman talked on, a radio that keeps drifting from one station to another completely at random. First the news, then some music, a three-six-three double play, then back to the latest bombing in Bosnia. Though not entirely at random, for it seemed to be words that set him off in one direction or another, like those word association tests psychiatrists use to see which way the mind jumps. *Wedding bells* had made him positively *leap,* race way back to a time when his wife put her hair up so elegantly before a dresser mirror. And getting him to jump back was going to be hard—for despite his impatience, despite his hunger, despite the fact that all he had was Mr. Koppleman, who didn't exactly have his faculties in full working order, he felt just a little callous here, like a burglar sifting through the family jewels, flinging them left and right in an effort to find the right one. Mr. Koppleman's memories might mean Jack crap to him, but to Mr. Koppleman they were pure gold. But there was no choice—those taillights were already rounding the corner, while William sat stuck at a traffic light. He'd have to lead Mr. Koppleman back. No two ways about it. He'd have to lay a few crumbs along the way maybe, then lead him back, the way you tempt a wary cat back into the house. *Here kitty . . . kitty . . .*

"So, Mr. Koppleman," he said now. "Your wife? She been gone long?"

"I don't remember."

"Losing our loved ones—that's tough . . ." trying to guide him back into the past, but suddenly bringing himself there first, imagine that, Rachel sitting there clear as day, and smiling at him too.

"I don't remember," Mr. Koppleman repeated.

"Take *me* again. I lost my wife too." Well, he *had,* hadn't he? Lost her in a motel on Utopia Parkway and never *could* find her again.

"Sorry to hear it."

"Yeah. And that's not even mentioning all the *friends* I've lost."

"I've got a bunch."

"That's good, Mr. Koppleman. Wish I did." And he *did* too.

"I've got a bunch of friends. The thing is, we keep missing each other. They come to visit me but I never *see* them."

"Sure. That happens."

"I've got to straighten that out."

"Yeah. You ever get to see *anybody?*"

"Sometimes."

"Like who . . . ?"

"I've got to straighten it out. Talk to the management here . . ."

"Tell you what," William said. "I'll talk to them for you."

"*What . . . ?*"

"Who came to visit you, Mr. Koppleman?"

"You'll talk to them for me?"

"Sure."

"About *what . . . ?*"

"I'll straighten it out for you."

"Somebody's got to."

"Who came to visit you?"

"What are you talking about?"

"You said sometimes you got to see visitors. *Who?*"

"What did your wife die of?"

"Loneliness, I think." And Rachel nodded, then finally left the room. So long, Rachel. So long.

"I don't remember," Mr. Koppleman said.

"You don't remember *what?*"

"Who came to visit me."

"I'll throw out a name here. Jean Goldblum."

"Who?"

"Jean. Jean Goldblum. He's dead now."

"Sorry to hear it."

"Yeah. But I think he came to see you."

"You said he's dead."

"*Before* he died."

"*What?*"

"Holy shit!" The orderly was dangling the *Hustler* centerfold in front of a glazed-eyed resident now. "Look at that." He turned it around and kissed it somewhere south of her belly button. "Sweet . . ."

"Mr. Koppleman?"

"Yes?"

"Hello."

"Hello."

"Jean Goldblum came to see you. Remember?"

"Maybe."

"What did he want?"

"I'm not sure."

"You're not sure?"

"I'm not sure he came to see me."

Okay, he'd never been very good at the tango. Now Santini, he could cut the rug like nobody's business. But *him*—he was in dire need of a few Arthur Murrays.

"Come on, Mr. Koppleman. Think. I'm in trouble here. I need your help."

"Okay."

"Jean Goldblum came to see you. They brought you in here just like this. You had no idea who he was maybe.

Maybe you said get me out of here. But he said wait a minute. Listen to me. I need to know something. Help me out here. So you did. Maybe he even thanked you afterward."

"Sure."

"You remember, don't you?"

"Maybe."

"Well then." He leaned forward now, close enough to whisper in his ear, close enough to kiss him. "What did he ask you? *What?*"

"He asked me why I'd been spared."

"What?"

"He asked me why I'd been spared. Me, out of everyone."

"Spared, Mr. Koppleman? By *who?*"

Do you go for the box, or what's behind curtain number two, the TV MC was saying. The black orderly had thrown his *Hustler* down on the chair and joined the other men by the television.

"Go for the curtain," he said now, and laughed, "go for the gold, baby."

"Good question," Mr. Koppleman said.

"What did he mean?"

"Good question."

"Come on, Alfred. Stay with me."

"He thought I knew something."

"That's right."

"He badgered me."

"What did he think you knew?"

"Good question."

"He asked you why were you spared. *You.* Out of everyone."

"He badgered me."

"Do you know who *everyone* was?"

"Good question."

"I do. I know who they are."

"Who?"

He pulled the map out of his pocket. "Alma Ross . . . Joseph Waldron . . . Arthur Shankin . . . Mrs. Winters . . ." ticking them off one by one, hoping the names, like sign-posts, might lead him home—might lead the both of them there.

"See, Mr. Koppleman. *Everyone.*"

"Okay."

"*They* weren't spared. That's what Jean knew. That's what Jean found out here, isn't it? But *you* were."

"*What?*"

"You were spared."

"By who?"

"Good question." He felt drained. Yes he did. A couple of times around the dance floor and he was ready for the oxygen tent. "Mr. Koppleman?"

"Yes."

"Hello."

"Hello."

"*Who* were they?"

"Who were who?"

"Those people. The ones who weren't spared. Do you know them?"

"Do I know *who?*"

"These people."

"What people?"

Okay, Mr. Koppleman had left him. Sure he had. Scurried up a telephone pole, danced along the wire, and was smiling at him—like the Cheshire Cat.

William kept at it—for a little while more he did, tried this and that to get him down, but although he tried every way he knew and for longer than he should've, it was no go. Even the fire department couldn't get him down now. So he gave up.

The black orderly was fiddling with the TV dial, switching it back and forth with a vengeance.

"I'm done," William called out to him. And, in a way, he was.

"Leave him there," the orderly said. "I told him to go for the curtain, so he keeps the box and gets skunked."

"Yeah," William said. "What a shame."

"Just leave him there . . ."

William looked down at Mr. Koppleman, *down,* because he'd already gotten up to go.

"Take it easy," he said. But he didn't think Mr. Koppleman heard him.

"I've got to straighten this out," he said.

You and me both, William thought. You and me both.

There were just a few more places to go before he left Miami.

He called the number again, the last place Koppleman had lived before he'd been put out to pasture in Golden Meadows. He told the woman he was coming to see her.

She was, it turned out, the landlord. But not of much. The neighborhood was, if anything, a step down from the one he'd just left—which was saying something. And the building she lorded it over didn't put up much of an argument to change your mind. It was a sort of transient hotel, what they used to refer to in the old days as a fleabag, back before roaches relegated fleas to second banana in the order of household pests. There was a big one just inside the front steps—about the size of a good Havana cigar. It was taking a midday stroll on a stained carpet the color of pea soup. Two men with paper bags in their hands sat there staring at it like handicappers watching the pre-race walk-through.

"Bless you," one of the men said to William when he walked by, his hand out for donations, echoing the girl in white shorts from earlier. William put a dollar bill in it, wondering what he was going to do with all those blessings; maybe he could hold some in reserve for a rainy day.

The woman sat inside a glass-enclosed cubicle, watching a small TV.

"Excuse me," William said, talking through a hole he assumed was for that purpose.

"Twelve-fifty a night," she said. "Just like it says outside. We close the doors at eleven sharp and no funny business in the rooms."

"I don't want a room," William said.

"Then you came to the wrong place," she said, irritatingly, looking at the TV. "If you were going to the beach, you're lost. If you were going to the dog races, you took the wrong turn."

William said, "I came to talk to you about Mr. Koppleman."

Now, at last, she looked up at him.

"So?" she said.

"So?"

"So what about Mr. Koppleman. This is a television.

This is the *Guiding Light*. I watch the *Guiding Light* every day—I've watched it every day for twenty years. So what about Mr. Koppleman?"

"When," William said, looking at his watch, "is it over?"

"Three."

"Fine. I'll wait."

He walked back to the only open chair in the lobby and sat down. There was a fan in the glass cubicle, but there wasn't a fan anywhere else. In five minutes he went from perspiration to actual rainfall. No kidding. He was slowly creating his own lake, Lake William; people would be able to rent rowboats on it and take a nice Sunday afternoon picnic by its shores. It would be listed in Mr. Leonati's guidebook under Florida attractions, right up there with Elmo's Alligator Farm and the Official Ripley's Believe It Or Not Museum. If he were especially lucky, it might even *make* the museum.

At three o'clock, he sloshed back over to the glass booth but the television was still on.

"*General Hospital*," she said.

"All right," William said, "all right." He took out his wallet and counted out twenty dollars, then held it up where she could see it.

"Great," she said. "I'll go right out and order the fur."

She took forty. (The equivalent, by the way, of six frozen Shakeys Pizzas, eight chicken pot pies, six cans of Chef Boyardee spaghetti, two loaves of bread, eleven cans of Bumble Bee tuna—or about two good weeks of eating. Not that he wasn't buying something nourishing here.)

He asked her how long Mr. Koppleman had lived there.

Long.

And who'd put him into Golden Meadows.

His son.

And why?

Have you seen Mr. Koppleman? He was starting to walk into walls.

And if he'd always lived in Florida?

Uh uh. New York.

And why'd he leave New York for here?

Because his doctor recommended it. Because he liked the Dolphins. Because he was old. Who knows. That's what old people do. Aren't you here?

And then just one more thing.

Yes?

What part of New York had Mr. Koppleman come from?

Flushing.

Yes, William said. Yes.

Now there was one place left to go. Just one.

He drove out of the city, out of the greater Miami area, down U.S. 1 to Homestead.

Years ago, someone had mentioned that that's where he'd gone. To Homestead. That you could find him almost any day of the week down at the public golf course practicing his short game.

William counted down the miles as he neared the city limits, and when he grew tired of counting down the miles, he started counting down the years.

Then he gave up.

The public golf course was easy to find—Florida was good about things like that. Lots of signs directing you to lots of places you really didn't want to go.

But when he got there, he was right where they'd said he be. Only today, he was practicing his drives, banging them this way and that, trying to get the club handle around a belly that was starting to resemble the Pills-bury Doughboy's. William wondered if he still drummed his fingers across it, still imitated all those tough guys that only popped up on late-night TV now.

Actually, William wondered about a lot of things.

He was trying to think of the right greeting. What you say to someone who you haven't seen in an eternity. What you say to someone who you used to work with, used to tail like Tinker Bell on his trips to Never-Never Land. And he was trying to think of something that he'd *never* been able to think of. What you say to someone who's fucked your wife.

But he needn't have bothered. Santini turned and saw him first.

"What do you know," he said. "It must be old home month."

Santini looked like an old duffer. Shocking. Except that's what *he* looked like too. Oh yeah.

"How are you, Santini?"

"Down to an eighteen handicap," he said. "Not too shabby. You play?"

"No."

"Sure. You can never get on a course up there. I re-member."

Santini turned and sliced another one into the tree line. "Shit. You'd think I wouldn't do that anymore."

"It's a hard game."

"You can say that again." Santini turned back around.

"You know, you don't look *too* terrible. Kept the weight off at least."

"Yeah."

"Want to grab a beer?"

"Why not."

Santini led him to a refreshment stand dotted with white plastic tables, almost all of them filled with other old duffers who looked just like him. "How's it goin'?" a few of them muttered as they passed by with two tepid beers.

They found a table to themselves at the back of the terrace.

"So," William said, "Jean came to say hello." *Old home month*, Santini had said. His first look at William in God knows how long and that's what he'd said.

"Yeah." Santini took a long swallow. "Ahhh."

"What did he want?"

"You know Jean. Who knows?"

"Yeah. I know Jean."

"He said he was working on a case."

"What did *you* say?"

"I laughed. I think."

"He *was*."

"Was *what?*"

"Working on a case."

"Well, what do you know." Santini took another swallow.

"Did he mention anything about anything?"

"I didn't ask. I don't play detective anymore. I play golf."

"Sure."

"How about you, William? You working on a case *too?*"

"He's dead, Santini. Jean died."

Santini took another swallow, but if the first one had been long, this one was longer, *real* long, and after he finished, he put the glass down slowly, *real* slow.

"Yeah, well, that seems to be happening to everybody I know, isn't it. What happened—he get hit by a bus?"

"Heart attack."

"Couldn't be. He didn't have one."

"Maybe he developed one right at the end."

"Not a chance. *You* were always the one with the heart. Remember?"

"I remember."

"And you still have it, I bet. Is that what this is all about? You taking over for Jean—for old times' sake?"

"For old times' sake."

"Well, be careful, William. When I laughed at him, Jean said he hadn't lost it. Maybe. But *you* never had it. Understand—one friend to another."

"Sure. I'll be careful."

Then they started talking about old times, lots of old times, all the old times except, of course, *one*. But then, after a half hour or so, it was as if the gulf of missing years began to widen, till they were both on opposite shores, shouting to be heard but too far away to be understood. And they were just two old guys who used to know each other.

Santini began to play with his driver, twisting it this way and that, executing phantom half swings at the slate tile floor. William finished his beer, wiped his mouth, and got up.

"Well, it was nice to see you, Santini."

"You too, William."

He turned to go.

."William?"

William turned back around, *all* the way back around, thirty-five years back around.

"It could've been anybody, William. Understand? Anybody. I'm just sorry it was me."

"Yeah," William said. "So am I, Santini. So am I."

SIXTEEN

To begin then, begin at the beginning.

The very beginning. Construct a scenario, one scene at a time, follow it through to the final curtain, and if you don't applaud—if you don't stand up and give it a goddamn ovation, start over.

If it's too much to swallow, Jean used to say, *spit it out.*

He was home now. Back in his apartment. And though he'd only been gone three days, it felt like three years. At *least.* He hadn't just come back older either, maybe wiser too.

No one had been there to greet him, which was just as well, since he hadn't been in the mood for it, and wouldn't have had anything to say. *They,* however, would have had a lot to say to him; Mr. Wilson had died. Chalk up another one for the carnivores. They weren't there because they were all at his funeral. It was, he heard later, a dignified, if sparsely attended, affair.

To begin then, begin at the beginning.

The first thing he'd done, the very first thing, even before unpacking or taking a shower or knocking one back, was enter Mr. Wilson's room like a thief in the night.

He knew Mr. Wilson had died the moment he walked into the room. Someone had put all of his possessions into boxes, one on top of the other, forming a kind of poor man's pyramid. His Harlequin collection took up two boxes by itself. His pictures had been taken off the walls, his clothing wrapped in plastic sheets, the floor swept clean. Mr. Wilson's death hadn't been tidy—he'd lasted for over a week, in and out, up and down—but what he'd left behind was. You could wrap it with a bow, you could give it the white glove test—it was suddenly as antiseptic as a newly available hospital bed.

William was there for a purpose, and even though his sudden knowledge of Mr. Wilson's death made him feel *more* like an intruder, and not less, and also, by the way, made him feel *diminished,* diminished by one fewer person who would ever share his bridge chair, purpose *stuck.* Mr. Wilson had been a collector of sorts, not just of Harlequins and Senior Citizen Workshop pamphlets, but of everything else. Like phone books, maybe. Not just this year's, but last year's, and even the years before that. That was his reason for being there, to see if Mr. Wilson's collection of knickknacks included Ma Bell.

He had to sift through several boxes, three in fact, before he found it *did.* The phone books went back fifteen years. Even the Yellow Pages. William put those aside, and carried the regular listings back to his room. He should've made two trips but he did it in one, groaning and grunting all the while (his shoulder was tormenting

him with particular vengeance today and arthritis had settled into his knee joints like an irritating relation that has
no intention of leaving).

To begin then, begin at the beginning.

It didn't take long to find what he was looking for.
Even though he had to go back ten years before the list
was complete. Then he had it, laid out before him in
black and white, another expression Santini was fond of
using, and understandably, since that was very much the
way he saw the world.

The phone book from ten years ago had them all. Koppleman to Winters—every last one of them. Shankin
dropped from the phone book a year later. Waldron and
Timinsky a year after that. Mrs. Winters—our lady of the
Christmas card—was next. Then a banner year—everyone exiting except Koppleman, who lasted until just two
years ago.

There—everyone present and accounted for, *sir.* Black
and white.

It suddenly seemed to him that he'd gone on a long
trip only to walk downstairs. They say a journey of a
thousand miles begins with one step, but he'd managed
to turn the aphorism on its head. His journey of one step
had *begun* with a thousand miles. The answer had been
in Mr. Wilson's phone books all the time, resting one floor
down while he sweated his way through southern Florida
like a tourist with a limited timetable. So much to see
and so little time to see it.

To begin then, begin at the beginning.

The beginning was Shankin. Chronologically speaking,
it began with him. So that's where he began too, starting
the very next day after a very bad night, beginning there,

then going through the list with chronological precision, excepting for Mrs. Winters, whom he tried third due to a hunch of his. By then, of course, the pattern was set in stone, and it wouldn't have mattered what order he'd gone in, the order being irrelevant, since the results were, in each and every case, the same.

They were all, each and every one of them, in Flushing. He took the same bus he'd taken a week before to Jean's funeral, and that he'd taken again to visit Rodriguez and Weeks. They were becoming old friends, the bus driver—a fat black woman—and him. She just about smiled at him when he climbed aboard. She nearly said hello and asked him where he got such a fancy tan. She almost refused to accept his money. Okay, so maybe they weren't *that* good friends, maybe he was taking a little license here, but a few more bus rides and who knew? This Flushing thing, after all, was getting to be a habit.

He walked down the same crowded streets, even recognized a few of the Chinese merchants, Korean fruit sellers, and Cambodian newsstand vendors. Old friends now, all of them. Even his fellow pedestrians seemed, well, a little *pedestrian* now, a little familiar, save for the fact they seemed to be moving a bit faster than before, as if they were running from the thunderstorm that was hiding somewhere in the inky clouds and cloying humidity. There were no shadows today, William noticed, but there should have been. Twelve shadows at least, maybe more.

Arthur Shankin. He'd lived in a modest building of red brick. A woman lay out in front on a green lawn chair; maybe once there'd even been a green lawn to go with it, but not now. It was all dirt and crabgrass now.

Yes, the woman said, she'd known Mr. Shankin. But *no,*

she hadn't known him well. *Try Mr. Greely,* she said, *Mr. Greely on the second floor—he and Mr. Shankin were friends.*

He checked for Mr. Greely's name on the mailboxes—2E—then went up the elevator.

"Glad to see you," Mr. Greely said, when he opened the door, a man of about eighty with a fairly nasty squint, "who are you?"

William explained: lawyer, inheritance, last address.

"Of course," Mr. Greely said. "Anything I can do."

Mr. Greely was, of course, his first stop of the day, but as it turned out he could've closed shop right then and there. For though he would make twelve other stops that day, twelve destinations on the William Express that would leave him tired and very wet—the rainstorm was but minutes away—he would learn no more and no less than he would from Mr. Greely. For each stop had its own Mr. Greely—the woman next door, the man downstairs, the friend down the hall, and the story Mr. Greely told would turn out to be pretty much the story they *all* told.

"He went to Florida," Greely said, "some time ago."

"Do you know where? Did he give you an address?"

"Oh sure." And Greely got it for him. It matched the address in Jean's file to a T, just as the other addresses he'd get from the other Mr. Greelys would too. Which wasn't really surprising, since that's precisely where Jean had gotten them from too.

"It seems like I did this before," Mr. Greely said, "but I don't know why? You know . . . déjà vu."

No, William thought, just *déjà Jean.*

It was Florida all over again. For he'd arrive at a place only to discover that Jean had been there first. He was still working backup, still following taillights in the dark.

"Do you keep in touch, Mr. Greely?" he asked. "Do you ever hear from Mr. Shankin?"

"Not really. He sent me a postcard after he got down there. The weather's fine, he said. The weather's fine and I'm fine."

"Was he?"

"Was he what?" Mr. Greely squinted at him.

"*Fine?*"

"I suppose."

"Did you answer him back?"

"What for? He knows what the weather's like up here."

William didn't know if Mr. Greely was trying to be funny or just *was*—funny in the head maybe, no one home, bats in the belfry, all those quaint terms for something so clearly terrifying. But he thought maybe Mr. Greely was neither—just funny by accident, like someone who's always slipping on banana peels.

"Is that why Mr. Shankin went down to Florida? For the weather?"

"I suppose."

"And you haven't heard from him since?"

"Nope."

"Why?"

"Why *what?*"

"Why do you think you haven't heard from him? After all, you were friends, weren't you? Wouldn't a friend write you again?"

Mr. Greely didn't seem to understand.

"I never thought about it. He's down in Florida. I'm here."

"Yes, you're here." But *he's* not in Florida, William wanted to add. I've been there, and he's *not*. You're here but he's *nowhere*. He's missing. But he didn't say that, any of it. Instead he asked: "Do you still have the postcard?"

"I suppose."

"Could I see it?"

"What for?"

"An example of his handwriting. A formality where large sums are concerned." Funny how lies came so easily now, lies that you speak out loud as opposed to lies that you tell yourself. He'd always been good at one, now he was good at the other, a complete liar now, becoming more polished with each "lawyer," "inheritance," and "sum."

"Arthur's gonna be rich, that it?"

"You never know."

"Hmmm . . ." Mr. Greely murmured, as if that explained a lot. Then he went looking for the postcard, which he returned with in his hand; he blew a layer of dust off it.

"All yours," he said.

Mr. Greely was right. *The weather's lovely*, Mr. Shankin had written. *And I'm doing fine*. That, more or less, was it. It was postmarked Florida—dated ten years ago almost to the day.

"How rich is Arthur going to be?" he asked.

William ignored him; he had another question.

"Mr. Greely, Arthur have any family?"

"Don't think so."

"There was just you then. And he sent you a postcard and he said *I'm fine*."

"Right," Mr. Greely said. "So how rich exactly . . . ?"

But William was already on his way.

The other Mr. Greelys:

Where Mrs. Timinsky used to live—stop two on the

Express to Nowhere—it was the lady in the next apartment over. One Mrs. Goldblatt, who offered him tea and cookies and two pillows which she insisted he put under his ass when he sat down on the couch.

She'd gotten a postcard too, but she didn't have it anymore and didn't remember what it said.

"It's the best thing for her," she told William.

He didn't understand.

"Florida. The very best thing."

Mrs. Timinsky had suffered from a liver disorder, she went on to say. Not to mention psoriasis, palsy, lumbago, and a general lack of anything to do.

"Florida's got lots of elderly people," she said, as if she was talking about people she had absolutely nothing in common with, though she couldn't have been younger than seventy. Well, age is a state of mind, they say. What they don't say is what that state of mind *is* exactly, which is generally poor, generally, unrelentingly miserable, as a state, akin to, say, the State of Nevada, half of which was bombed out and chock-full of radioactive half lives. Mrs. Goldblatt however was still in the state of cheeriness, or perhaps in the state of self-denial, just passing through on the way to the state of lunacy where Mr. Koppleman now resided.

"She'll fit right in there," Mrs. Goldblatt said, still talking about the State of Florida.

"She went there for her health, then?"

"Thank you very much—you look in good health too." Mrs. Goldblatt, apparently, was blessed with the one ailment that came in handy in the New York of the late twentieth century: encroaching deafness.

William finished off his lemon butter cookies and his cup of tea; he left.

And so it went.

Halfway between Mrs. Goldblatt and the place where Mrs. Winters used to live, the rainstorm hit. It came like a slap in the middle of a quiet conversation, followed by deathly silence, then tears. Marble-sized raindrops knocked him back and forth across the sidewalk; he began to stagger.

When he finally reached Mrs. Winters's old haunt, a boarding house not unlike the one he lived in, he was very cold, very wet, but also, he supposed, very pitiable. And pity wasn't too bad a thing to have going for him, he thought—it was, after all, a staple of beggars, and what was he but a beggar in nice clothes. Okay—decent clothes, clothes just this side of Goodwill.

He'd picked Mrs. Winters third because of his hunch that if there was a Mr. Greely here, his name would be *Raoul,* instead of say, Sam.

It was.

He was, as it turned out, the landlord.

Sure, he remembered Doris, he said, as he worked on a washing machine in the basement. Doris Winters. Nice old lady. She'd lived there for years.

Then?

She took off to Florida.

He was a sort of friend of hers?

No, not really.

But they kept in touch?

No, not really.

Never wrote her a postcard? Not *once?*

Well, now that he mentioned it, yes, once. A Christmas card.

Any answer?

No, now that he mentioned it, no answer. Not that he remembered, anyway. Though he did remember someone else asking him about Mrs. Winters—friend of his, perhaps?

Perhaps.

Washing machines were the worst, he said. Can't fix them. Never could.

Any idea why she went to Florida in the first place?

In the first place, it wasn't his business. In the second place—he thought her doctor had recommended it. That's what he thought.

And any family to speak of?

There was family. But not to speak of. A kid on the West Coast somewhere, maybe some grandkids too. A Christmas card every year and maybe they called her if she was lucky. Family, but not to speak of. So she didn't.

Just another old person with nobody.

He told Raoul thank you. He told him he'd been very helpful.

If you say so, Raoul said, going back to his washing machine. William went back to the street.

SEVENTEEN

A lawyer William used to see a great deal of once said to him: Never ask a question you don't know the answer to. Not in court and not in bed either. *Especially* in bed.

For the rest of the day then, William felt like a lawyer. A good one too. He asked questions but he already knew the answers, and by heart. The questions differed a little, here and there they did, but the answers were always the same. It was like interrogating the same witness twelve times, or perhaps twelve different witnesses, but to the same crime. The problem was, of course, that no one had actually seen a crime.

All they'd seen were twelve old people going off to Florida—innocuous enough, because they'd seen that every day. They didn't know that they'd never—with the exception, of course, of Mr. Koppleman—*arrived* there, that when they'd disappeared from the White Pages, they'd disappeared from the earth. *If you were headed to the dog races,* the woman had said to him, *you took the wrong turn.* Only there were twelve wrong turns here, and at the end of the street, something waiting.

Something that had taken all of them, but *spared* one.

Why were you spared? Jean had asked Koppleman. *Why you?*

Okay, this was something Jean had known, something Florida had just affirmed for him. *You find what you look for.* And he had, he had.

And now, sitting in his room at the end of the day, William was trying to find something too. A beginning.

Because that's where you begin. At the beginning.

It was still raining out. The sound was almost numbing; on another day, in another life—for instance, last week's—he might have slept to its simple rhythm. Dreamed about Rachel, wrestled a few demons, sawed a few logs. But this was *this* week, and this week he was William the Conquerer as opposed to William the Meek, William with the emphasis on *will.* In that he *had* one, in that it had allowed him to get on a plane to Florida and do a little old-fashioned gumshoeing in Flushing. Okay, the humidity in the room felt a little like tension— yes it did. His upper lip *was* stained with sweat, his palms *were* a trifle slippery. His shoulder was crying uncle— that too. But here he was, present and accounted for.

Here he was with two lists spread out in front of him— one with the names of the unspared—the unspared and Koppleman, the other with the ambiguous numbers in Jean's file, trying like mad to make a connection.

It was Koppleman, however, that kept taking the brunt of his scrutiny. The odd man out. And it was the odd that gave you an even chance, wasn't it. Like those grade school primers where five farm animals were followed by a clock. Which one didn't belong? Which one and why? The truth was, he hadn't been very good at those kind of questions. He was too left brain, maybe—he kept thinking the clock was too easy, that there *were* clocks on farms, that it might be the pig or the chicken. He hadn't been good at questions like that, and he still wasn't.

If Koppleman stood out, it was hard to see why, maybe even impossible. Beside each name he'd listed all that he'd learned about that particular person. They were all old; they'd all gone to Florida; they all had either no family or none worth mentioning; they'd all disappeared. Excepting Koppleman. The similarities ended there.

Some of them were Jewish. Some of them weren't. Some were born abroad. Most weren't. Some had sent postcards. Some hadn't.

Now the postcards, here's where things got interesting. He'd been able to collect two more—one from a next-door neighbor of Mr. Waldron's, the other from Sarah Dillon's companion—a spinsterish woman of fifty-five who'd lived below Mrs. Dillon and had, for a salary of twenty-five dollars a week, cleaned, cooked, and cared for her.

At first glance the postcards were entirely ordinary. One was of Miami Beach circa 1960. Two were of Sea World—Shamu and a couple of dazed-looking sea lions. Even what was written on them was ordinary, as dull and predictable as most postcards are. But here, ladies and gentlemen, was what was *extraordinary*. Ready, sitting up now? What was extraordinary, extraordinarily strange—okay, a little redundant, but so what—and extraordinarily chilling, was that the dull and predictable things

Arthur Shankin had written to Mr. Greely were the same dull and predictable things Joseph Waldron had written to his next-door neighbor and the *very* same dull and predictable things Sarah Dillon had written to her companion. Not sort of the same. Not kind of the same. The same. Exactly the same. Word for word. Period for period.

The weather's lovely. And I'm doing fine.

Times three.

And yet the handwriting was different on each card— in fact, both Mrs. Dillon's companion and Mr. Waldron's next-door neighbor had sworn the handwriting genuine. The message was the same, but the authors weren't.

What to do. Call Ripley maybe and have it put under Strangest Coincidences. Call Mr. Brickman and listen to everything he didn't want to know about Mr. Wilson's funeral. Call Elsa the She Wolf of the SS and pay homage to her tattoo. Call a good private investigator.

Call it quits.

After all, William the Meek would be delighted by that, might even throw a party and invite the whole house in for cheese dip and Mantovani. This William the Conquerer fellow was getting annoying lately, was making him go on trips and stay in broiling hotel rooms and talk to all sorts of people he didn't like. He was making him puzzle things out, and he wasn't good at that stuff; why you had to *spell* things out for this guy, fling open the curtains at the Par Central Motel and say *see* before he even suspected his wife was employing the services of the Three Eyes Detective Agency on a regular basis. And it's not like he got around so good anymore either, he had some physical limitations here, he had *pain*. Maybe calling it quits was just what the doctor ordered.

But William the Conquerer would have none of that— he could tell; he'd heard the arguments but he wasn't buying. After all, he was *still* staring down at the lists— he hadn't put them away, they were still there. He was stymied by one, fine, but he'd gone on to the other— those numbers, which despite a modest proclivity for mathematics, were proving hard to figure.

He'd at least, okay the *very* least, matched a person to the names, but he'd matched the numbers to zilch, to the sorriest number there was, to zero. Even their appearance had him stumped; the names and addresses had been as neat and orderly as wedding invitations, but the numbers had been written down haphazardly, as if Jean had been jotting down the license plates of a speeding car. That, of course, had been his first guess: license plates—*buzzzz*, oh, we're sorry, care to try again? (They were too long for license plates.) Okay, zip codes. *Buzzz*. Telephone numbers. *Buzzz*. Social Security numbers. *Buzzz*. Credit card numbers. *Buzzz*. And they weren't passport numbers, driver's license numbers, model numbers, combination numbers, lottery numbers, prison numbers, or even Numbers numbers. He knew only that they were *annoying* numbers.

The phone rang.

William stared at it as if it were something strange, a meteorite perhaps, a moon rock, perhaps even a blue moon rock, for that's about as often as it rang these days—once in a blue moon. And when it did, more often than not it was a wrong number, the caller embarrassed

by his mistake, William embarrassed at knowing it before even picking up the phone.

But this time, it wasn't a wrong number.

"Is this, uh . . . William?" the caller said.

William said that it was.

"But who's *this?*" he asked, thinking that it was probably someone trying to sell him a subscription, or a time
share in the Poconos, or even that it was someone looking for William, but not *this* William. That's what he
thought, that's what he would have bet on—but conform-
ing to his track record at every track in the metropolitan
area, he was wrong. In fact, he could have guessed all day,
and guessed all night, and taken a slow boat to China and
back and continued guessing, and he wouldn't have come
close. The fact was, the person on the other end of the
line was the very last person on earth he would've expected. At least, one of the twelve last people on earth.
Mainly because he didn't think that person was actually
still *on* the earth.

"This is Arthur," the caller said. "Arthur Shankin. I've
heard you've been looking for me."

"Yes," William said, once he could form the words and
actually get them out, "I have."

Yes. I have.

Three small words, but under the circumstances, a
speech. I have been looking for you, I've been looking
for you in Florida, and I've been looking for you here,
and I didn't find you and I thought you were dead, you
and eleven others of you. Of course, he didn't say that,
or anything close to that. What he said was: "How did
you get my number?"

"It's in the book."

"Yeah. But who—?"

"What kind of inheritance?" Mr. Shankin interrupted. "A relative or something? What about it, am I rich or what?"

"Mr. Shankin, is this a local call?"

"That's right."

"So you're not in Florida anymore?"

"Not unless Florida's local."

"But you *were* in Florida?"

"Sure. Why?"

"You sent a postcard to a friend. Mr. Greeman—"

"Greely."

"Of course, Greely, and you put a return address on it."

"So?"

"That address doesn't *exist*."

"So I made a mistake. What's the difference. Do I have money coming to me or don't I . . . ?"

"How long you been back?"

"Oh . . . six months I suppose."

"Six months—and not even a hello to your old friend Mr. Greely?"

"As a matter of fact, I said hello to my *old friend* Mr. Greely today. And *old friend* Mr. Greely told me about *new friend* William. He said you were a lawyer and that you had a nice present for me. An inheritance. So what about it, what about this inheritance . . . ?"

"There isn't any."

"Come again?"

"I'm not a lawyer. There isn't any inheritance."

"Okay. There isn't any inheritance. You just like to tell

people there's an inheritance. Why do you *do* that exactly?"

"It's just a story I made up. I needed to find you. I have."

"*Find* me. What for?"

"For the same reason Jean Goldblum wanted to find you. *Did* he?"

"Who's Jean Goldblum?"

"Guess not."

"Who's Jean Goldblum? And who are *you*? You're not a lawyer, fine. Who are you?"

"Could we meet someplace and talk about it?" He wanted to see him in the flesh; he suddenly felt a real need to do that.

"What's wrong with talking on the phone?"

Yes, what *was* wrong with talking on the phone? People talked on the phone every day, all sorts of things got done on the phone. And it was raining cats and dogs outside, that too. It's just that he'd been out chasing phantoms in places called Magnolia Drive and Coral Avenue and Beaumont Street, and now he wanted to press some flesh.

"It's a little complicated, Mr. Shankin. I've got a lot of questions."

"Oh yeah?" A drawn-in breath, a slight grunt, William could almost hear his fingers drumming on an armrest. "Okay—but you'll have to come here—I've got a bum leg. You want to talk to me about something, you've got to come here."

"Sure. Where are you?"

"Ten-thirty-two Cherry Avenue in Whitestone. Know

where that is? The house at the end of the block. You know where Whitestone is?"

"Yeah, I'll find it. In an hour?"

"Okay, in an hour. Why not?"

Yeah, why not.

William put away his lists and tucked away his theories, each and every one of them, from the half-baked ones to the seriously delusional ones. Perhaps he wouldn't need to search for a beginning after all. Perhaps he was being given the ending. Maybe he'd been on the proverbial wild-goose chase and perhaps everyone had known it but him. Arthur Shankin was alive and well and living in Whitestone. Maybe they all were—maybe they all were alive and well and living somewhere—in Whitestone or Florida or Pango Pango. Maybe Jean had just been an old man telling tales and he'd just been an old man *listening* to them. The truth was, he felt foolish, as foolish as old fools are supposed to feel he guessed, which is *very* foolish. Maybe it was time to put an end to it, to order the cheese and crackers and lay on the Mantovani. So let's.

He called a cab company; he was becoming quite the spendthrift these days, plane rides and taxis and all in the same week. Then again, it wasn't every day someone came back from the dead—the last time it happened they'd gone and started a religion about it. Besides, from the sound of it, the rain had gotten nastier—not just cats and dogs anymore, but alley cats and rottweilers maybe.

He heard the beep of the Dial-A-Cab just as he was leaving his room. Mr. Leonati opened his door and peered out at him.

"Off again?" he whispered.

"Just for an hour."

"It's raining," he said.

"Yeah?"

"Where's your umbrella?"

Good question. Where *was* his umbrella? Better yet, did he actually have an umbrella, or did he just used to have one but not any longer?

"Take mine," Mr. Leonati said, ever generous with his suitcases, travel tips, and now umbrellas. "Five bucks from a guy on the corner."

"Thanks."

When William finally arrived downstairs, then finally opened and closed his five-dollar umbrella, and finally crawled into the backseat of the taxi, it looked very much like William was finally going to become the victim of urban angst. One of those unfortunate people who happen to get on the nerves or get on the bad side of or just get in the way of a seriously pissed-off member of a service industry. The taxi driver was upset with him, with him or with his day or his job or with all of the above. He glared at William and cursed at him in an unfamiliar language, Turkish maybe or Russian or Romanian—something, anyway, that was Greek to him. You couldn't mistake the tone though: The tone said if I had a gun I would shoot you with it. It made William wonder if they put those bulletproof dividers in taxis to protect the drivers from the passengers or vice versa. He was glad, anyway, that it was there.

He told him the address, which seemed to calm him down a little, or at least shut him up. The rain swept across the windshield like runoff from a flood, bubbling up against the back window like seltzer. The cab didn't so much as drive its way there as *slosh* its way there, through knee-high puddles black as oil. And the humidity seemed to have followed him from Florida; it felt like he was pasted to the seat.

"Cherry Avenue," the driver said after fifteen minutes or so, or actually *Cherkavy* or *Sherrynue* or something anyway that sounded enough like Cherry Avenue for William to think that it actually was. William paid him, making sure to leave a healthy tip, so that *he* might stay that way too. He got out.

Right into a puddle. It was up to his ankles and surprisingly cold. He dodged the cab's ensuing wake, for that was the only word to describe it, and opened up Mr. Leonati's umbrella again.

Ten-thirty-two Cherry Avenue *was* at the end of the block. It was too dark to make out much of it, but the address was clearly decipherable on the tin mailbox by the garden gate.

William walked into the garden arborvitaes and azaleas—and up to the front door. He knocked.

"Come in," he heard Mr. Shankin say.

William opened the door onto pitch blackness.

"Let me turn the light on," Mr. Shankin said. "Come on in."

William stepped in, and then remembered, just a bit embarrassed now, that he'd forgotten to close Mr. Leonati's umbrella. Which, as it turned out, might have been bad manners but wasn't too bad a thing. After all, according to those who would later piece it together, it saved his life.

EIGHTEEN

Someone had been walking their dog, a gray Chihuahua named Mitzi, extremely fussy about where it deposited its Chihuahua-sized excrement. It liked to deposit it after ten, and it liked to deposit it on Cherry Avenue—just about where the last house stood, because its owner let Mitzi do it on the lawn there. No one ever complained because no one lived in that house anymore. Because of the fire. Which had gutted its insides and left a hole about thirty feet deep.

Which is why, when the owner of the gray Chihuahua saw William walk in the front door, she thought *that man must be lost* or *that man must be mistaken* or just *that man must be crazy.* And went off to investigate. Which, like the open umbrella, was a good thing—for that too helped save William's life.

The umbrella first—five dollars off some guy on the

corner—but in its own fashion, sturdy enough. Which, as it turned out, it had to be.

For when William took his second step into the house, he thought, for the briefest moment, that he was stepping onto the softest carpet. Carpet soft as air, which unfortunately, it was. He fell—just like in those *dreams* of falling, where it seems to take forever to reach the bottom, as if you're suspended by parachutes. In this case he was suspended by Mr. Leonati's five-dollar umbrella, which, half closed when he stepped into air, sprouted into full flower a quarter into his descent and helped, ever so slightly, but ever so critically, to deaden his fall. He landed with a thud on a pile of mud and lumber. And mercifully, blacked out.

And if it wasn't for the owner of Mitzi the Chihuahua, who arrived at the door about a minute later, he no doubt would have stayed that way. Permanently. She, of course, couldn't see anything at first. But she'd seen him go in and she hadn't seen him come out, which meant there was only one place he could've gone: down. She left, yapping Chihuahua in tow, to find, one: flashlight. And, two: husband. Which, by the way, allowed the inhospitable *Mr. Shankin* to leave unnoticed. That, however, was figured out later when William was bandaged up and conscious. For the moment, he was neither.

The owner of the yapping Mitzi—whose toilet routine was in the process of being royally screwed up and was letting everybody but *everybody* know it—returned not only with flashlight and husband, but husband's friend as well, both of whom thought she was crazy and both of whom said so. But when she shone her flashlight into the pit, revealing the what-must-have-been-ghastly sight,

they apologized, sort of, which means they stopped calling her *crazy bitch* and starting calling the fire department.

It took six firemen to get him out, two to lower themselves down into the hole attached to safety lines, two
to pull him out—tightly strapped to a canvas stretcher—
and two to complain about it. About the heat in there,
about the rain *out* there, about the spaced-out geezer
down there. All in all, they would have rather been fighting fires. Anyway, William slowly surfaced, like the disappeared person in a magic act come back to the stage,
still, by the way, mercifully unconscious.

Mercifully, because the fall had broken two ribs, one
navicular bone, and one toe, not to mention given him
a nasty bruise on the head. This they ascertained at Booth
Memorial Hospital after a half a dozen X rays. Which is
just about where he woke up. And screamed. They
quickly shot him with painkiller and back he went, back
to dreamland.

They never took a police report. He told them—the
doctors and admitting administrators—that he'd gotten
the wrong house, that's all; he'd gotten confused, entered
the wrong house, and paid for it. *Honest.* One look at
the birth date on his out-of-date driver's license and they
had no trouble believing him. They asked him a lot of
questions having to do with his memory and a few more
about Farmer Brown having two dozen eggs and need-
ing to give half a dozen to one neighbor and *two* or *four*
or a *dozen* more to his other. Farmer Brown was one generous farmer, William thought. At the rate he was giving out eggs, he'd be on a federal subsidy program in no

time. Perhaps if *he,* William, didn't have Alzheimer's, Farmer Brown did. Sooner or later they were going to find him sleeping with his cattle. Or just walking into the wrong farmhouse in the middle of the night and knocking himself unconscious.

The question, the *real* question here, the question they should have been asking if they'd known enough to ask it, was *why* William was lying. That was an interesting one, absolutely. After all, he could have told them the literal truth, that he was in the middle of an investigation and that he was just trying to get to the bottom of things—ha, ha. Or he could have told them a half-truth, or maybe a quarter or sixteenth—which would have merely mentioned a particular or two maybe: phone call, taxi, and free fall. But he didn't. Maybe he didn't because they'd *really* think he was crazy then—*who's the old guy think he is, Mickey Spillane?* Or maybe he didn't because he really didn't have that much to tell anyway. Much that made any *sense* at least. Or maybe he didn't because he was determined to finish it just the way he'd started it. By himself. Those were good reasons, each and every one of them. Sure they were. They just didn't happen to be the *right* reasons. The actual reason he hadn't told them the truth had nothing to do with finishing what he'd started, because it had *everything* to do with his recent decision to not finish at all. His *very* recent decision. So recent, in fact, he'd barely had time to tell himself. Himself was pleased though. The road had been exhilarating, at the very least interesting, but he was getting off. In fact, there was the exit sign straight up ahead.

Someone had tried to kill him. He'd gotten too close to something or someone and they'd tried to kill him.

That might've made him defiant, or real determined, or plain stubborn, or just pissed off, but what it actually made him was scared to death. The real world had given him back his fear of death. So okay, he'd keep it. Besides, he owed nothing to nobody—certainly not to Jean, whom he hadn't worked with in years and hadn't liked when he had, and certainly not to those twelve old people who'd gone to Florida by way of the Bermuda Triangle—none of whom he'd seen, *ever.*

William the Conquerer was going back into mothballs. William the *Meek* was now taking calls.

One from Jilly—*all the boys down at OTB say hello, and don't worry, your job's still waiting here for you when you get back on your feet.* One from Mr. Brickman—*you sound groggy, William, just wanted to say I'll be stopping by.*

And making calls too. At least *one* call, just to tidy things up a little. A week after his admittance, wrapped in a soft cocoon of bandages and morphine-induced haze, he rang up Mr. Greely.

"No," Mr. Greely said, "no one called me. But I put out the word."

"The word?" thinking that Mr. Greely sounded like a missionary.

"Sure. The word. I said you were looking for Arthur. You understand, in case anybody heard from him."

"Who did you put out the word *to?*"

"Who remembers. You know, *people.* In the building. Whatever. So did you find him or didn't you?"

"Didn't."

"Too bad."

"Yeah."

End of inquiry, end of the road. He owed nothing to nobody.

So he kept reminding himself, as the nurses dressed and redressed his bandages. *The neck bone's connected to the chest bone,* he sang in his head, *the chest bone's connected to the rib bone,* the rib bone's connected to a twenty-four-volt battery that was mercilessly sending rivers of pain down his body. That's what it felt like. Question: How do you make your arthritis feel better? Answer: You fall down a thirty-foot hole and smash your ribs to bits. Which guarantees that you won't even notice your arthritis; *arthritis,* what arthritis? Old bones, that's what the nurses said he had. And old bones take a long time to mend. He needed time to recuperate—that's what the rest of his life was perfect for. If he needed purpose, he'd found one. To mend.

And yet he kept thinking about Jean. How he didn't owe him anything. It was the shots that did it, he thought. Painkillers, mind-numbers, narcotics of one form or another, they kept him dreaming. One minute he was stuck painfully in the present, the whoosh of the air conditioner, the wheeze of the bronchial patient in the next bed, the whine of the TV. And he did mean whine. My Wife Doesn't Dress Sexy Enough. My Wife Dresses Like A Slut. My Husband's A Drag. My Husband's *In* Drag. She's Vain. He's Stupid. She Eats Too Much. He Cheats Too Much. A nonstop litany of peeves, complaints, potshots, and outright humiliations. One minute he was *there,* wondering if Caught My Husband Wearing My Shoes should go a little easier on Thinks Wife Should Share. The next minute he was back fifty years or so and staring at Lost My Soul In Nazi Death Camp, at Jean, for the first time.

It was Santini who first brought Jean in. William had just left Mutual of Omaha—five years of being a claims investigator and he'd had it. Santini had left over a year ago—or been asked to. Something about a fraudulent claim that he'd either engineered, overlooked, or just plain screwed up. It didn't matter to William. They'd worked together a couple of times over the years and they'd gotten along fine. So they were going to start a detective agency together. Which is what ex-claims investigators did in those days if they didn't stay for the gold watch. William and Santini, the Two Eyes. Except Santini had somebody else he wanted to bring aboard.

Jean was a charity case. Which isn't what Santini *said*—but is what he was. What he said was that Jean had been doing the legwork for a highly disreputable agency downtown—highly *disreputable* in Santini's book being a euphemism for highly successful. Highly successful being the exact opposite of his recent forays into betting the over-unders in college basketball, bets that he'd placed with a certain Mr. Klein. Who *was* highly successful, not to mention highly fortunate, having sat out the Holocaust comfortably ensconced in a 32nd Street brownstone, and not somewhere in Poland like his late uncle Lou. Which, the truth be told, made him feel just a little guilty, which caused him to actually chair a number of very legitimate refugee programs after the war. America, which was feeling just a bit guilty itself, had finally opened its doors to a number of Jews who were still breathing. Not a large number, not a number with a lot of zeros behind it, but a decent number. And a suddenly decent Klein was there waiting for them, with warm clothing and hot soup. And in Jean's case, a job. Jean, whom he'd found with just the shirt on his back, that faded snapshot in his pocket, and some ugly blue numbers on his arm. Not to mention a chip the size of Mauthausen on his shoulder. Mr. Klein had apparently taken to Jean, to his story anyway, which was of someone who'd actually tried to do something in a time and place where everyone mostly did nothing. Everyone, that is, who wasn't committing crimes against humanity on a regular basis. Jean had helped smuggle Jews out of occupied France, onto ships in Marseilles and then south, to Argentina maybe. But Jean had been seized, been tortured, and nearly been killed. That he wasn't, that he'd survived all that, was something of a miracle. That Santini was into Mr. Klein for four figures was something of a pain. Giving Jean gainful employment was something of a solution.

Not that Santini had been thrilled about it, at least, not at first, especially after they'd received a notice from Bellevue—or at least Jean had, a notice which had somehow been intercepted by Santini, who'd placed it on William's desk with a mournful look of dread.

"Jesus," he told William. "The guy's wacko."

"What?"

"Jean. He's nuts. They had him in Bellevue. Jesus Christ. Look at the notice, for Chrissakes. *Due for a follow-up*. Do you see that? We've got a nut on our hands."

Which was true and not true. The actual story, the one Santini pieced together later after he'd paid Mr. Klein a visit, was a lot less alarming. All survivors in this particular refugee program had been offered psychiatric therapy; Jean had apparently accepted it. Which didn't much mollify Santini any—crazy was crazy. What *did* mollify Santini was that Jean began to show how good he was, that his hard-won knowledge of the darker impulses of humankind was paying dividends. Jean wasn't making any friends but he was making lots of clients. So while crazy was crazy—money was money. His place was secure, even though one of the friends he wasn't making, was William.

Though William, of course, had tried. He'd greeted the frail, wasted soul before him with pity and been met squarely with a roundhouse right of scorn. Of course, he understood—Mauthausen and all. He'd tried flattery too, told Jean how proud he was of what Jean had attempted, told him how special heroism was in a world with so little of it. Jean told him to shut up. If Jean was a hero, he was a reluctant one. He'd seen the *real* human spirit at work; he'd seen it man an assembly line of death with crackerjack efficiency. Heroism—he wanted no part of it. And he wanted no part of William either—William, whom he saw as just one more bleeding heart. And maybe, William thought now, stuck back in the present with its wheezes, whooshes, and whines, he was right.

But not now; now's different. Jean would have approved, he thought. He was giving up the ghost, and even though it was *Jean's* ghost, he would've approved. Heal thyself, William thought, then whispered it aloud. Heal thyself.

Mr. Brickman came to see him on a Tuesday.

"I never walk out alone anymore," he said, "but in your case I made an exception."

"Thank you."

"So"—Mr. Brickman peered at him—"what transpired here?"

"I didn't look where I was going."

"Obviously. Where *were* you going?"

"To see a friend. Wrong house," the words springing out of him as if on their own, like trained circus animals used to pirouetting on cue.

"I'll say," Mr. Brickman said. "By the way—*what* friend?"

"You don't know him," William said, thinking that neither did he—*know* him. And also thinking that this wasn't bad at all, lying around pasha-like, chatting with friends, that it passed the time in a painless sort of way. And painless was what he was after, yessiree—just what the doctor ordered. Sometimes when he looked down at his body, at that mountain of gauze and plaster, he actually scared himself. It was like looking at his reflection in the mirror of the National Inn, only times squared. There he just looked like he was deteriorating; here he looked like he'd finished. A little like a rag doll with the stuffing all torn out. And it hurt—in between the narcotics, it hurt even to breathe.

"When are they going to let you out?"

"They keep saying when my medical condition improves. Either that, or when my Medicare condition doesn't."

"They *said* that?" Mr. Brickman looked appropriately shocked.

"Just kidding, Mr. Brickman." Though he wasn't, not really. Sometimes he got the feeling the doctors weren't consulting his chart so much as consulting his coverage plan. He got that feeling because they kept looking at his bed as if they were tired and wanted to sleep in it. No doubt about it, they *wanted* that bed. The problem was, he was still in it.

His next-door neighbor in the bed over, which in this room meant about the width of a bathroom stall, was wheezing something awful.

"Anyway," Mr. Brickman said, followed by a sigh positively dripping with insincerity, "this is the life."

"If you say so."

"Sure I do. You know, I was thinking about Eddie the other day."

"What about Eddie?"

"Nothing. Just about him. About how he's dead."

"Yeah. He's certainly dead."

"Strange thing, isn't it?"

"What?"

"Being dead."

"Yeah. It's a strange thing."

"You shouldn't think about it," Mr. Brickman said, patting his arm—or actually, his sling. "Not in your condition."

"I *wasn't* thinking about it."

"That's the spirit. You know, someone called. He wanted to know how you were."

But I don't know a *someone,* William started to say. Then stopped, feeling all of a sudden very cold, cold like death. Okay, stupid me.

"Someone," William echoed. "He wanted to know how I was. That's it?"

"That's it. I assured him you were mending."

"Was he happy about that?"

"Well, sure, I guess. Like I said, he was concerned."

"I'm sure he was. Didn't leave a number, did he?"

"Number? No. But if he calls again . . ."

"Sure, Mr. Brickman. If he calls again, you'll ask."

"Naturally."

Conversation withered after that, took a definite turn into small talk and then very small talk, and then talk that was just about infinitesimal. William, still thinking about his anonymous well-wisher, felt as if all those bandages that were wrapped around his body had suddenly wrapped themselves around his throat. Mr. Brickman, who wasn't exactly leading an exciting life these days as a virtual shut-in, seemed to run out of things to say. So he said goodbye.

"Thanks for coming," William said, although he wasn't altogether sure now that he was.

Fifteen minutes after Mr. Brickman left, the day nurse—a large black woman who tended to talk to him as if he were under the age of ten—gave him his daily dose of nirvana. It worked too; a minute later he was in the middle of a strange dream.

A doctor was standing over his bed. The strangest-looking doctor he'd ever seen, his pupils black as a negative of snow, *that* black, framed by eyebrows the color of steel. He was an old doctor to be sure, but *not a kindly* old doctor. He wore an air of detachment about him, as stiff and starched and antiseptic as his smock.

"For you," the doctor said, "to help you sleep." Something was in his hand—more painkiller perhaps?

"I'd like to talk," William replied. "I'd like to tell you something."

"Yes . . ." The doctor hesitated. "Well, why not."

"It's just this. I'm off the case. That's all. Someone tried to kill me and then he called Mr. Brickman to see if he'd finished the job. I'd like whoever it is to know that I'm off the case. That there's no hard feelings. Could you arrange that?"

"Of course. But maybe he thinks you know too much. Did you consider that?"

"Actually, I have. But you see, he's wrong there. I know very little, almost nothing."

"Ah well, in that case, maybe he'll listen. Don't you want to sleep now?"

"No. I want to talk. I told you."

"But you're in pain. Aren't you in pain?"

"Yeah, I'm in pain. But I don't want to sleep. I'm . . . well . . . afraid."

"Afraid? Afraid of *what?*"

"Of sleep. I'm afraid that if you put me to sleep, I won't wake up again."

"Is that so bad a thing?"

"Maybe not. But all the same . . ."

Then the dream turned murky, that is, murkier than dreams usually are. It seemed to him that the door opened, that the door opened or a window did, that a television was turned off or turned on, and then the doctor was gone.

End of dream. He woke up what must have been hours later with a headache and a dry mouth, a little like a hangover without the fun.

NINETEEN

They let him out one week later. By that time his burden of gauze and plaster had been reduced to two small casts on his little toe and right wrist and three fat bandages wrapped around his chest. He was given a large bottle of codeine tablets to take with him, that and a set of orders, the major one being to stay put and not walk into burnt-out houses in the middle of the night.

"Don't worry," he told the doctor, leaning on a two-pronged cane that he'd been given, or actually been made to purchase, "I have no intention of walking anywhere."

"Good boy," said the doctor.

William didn't know if he was supposed to say thank you or just wag his tail.

A car service was waiting for him in the circular driveway—courtesy of Medicare. The driver peered out at him with unmistakable distaste; one old man and one new cane meant he'd actually have to get out and help once they'd arrived wherever it is they were going. He didn't look quite as homicidal as the driver from the other night, *that* night, but he looked like he wouldn't mind tripping William on the way in. William sympathized—after all, it was hot.

When they arrived at their destination, Mr. Brickman was waiting, Mr. Brickman and Mr. Leonati too, so the driver was able to stay where he was, his only manual labor the handing back of change. This brightened his mood considerably, leading him to actually say something solicitous.

William thought it must be something solicitous, because of the tone—the words were in Russian or Greek or Lithuanian or maybe pig Latin. Not speaking English seemed to be the taxi driver's rule of thumb these days.

Mr. Brickman and Mr. Leonati *did* speak English though.

"You don't look too good," Mr. Leonati said as he helped him out of the car. "What do you think?" he asked Mr. Brickman, who'd flanked him on his other side and was already grunting from the exertion. "You think he looks good?"

"Better than when I saw him before. You should have seen him then. He looked awful."

William felt as if he was caught in the middle of a stage routine—Leonati and Brickman, Brickman and Leonati—and him, the stooge, the butt of their hilarity. What next, he wondered—a pie in the face?

They helped him upstairs, one stair at a time, as if he were an infant learning to walk. Mr. Brickman appointed himself cheerleader and surrogate dad.

"Whoa . . . that was a nice big step. A very nice step.

Now let's go for another. Whoa, what a step that was. A beauty of a step. Think you can do another."

Finally they got him to the top of the stairs and then to his room. They'd added pillows to his bed to make it more comfortable, and Mr. Brickman even had a card for him.

Roses are red, violets are blue, I here your sick, get well soon. Signed *Laurie.*

"So," Mr. Brickman shrugged, "she's not too good with rhymes. But it's the thought that counts."

"Yes, it's a nice thought. Thank her for me."

"I already did."

Mr. Leonati said, "Look, if you want food or anything, anything at all, I'll go out for you. Till you get back on your feet."

"I appreciate that, Mr. Leonati." And he did. He appreciated everything: them helping him up the stairs, the extra pillows, even the card—he appreciated that too. Being alive—he had a little appreciation left over for that too. In fact, he'd like to give being alive his *sincere* appreciation. This was okay, all of it, okay. They were playing house here, him, Mr. Brickman, and Mr. Leonati, and they were all doing a bang-up job. It suddenly occurred to him that if you acted like a family, you became one, enough of one anyway, to take the chill off. And it was cold out there, colder even than he'd remembered.

But now he was back inside. And just as before, when he'd left a hospital to go back to his room, left it with a bullet lodged in his shoulder and a certain hard-won understanding of his place in the scheme of things, he felt as if an elephantine weight had been lifted from his shoulders. *Atlas* hadn't had such a weight. Okay—so there was a certain dignity in bearing a thing like that, even, occasionally, a thrill or two, but by and large it was just plain wearisome. When you let it go, you realized that.

But now he was back in the bosom of his little family, safely ensconced in his bed, surrounded by pillows and well-wishers. A veritable oasis of peace. The only thing, in fact, that marred this oasis of peace, marred it at all, was the box still sitting by the doorway, *that* box, and occasional names that came flitting into his head like a list of items he'd forgotten to pick up at the store. Mr. Waldron, Mrs. Ross, Mr. Shankin. Okay—a pretty long list maybe, but every one of them a luxury item, not part of the four basic food groups at all. You'd have to *pay* for those little items, they'd cost an arm and a leg—at least two ribs and a navicular bone. And he was a little strapped now, now and for the completely foreseeable future. The box would have to be thrown out. And the names? He'd forget them, the way old people always forget names—after all, names are the first to go.

He didn't, of course—though not through lack of trying. If he was graded on trying, it'd be strictly A plus. He watched a lot of television—became quite fond of television—the game shows, those talk shows, even the commercials, all of them like gabby friends absolutely intent on keeping his mind from wandering into dangerous waters. They *did* keep his mind from wandering into dangerous waters. Well, maybe he waded in a little here and there, strictly up-to-the-knees stuff. But then his attention would be grabbed, absolutely yanked, by House-

wife Hookers or Stripper Postmen or that ever spinning
Wheel of Fortune or the latest Shaq-A-Tack.

And the time television couldn't fill was taken up by
Mr. Brickman, who showed up with alarming regularity
as if he were pulling guard duty. In *his* mind, he probably was on a guard duty of sorts, for Mr. Wilson's death
had turned him into a sentinel of vigilance. Not to mention a general purveyor of doom. The actual *doomed* here
were the elderly—whom he'd elected himself guardian of
in the general, and of William in the specific. In his
mind, they were an endangered species, threatened on
all sides by a host of evils. And William, newly back in
the fold as he was, found Mr. Brickman's attitude almost
pleasing, comforting even, an affirmation of his own new
credo.

Mr. Brickman kept a running score of the ongoing
holocaust, replete with some of the more lurid stories
concerning their fellow brethren.

"An eighty-eight-year-old woman," he read to William
one day, "found gagged and beaten in the closet of her
Brownsville apartment. *And* raped."

Another day's lead story: "An elderly married couple
in Washington Heights threw themselves out the window in a suicide pact. Couldn't take the constant mug-
gings."

There were a lot of stories like those, and Mr. Brickman found all of them. Senior citizen set on by guard
dogs, elderly couple dead of dehydration, ninety-year-old
poisoned by pet food, elderly people beaten, robbed,
stabbed, garroted, evicted, raped, sodomized, run over,
and euthanized. See, Mr. Brickman was saying, one by
one the herd is being decimated.

And William listened, listened and nodded in soulful agreement. An old man's place is in bed, in bed with the television on. He understood that again; he'd be sure to remember it.

And yet he couldn't forget everything. He could forget a lot, but not everything. So there he'd be, glued to Men Who Date Canines, or listening peacefully to Mr. Brickman recount the latest atrocity against some elderly woman, when he'd remember some *other* elderly woman—Mrs. Ross maybe. Tiptoeing into the room and tapping him on the shoulder like a little sister he'd been ignoring, the one whom he'd been told to look after. And even though he'd say *go away,* sometimes she didn't listen to him, and she'd stay there, right by his shoulder, breathing down his neck. Of course, then, more often than not, he'd remember something else—that house on Cherry Avenue for instance. He'd remember that voice telling him to come right in, and how it felt to fall into absolute nothingness. He'd listen to his old bones going ouch, and then, before you could say *codeine,* she'd be gone, poof, vanished. Memory, then, could be your friend. It could sometimes kick the crap out of other memories you didn't want to deal with.

One day he asked Mr. Leonati to get rid of the box, for he thought that it was deliberately staring at him. Anyway, every time he opened his eyes, it was *there.* Sitting there like some icon of a religion he'd lost his faith in. He wanted it thrown out. But just as Mr. Leonati was lifting it, he said *no, never mind,* maybe he should look through it once more and Mr. Leonati said *fine, whatever,* and put it back down.

But William didn't look through it. He turned on Nuns

Who Strip instead. He played checkers with Mr. Brickman. He puttered around with his two-pronged cane. He taught himself *old* again, not that he'd actually forgotten how. It was like falling off a bicycle—that easy.

But in the corner of the room was that box, and that box kept bothering him. There was no place in the oasis for that box. So one day he decided, *really* decided, to throw it out.

This time he asked Mr. Brickman to do it, and though Mr. Brickman wasn't happy about it, he agreed. He tried lifting it from several angles, like a golfer lining up a particularly difficult putt. When he finally decided on his approach, he dug in with both hands, grimaced for his audience of one, and lifted it slowly up off the carpet. And dropped it.

The box opened and almost everything came spilling out of it.

And that's how it happened, the way most things happen—not by design, but by simple, stupid accident—that William finally discovered what the numbers meant.

It was so simple, so ridiculously obvious, that for a good half minute or so he thought he must be mistaken, that it would dissolve like a thirst-induced mirage as soon as he gave it a second look.

But it didn't.

And he remembered again how there's two kinds of seeing, just like there's two kinds of reading. By rote, where every letter's letter-perfect, every word sounded out just the way *Webster's* tells you, but with just the most rudimentary understanding, without any real comprehension at all. And the second kind of reading, which is like reading with a third eye, like reading *between* the lines, where you suddenly understand everything. And William had been reading things the first way, not the second, so though he'd gone through Jean's box and made note of everything, he'd seen *nothing*.

And he hadn't been listening either, not really. What had Weeks said?

For a long while he did nothing, really nothing.

That's right. He did nothing.

Because *he didn't read or have a television or even an interest.*

He didn't read. Or have a television, or an interest, or a hobby, or maybe even a friend.

But he did have something. A baseball program, a little black book, two salt and pepper shakers, a couple of flyers. And a library card.

He didn't read. But he had *that.*

"Mr. Brickman," William said, "could you do me a favor and pick up that library card for me."

Mr. Brickman, still smarting from his previous blunder, smiled meekly and picked up the card.

"Does it have a date?"

"A *date?*"

"A date of issue?"

"Oh . . . let's see . . ." Mr. Brickman peered at it. "Yep . . . March, of this year. Expires in 2000. Made out to—"

"So it's a new card," William said, "*brand*-new," cutting him off, but not so much speaking to Brickman as to himself.

"Yeah. It's a new card. So?"

"So . . . ?" So. So we stay in bed, so we turn on

Teenagers Who Marry Their Fathers, so we bet the OTB, so we stay put. Or so we start over.

"Want to go to the library, Mr. Brickman?"

Mr. Brickman said okay.

Why the Flushing library, Mr. Brickman wanted to know, once they caught the bus on Northern Boulevard—William waving hello to his old friend, the black woman driver. Why the Flushing library when there was a perfectly good one right in Astoria—no more than ten blocks from them? *And*—if he hadn't noticed, it was hot outside, *and*—if he hadn't noticed, he could still hardly walk, so why then go all the way to *Flushing?*

"Because *that's* the library that's got what I want," William said.

That shut Mr. Brickman up—but only temporarily. He began, instead, to point out all the probable muggers among their fellow bus passengers—which was every man between fifteen and fifty who exhibited the slightest signs of antisocial behavior: not talking to the person next to them, or talking too much to the person next to them, or rolling their eyes, or dropping their chin, or cracking their knuckles, or biting their nails, or sleeping, or, more ominously, *pretending* to sleep—which just about, ladies and gentlemen, convicted each and every man on the bus. Muggers all.

And ladies and gentlemen, here's the amazing thing. William might have dismissed it with a condescending smile, he *might* have, all things being equal, but all things weren't equal; Mr. Brickman was old and they weren't, Mr. Brickman was old and so was he. And now that he'd been suitably reminded of that, he found himself scan-

ning the would-be Murderers Row right along with Mr.
Brickman, listening to his commentary with a judicious
ear, and wondering if maybe *that* one did look a little
suspicious, if that *other* one did have some bad intentions hiding somewhere behind his seemingly harmless
demeanor. The problem with the younger ones was they
all looked like that now—like hoods, they all had the
hood look. Looking dangerous was in fashion—even your
face had to look dangerous, you had to have the *sneer.*
The problem was, some of those sneering delinquents
were grade A honor students, but okay, some weren't—
some of them were the Puerto Rican kid who'd spit in
his face. The problem *was,* the only way to tell them
apart was to wait until one of them knocked you down
and the other one picked you up and walked you across
the street. No doubt about it, this getting-old thing was
tough—you had to be able to see a little keener just when
your eyesight was walking out the door.

Then too, there was the way *they* looked at you. Or
didn't. William had become aware of that only gradually,
the way you gradually become aware that you've grown
fat—one article of clothing after another growing tighter
till suddenly they're all tight, too tight to wear, and you
have to stop blaming it on shrinkage, on that stupid Chinese cleaners down the block, and face facts. That's sort
of the way William discovered that he'd grown invisible.
That he'd become, without the slightest help from Claude
Rains, the Invisible Man. No doubt about it. He'd walk
down the street and no one saw him. No one. And the
older he got, the more invisible he became. To pretty
girls, attractive women, to *homely* women, to just about
every variety of woman there was, he'd suddenly ceased

to exist. That's what he'd noticed first. Then he noticed
men weren't seeing him either. Most men. They saw
through him, around him, behind him, but not *him*.
Which is just the way most people see the old—they
don't, and the ones that do generally have something bad
on their minds, like rearranging your face.

Back to Mr. Brickman's fear then; it was a real fear.
William felt it, and being old, he caught it, and catching it, he was forced to sit with it for the entire twenty-
minute ride into Flushing. Right now they were passing
over Flushing Bridge, the river beneath them so pumped
full of pollutants it resembled one of those tar pits, handy
graveyards for numerous woolly mammoths. This one
had swallowed cars though, cars and washing machines
and garden hoses and rusted train tracks. There was a
sandpit warehouse right at its edge, but the river refused
to reflect it, *or* its clock, which was frozen, had been
frozen for years, at precisely 2:17. It was like a reminder,
that clock—that the only way to stop time was to drop
dead.

The library was dim, and considering the lack of working air-conditioning, surprisingly cool. It had the look
and feel of a church—the same portentous quiet, the
same expression of serene contemplation on the faces of
the adults there. The non-adults looked about the same
too—they looked like they'd rather be somewhere else.
Mr. Brickman looked like he'd rather be somewhere else
too—back in Astoria on his home turf. William felt a little like a transgressor here himself—he hadn't been to a
library in years, or, in fact, to a church either. The sound
of his cane echoed through the rows of books causing

reader after reader to look up at him as if he'd made a particularly rude noise. Once they'd seen him though, or *not* seen him, it was back to the books in a flash.

The librarian, a long-haired young man who seemed imprisoned by his tie and jacket, walked over to offer his assistance—either that, or to tell him to get out. It was hard to tell from his expression, which was decidedly neutral. But courtesy won out.

"What can I do for you?" he asked.

Everything, William was tempted to say. Only everything. But he restrained himself. Instead, he took the list of numbers that was folded in his hand, Jean's numbers, and dropped it onto the counter, flattening it out as if it were a road map and he was in need of directions. Which, as a matter of fact, he was. *For I'm lost,* he might have said. *I'm lost and I need to know where I am and where the place is that I'm looking for. And I have to know how to get there, that too, I have to know the route.*

But what he actually said was: "These are call numbers. Do you think you can tell me where they are?"

Mr. Brickman, who was peeking over his shoulder said: "What are they . . . novels?"

"Periodicals," the librarian said. "I'll have to look downstairs. Take a seat."

So they sat. Mr. Brickman drumming his fingers on the table, William doing his own sort of rat-ta-tat-tat in his head, Shankin to Waldron to Ross, wondering exactly what periodicals Jean had been so interested in, and why.

Then the librarian was back upstairs, two magazines in his hand and an apologetic expression on his bemused face. No doubt about it—if it was possible to be both, both amused and sorry, he was.

"One magazine isn't here anymore," he said.

Okay, William thought, that took care of the *I'm sorry* part.

"Here's the other two," he said, dropping them on the table.

Which took care of the *I'm amused* part.

The first magazine was called *Tattoo* and had some sort of biker chick on the cover. The second magazine was called *Healthy Skin* and had some sort of Swedish chick on the cover. Those were the periodicals he'd asked for. He'd have been amused himself, if he hadn't been in pain and hadn't been in need of answers and hadn't been at the short end of the rope. He'd have smiled too—the way Mr. Brickman was smiling, or trying not to.

"What gives?" Mr. Brickman said.

Yes, what gives? The Table of Contents—that *gives*. It gives the contents. The contents it gave of *Tattoo* were "Biker Babe of the Month—Inside Foldout." "Snakes, Scorpions, and Scythes—The Tattoo Artists of San Fran." And "Getting Your Last Year's Girlfriend Out of Your Heart and Off of Your Chest—The Off and Ons of Tattoo Removal."

And what did the Table of Contents of *Healthy Skin* give? It gave these contents: "Sun or No Sun—The Latest Facts." "Cucumbers—Myth or Miracle?" "How to Pamper Your Derriere." And "Tattoos—The Newest in Laser Removal."

So, all in all, they gave a lot. They gave William what he'd asked for back in that Florida hotel room. For Jean to show him the way. And Jean had, he had. He'd tapped him on the elbow and said *I will talk to you. If you listen, I will tell.*

TWENTY

Mr. Weeks looked even paler than before, like fine white china, the kind your aunt makes you eat from on Sunday visits, the kind that breaks into bits at the slightest pressure of your hand. You've got to be careful with china like that. He let William in without a word, as if he'd been expecting him to show up at any moment, as if they visited each other on a regular basis to discuss what's wrong with the world. Mr. Brickman had been left downstairs to wait for him, partly because he still had no idea what William was up to, and partly because strangers weren't exactly welcome in *Weeksville*.

"Your leg . . . ?" Mr. Weeks said, after William had gently eased himself into a chair.

"Something's broken," William answered.

"Ah." Mr. Weeks nodded, as if he'd expected as much.

The room felt pretty much like it did the last time he was here, like a crawl space; William had to resist the temptation to duck. The air tasted medicinal, gritty as soot, and William noticed yet another drape had been plastered against the window Mr. Weeks was fighting a war, William thought, but Mr. Weeks was losing. It was World—*100*. Weeks—*0*.

"What can I do for you?" Weeks said.

"Well, I've got a question."

"Sure."

"Just a little one."

"Okay."

"Just a little one about something you said last time."

"I'm listening."

"You were talking about that night he came in looking like a ghost, the night he told you he had the biggest case of his life. Remember?"

"Yes. I remember."

"Then you said you didn't see much of him after that. That's the way you put it. Right so far? You saw a lot less of him, you said. Except for *twice*. Once, when he came back from Miami and dumped that file on you. And one other time. Before that. When he came in to borrow some *medicine*. Recall that, Mr. Weeks? Those were your words, right? That he came in to borrow some medicine because he'd burnt himself *cooking*."

"Yeah."

Mr. Weeks was looking just a little edgy now, not like he was going to make a dash for it or anything. Just like he was thinking about it. But then, there wasn't anywhere to go.

"Jean cooked a lot then?"

"Now and again."

"Really? What was he cooking *that* night?"

"Don't know."

"Well, what did he burn himself on? The hot plate maybe? The stove?"

"He didn't say."

"Okay, he didn't say. What *did* he say?"

"I'm not following . . ."

"Sure you are. You're following along fine. He came in to borrow some medicine. Because he'd burnt himself. That's what he said, right?"

"Right."

"He burnt himself *cooking*."

"Uh huh."

"But who knows what he was cooking that night. Could've been anything, right? Maybe his specialty."

"I didn't ask."

"What *did* you ask?"

"I asked him how I could help him."

"Sure. You were good at helping him, weren't you. That was *your* specialty. Take my file, Weeks, he said, and you did. Like that. Tell no one, he said. And you didn't. Until me of course. What did he want you to help him with *that* night?"

"I told you. He burnt himself. He wanted medicine."

"That's right. Bet it was a bad burn too. How did he burn himself so *badly*?"

"I *told* you." Yeah, Mr. Weeks was definitely not a happy camper now. "He burnt himself cooking."

"Okay. When I went to Jean's funeral, know what I did, Mr. Weeks?"

Mr. Weeks shook his head. He didn't know.

"I shook his hand. Honest to God. I wasn't supposed to open the coffin either. It was closed—those were the

directions. So why did I do it? Why? There's a famous
line about this old Brooklyn Dodger—I forget his name—
Max something. No one liked this guy. He was a bully
and a drunk and he used to piss off the sportswriters no
end. Until the day he got old and was told he was traded,
gone, just like that. Then he all of a sudden got friendly.
And you know what one of these writers said? He said,
*Poor old Max. He's finally saying hello when he ought to
be saying goodbye.* Well, I guess I was saying hello. Understand?"

Mr. Weeks nodded this time. He understood.

"I was saying hello, fine. Only I had this weird feel-
ing that it wasn't Jean in there. Yeah, I know it's crazy—
I know it *was* Jean in there. But he didn't *look* like Jean.
I couldn't figure out why. Not really. Not until today."

Mr. Weeks was looking down at his wrist. *That's right,*
Mr. Weeks. *That's right.*

"You know, Jean never, ever, hid it. Just the opposite.
He wore short sleeves in summer. Always. Even in winter he'd roll his sleeves up to the elbow—screw the tem-
perature. So it was always there for anyone to see. Anyone
did. If you met him, or talked to him, or *hired* him, you
saw them. His numbers were out in the open, his sou-
venir from the Germans, yes? But here's what I remembered today. *Here's* why he looked funny to me. When I
shook his hand at the funeral home, they weren't there.
That's right. Gone, poof, not a sign of them. Okay, I admit
it—the other funny thing was I didn't even notice it. Not
at first, not *then.* Not until today. But today I did. Today
I remembered. Jean burnt himself, sure he did—but he
didn't burn himself broiling a fillet, did he? Did he, Mr.
Weeks? He burnt off his *numbers.* Jean went somewhere.

Jean went somewhere and had those numbers burnt off his arm."

Mr. Weeks remained silent, like his tomb of a room, dead quiet. But among the things he didn't say was *you're wrong. You're mistaken. You're telling tales.* Mr. Weeks was quiet, but Mr. Weeks wouldn't shut up.

"Okay," William said. "Okay. So where'd he go? The family doctor, the neighborhood dermatologist, the local tattoo parlor. Where?"

"A clinic."

So. Weeks speaks.

"A *clinic?* What kind of clinic?"

Mr. Weeks sighed, a good and heavy sigh, a sigh that sounded like the last gust of a passing thunderstorm.

"A *bad* kind," he said, "that's what kind. They did some job on him. They used *acid*—okay."

"Did he tell you he was going to do that?"

"No." Weeks shook his head. "It was just like I told you. I *hadn't* seen him for weeks. Then one night he knocked on my door. He was in a lot of pain. He showed me his arm and told me what he'd done. I was a medic in the war so I knew it was bad. Even if I hadn't been a medic, I'd have known. It was infected. They'd burnt his skin off but they'd left it exposed. He needed attention."

"So you gave it to him."

"I told him to go to a doctor. I told him to go to one immediately."

"But he didn't."

"No. He thought that was funny. *I've already been to a doctor,* he said. He thought everything was funny that

night. He was . . . manic, possessed almost, you understand? He wanted *me* to fix him up, no one else."

"So you did."

"Yeah. As best I could. I have a first aid kit here, quite
a large one. I don't go out, so I have to, you understand.
Just in case."

Just in case the gumshoe gourmet had a cooking accident.

"I cleaned it out and put a salve on it. Then I wrapped
it up good and gave him some penicillin. He was lucky,
that's all. It worked."

"Yeah," William said. "He died, but not of that." Mr.
Weeks didn't have the fans going today; it felt as if he
were sitting inside a collapsed tent—that's what it felt
like. "Okay, Mr. Weeks. He came to you screaming in
pain and you fixed him up and you sent him on his
merry way. Now bear with me—here's the sixty-four-
thousand-dollar question. *Why?* Why, after all those years,
did Jean go and *do* that?"

"He said he'd earned it. That's what he said."

He'd earned it.

"Okay—I give up. Earned it how?"

"He didn't say"

"What *did* he say? Don't tell a soul, Weeks? It's between you and me? Be a pal? Let's just say I burnt my-
self cooking?"

"He said he'd earned it. I thought he'd earned the right
to keep it to himself."

So, William thought. It hadn't been Jean who'd made
him promise. Weeks had made a promise to himself, and
Weeks had gone and kept it.

"I don't know why he burnt his numbers off," Weeks

said. "I don't know why after fifty years it was suddenly
so important to him. He didn't ask me to understand
him. He just asked me to listen to him."

Mr. Weeks was certainly odd and maybe even crazy,
William thought, but he was loyal as they come. And in
this world, at this time, that had to count for something.
Sure it did. He couldn't imagine what Jean had done to
deserve Mr. Weeks's loyalty, probably not much, other
than to visit him occasionally and remain careful not to
laugh at him. But it had been enough, more than enough
for Weeks, who'd gone in like a faithful hound to bury
his master's secrets. He'd taken the photos and he'd taken
the file, and he would have taken this last secret to the
grave with him. That too. The only thing more surprising than humanity, William thought, is the human be-
ings it's wasted on.

He used the cane to lift himself up off the chair.

"Thanks, Mr. Weeks."

Weeks blinked at him. "What for?"

"When I find out, I'll tell you."

This time, the doorman didn't wave him through like
a ticket-taker. This time he made him wait.

"Miss Coutrino has company," he said, with something
resembling a sneer, then went back to his newspaper.

Okay, the sneer spoke volumes. Thin ones though, with
titles like *People I Am Better Than* and *People I Look Down
On*. People like Johns, and old Johns doubly so. And
even though William was a William, and not a John, he
had no intention of protesting today. He was tired, okay,
he was tired and he was hot and he was old. Yes he was,
no doubt about it, and getting older by the second.

His reflection sat directly across from him framed in gilt, like a still outside the old Bijou, from a horror matinee perhaps. The *Creature from Astoria* maybe, or the *Phantom of Forest Hills*. Okay, maybe he was being a bit too harsh here, he didn't look quite *that* bad. Not like the monster yet, just the monster's assistant—the one who limps after the mad doctor with a hump on his back. Only William was carrying something else on *his* back, a burden of a slightly different kind, although every bit as debilitating.

Among his burdens, in fact, was Mr. Brickman, who'd been dumped off again like an unwanted child. At an ice cream parlor this time, with instructions to wait, his suspicions only half mollified by William's insistence that he was simply visiting a shut-in who disliked company. Which described Mr. Weeks to a T, though not Miss Eat Your Heart Out at all. These things were getting pretty interchangeable though, his bag of lies, getting where one would do just as well as the other.

He waited over twenty minutes, or until a rather flushed-looking businessman came striding out through the lobby, or actually *slinking* through it, looking neither left or right, but more or less down at his shoes. Maybe business hadn't been good today, maybe he hadn't closed the deal quite the way he'd imagined, or maybe like any good businessman he was just wary of competitors.

The doorman let him through now, the sneer still amazingly intact, as if it were frozen on.

"Oh," was the very first thing she said. "It's *you*."

She was dressed for business too, which meant half dressed, black spike heels and a leather skirt up to there.

Her blouse was unbuttoned to her navel, and the faintest sweat covered her cheeks.

"Back as a customer this time?" she said, half sarcastically, but half not. He had the impression she'd thrust just a little more white thigh out at him.

"Afraid not." Not as a customer, or as a drunken mourner, or as a new acquaintance here to talk about the latest developments in Chechnya. "This time I'm here as a detective." And if he'd shocked her with that simple declarative statement, just imagine how it sounded to him. Faintly ridiculous, is the way it sounded, especially given that reflection of someone light-years past his prime that he'd just torn himself away from—faintly ridiculous and more than faintly pathetic. Well, in for a penny, in for a pound, he thought. Besides, he could be mistaken, but he didn't believe he'd actually heard her laugh.

What she actually did, was say "Who hired you—Rip Van Winkle?" So, okay, maybe she did yuk-yuk just a little.

She swung the door open though at the very same time, and let him in.

The first thing he noticed was that she had a new carpet. Then she noticed him noticing.

"Don't worry," she said, "I needed a new one anyway." Then she said, "You are sober this time, aren't you?"

"Completely."

"Of course you are. You're here as a *detective* this time, isn't that what you said—correct me if I'm wrong."

Okay, he didn't much like her tone now. Laugh's a laugh, but she was starting to erode what little self-confidence he had left—her and that reflection, a brutal tag team.

"What exactly can I do for you, *detective?*"

"For starters, you can stop making fun of me. Okay—I'm old, I'm Methuselah, okay. I should be playing mahjongg, I know. I should be in a retirement community asking Ethel how the chicken was last night. I'm not. I'm here. I've got some broken ribs and a bum toe, and that's not even going into the usual aches and pains. No one's hired me but *me*, but here I am and I'm pretty serious." All that was what he *wanted* to say.

What he really said was: "I saw those pictures Jean took of you." Half because he felt like pricking that smug veneer and half because he needed to ask her something.

But it didn't seem to work. She didn't look happy, okay, but she didn't look unhappy either. She looked like someone who'd just spent half an hour on her knees to some guy she despised, and was now having to listen to some other guy she didn't much care for either. It was a chore.

"Congratulations," she said. "Did you get off on them?"

"No."

"Oh come on, sure you did. I've got primo legs. You haven't seen legs like that since when . . . ?"

"I've got a question for you, okay?"

"Not okay. See, that's how it works in here. I tell you what's okay, and you say May I."

"I've got a question for you."

"I've got a question for *you*. Why don't you take that cane and fuck yourself with it."

"You mad at everyone today or just me?"

"Just you."

"Maybe I should come back."

"Maybe you should retire again."

"I've got a question for you."

"You said that already."

"Whose idea was it?"

"Whose idea was *what?*"

"How does it work exactly? You just go pick out that outfit because you feel like Eva Braun that day. It could be the school mistress or the lady cop but you're feeling a little Aryan, so you say what the hell, I'll go for the swastika today?"

"You *did* get off on those pictures, Grandpa, didn't you?"

"Or was it him? Did he give you the day's script and say I'll play the Holocaust victim and you'll play the SS?"

"This getting you hot?"

"How did it *work?*"

"You didn't say May I."

"Who set the roles? Who said I'll be this and you'll be that?"

"Who said I have to tell you?"

"He was on a case," William said. "Remember? He was old, like me. He talked a lot, he was maybe going dotty. But he was on a case. The biggest case of his life—that's what he told you."

"He told me a lot of things."

"That's right. A lot of things. But *this* thing he told you was true. Just like his selling runaway kids, just like his giving that up. He didn't always tell the truth, but he always told the truth to you."

"So what?"

"Whose idea was it?"

"I don't remember. Maybe it was mine."

"Yours?"

"Maybe it wasn't."

"How did it work?"

"I think it was his."

"He told you how to do it? He said let's play Nazi. He said—"

"Yeah, I almost forgot. Silly me. The customer's always right. Right?"

"Maybe not *this* customer. This customer had a number tattooed on his arm—sure, you saw it. This customer was in a *concentration camp*. This customer's family *died* in a camp. So what was this customer doing asking you to dress up as the family executioner?"

"Who do you think I am—*Dr. Ruth?* The guy who walked out of here ten minutes ago is wearing my *panties.* I don't ask them *why.* I tell them *how much.* Understand how it works?"

"Yeah. I was just wondering how it worked with *him.*"

"Sometimes he asked for that. Sometimes he didn't. Sometimes we just talked. At the end, we just talked."

"At the end?"

"Yeah."

"At the end, when?" Something had just occurred to him. "The night he told you about the case—the biggest case of his life? *That* night?"

"Sure. Who the fuck remembers. Why not."

Yes, why not.

"He burnt off his numbers," William said. "When he got this case he went and burnt off his numbers and when someone asked him why he did it, he said he'd *earned* it. And then he came to you and he said kick off those boots why don't you and let's chat. I just want to *talk* now—about things, the weather maybe, the unemployment rate, oh yeah, and this *case,* did you know it's the biggest one I've ever had—can't tell you what it is, but it is."

I've earned it.

That's what Jean said, it was becoming clearer now, even if Miss Coutrino—see, he knew her name now—was only half listening, even if he was half wrong, it was becoming clearer.

"Jean comes to you for who knows how long and he positively licks your boots. He pinches runaways off the streets and hits up their parents for payoffs. Then something happens . . ."

I've earned it.

"He stops. He stops selling kids, he stops playing kneel-to-the-Nazi. He goes and burns his numbers off. Why . . . ?"

I understand, Jean. I do.

"Because he's earned it. Because he's earned the right. Because this *case* has earned it for him."

There. He'd put two and two and two together and it sounded suspiciously like six, like it added up. Even she looked impressed now, okay, maybe just curious, about where he was going with all this maybe, and whether or not he was going to throw up on her carpet again. He was a little curious about that himself; even stone sober he felt more than a tinge of nausea here. Maybe it was the smell—the smell of sex, of sweat and semen and crisp dollar bills, or maybe it was this other nagging notion. This strange idea that the closer he got to making sense of all this, the closer he got to Cherry Avenue. This call-me-crazy feeling that getting to the bottom of one was going to land him at the bottom of the other. Again. Okay—*call* him crazy. He'd answer to it—to Crazy, to Hopeless, to Old Man, to Will.

Which is what Rachel used to call him. Only Rachel.

He wouldn't mind answering to that at all right now. She could call him Will or Sam or Joe or Tiny Tim. But she wouldn't call him *anything* because she wouldn't call at all. Because she was dead, possibly, or surrounded by grandchildren, probably, or maybe just sitting next to whoever it was that had finally given her a life. Definitely.

Okay, Rachel, this one's for you. Even if you don't want it, even if you won't know about it. It's for you too.

The woman, Miss Coutrino, was staring at him.

"Finished?" she said.

"No."

He'd been looking ahead. All this time he'd been looking in the here and now. But he'd gotten it backward. He'd been looking the wrong way. About-face.

"No."

When you looked the other way you saw a bunch of old friends. Sure. There was Santini and Jean and Three Eyes and Mr. Klein.

"No."

And the hospital. The hospital was there too. The one that had taken a walking dead man and tried to make him forget the unforgivable.

"I ought to be saying goodbye," he said.

"Goodbye."

But I'm saying hello.

TWENTY-ONE

They had a lot in common, William thought. Old age homes and mental hospitals. If he didn't know any better, he'd say they were almost interchangeable. And he didn't know any better. For example, you could put on your gravestone *I'd Rather Be Here Than In A Mental Hospital* or *I'd Rather Be Here Than In An Old Age Home.* I'd rather be shut away *here* than *there,* than either one of them. People would get your drift, no question.

Though this was, more technically, one wing in a many-winged hospital. And the wings were strikingly different; they didn't belong to the same animal. While one wing was dead and going nowhere—an ostrich wing, say—another wing was pumping with energy—a stork wing. He'd walked into that wing first—pediatrics and obstetrics, the pacing of fathers-to-be creating actual breezes. And like spring breezes, they carried the definite odor of hope, of things to come—in this case, talcum, formula, and lots of strong coffee. One whiff and William knew he'd entered the wrong place, that he couldn't be further from where he was going.

"Ward B's that way," a nurse told him, pointing in the opposite direction, as if he were an extra that had wandered onto the wrong stage, dressed for Greek tragedy in the middle of a chorus from Rodgers and Hammerstein—the kind where all the actors are doing cartwheels and do-si-dos.

Which brought him to the dead wing. Where there were no cartwheels, no breezes to speak of, and not the faintest sign of hope. You could search every inch of the place, turn it upside down and inside out and you'd never find hope at all. It wasn't allowed in. It couldn't get through the wired windows, or the electronically shut doors, and even if it did, the smell of disinfectant and urine would kill it.

On the other hand, *he* felt right at home. He'd had a hard night, the kind of night he used to have most nights, kept awake by clients who'd ceased to be customers and had become his responsibilities instead. After all, in the Three Eyes Detective Agency, he'd been the Third Eye— the one that never shuts, that doesn't even blink except to shed tears now and then. So while Jean and Santini slept, or Jean slept, and Santini slept with Rachel—he'd lain with his eyes wide open, all three of them. And last night had been like one of *those* nights, slumped before an infomercial for the Amazing Vacuum Sucker, which promised to suck up everything one, two, three—especially your four easy payments of $39.95. No doubt about it though, those infomercials were good. Ten minutes in and you were starting to wonder where the Amazing Vacuum Sucker had been all your life; by twenty minutes you were as good as sold. It was the audiences that put it over the top though, all those wowed faces cheering like mad every time the Sucker went to work. Everyone could use an audience like that, William thought. Do something good—sell a used car, mow the lawn, fix the plunger in the toilet and there they'd be, oohing and ahhing just for you. Take *his* situation, gumshoeing in his seventies and the only one who's noticed is the guy who invited him to drop in at Cherry Avenue. That's gratitude for you.

And last night—no sleep, out at the crack of dawn, limping to a subway station inhabited by bag ladies. He had to step over them to buy a token, then transfer twice, one train worse than the next, the cars empty of everything but garbage and the occasional homeless person. Urban art covered the walls and windows though, urban art being what he'd heard someone on TV call graffiti. This urban art said *Melissa Sucks Cock* and *Jews Eat Shit* and *Motherfucker* in several colors. Compared to most modern art, it was at least understandable, there was no denying the artist's intent here. The artist hated Melissa, he hated Jews, and he probably wasn't too fond of William either.

By the time he surfaced in Manhattan, he felt bruised and battered. The streets were empty—as empty as the train cars, and it was only then that he realized it must be Saturday. That was another thing about aging; it didn't so much free you from routine as set you adrift from it. Days lost their meaning—those Monday Morning Blues started showing up on Friday. Those Sunday Night Jitters started popping up on Tuesdays. One day was like any other day, no better and no worse. Today was Saturday, but it could have been Wednesday or Thursday or Christmas Day.

Especially here on Ward B. William didn't think days mattered much here either. There wasn't a calendar in sight here by the reception desk. No *reception* in sight either. He had to wait over five minutes till someone showed up. Then someone did—Hispanic, sleepy-looking, very girlish. And male. He didn't walk in so much as sashay, executing a sort of rhumba on his way to the desk. That kind of walk stood out, especially here, especially within the walls of Ward B, which were very unlike the walls in Ward A. The walls in Ward A were yellow and blue and dotted with plastic sunflowers. The walls in Ward B were dull pink and chipped, like bitten-down nails. The male nurse in Ward B had *nice* nails though, freshly manicured, with just a hint of lavender.

"Yesss . . . ?" he said.

"The thing is . . ." William said, yes—what *was* that ever elusive thing? "I need a little information. About a patient who was here a long time ago."

"What *kind* of information?" He had a breathy voice, no doubt about it— Mae West maybe—or Lizabeth Scott.

"I'm tying up an estate," William said, trotting out a new one, and why not. "We don't have a single living relative here. I was hoping his records might mention someone so we can get this thing taken care of."

"Uh huh. How long ago are we talking about here?"

"Oh, fifty years maybe."

"Are you *serious?*"

William said that he was—very serious.

The nurse said that he was *very* too. Very sorry that William had come all the way here thinking they'd still have records from over fifty years ago. Because if he thought they would, he was very mistaken. Very, very mistaken. And have a very nice day.

William said he was very disappointed. Very, very disappointed. Was he sure there were no records of any kind for patients from that time? It was a special program for Holocaust survivors. Maybe he could check with someone else?

"Maybe I could, or maybe I can't," he said. "I don't even know who's around today."

William said his nail polish was unmistakably attractive—what was the color?

"Thank you," he said, brightening considerably. "Purple Passion."

William said he didn't think he'd ever seen a color quite that nice. Nope, never.

"Maybe I *can* find someone," he said, as he picked up the phone. "Hold on."

A minute later—a minute William spent complimenting the nurse on his choice of shoes and lovely stockings—a woman close to sixty walked in. The opened door leaked in the sounds of soft wailing, of what sounded like several heads banging against several bars, of sniffling, and sobbing, and maniacal snickering, the sounds of undistilled human misery. William suddenly wished he was anywhere but here. Back in the hospital maybe, on morphine and talk shows. Not here.

"Yes," said the woman. "What exactly can I do for you?"

William took the story out for another spin around the room. Not a bad story at all, a good, solid story, a story you could depend on in a pinch. A story she wasn't buying for a New York City second.

"Are you a lawyer?" she asked.

"Not exactly," he answered, convinced if he said he was, she was going to make him prove it.

"Then what *are* you, exactly?"

"A private investigator for the concerned parties." When in doubt, why not try the truth? Pretty close to the truth anyway—the only thing *not* being the truth being the fact that the concerned parties were, of course, *him*. Though he certainly was concerned, no doubt about it. Especially when he realized that the truth, in this case, sounded even more like a lie than the lie. At least to her. Who was looking at him, at his *seventy-something-year-old* him, and probably sizing him up for one of those nice straitjackets. The next thing he was going to tell her was that he was Napoleon and that Josephine was outside waiting in the car.

"First of all," she said, "we don't keep records from that long ago. Second of all, if I *did* have those records, I wouldn't give them to you. They would be confidential, understand. And besides, I'm not at all sure about you anyway. Sorry."

She exited, back through the electronically opened door into the heart of Ward B, leaving William like a groom before the altar—*this* close to the honeymoon, and jilted just like that.

But then again, there was always the maid of honor.

Who was staring at him now with what looked like genuine compassion.

William mentioned how nicely his hair was groomed. And what a nice choice in rouge.

The male nurse said: "Look, I have no idea if he can help you, but there was a doctor who practiced here *forever*. He's retired now, but he still comes in to visit his old patients, okay."

William asked where this doctor lived.

"Real close to here. Five blocks maybe. I don't know if he was here that far back, but you never know, right?"

William said right. And thanks. And what a lovely pocketbook he had.

He gave William the doctor's address.

The doctor lived in a rose-brick town house. Lots of ivy trailing down the walls. Lots of shuttered windows— eight of them. Lots of cat shit by the front door in three, yes, *three* large litter boxes. William got to know the features of the town house intimately, for he worried that he was just a bit early and didn't want to wake the doctor from the wrong side of the bed. So he stood there like a night watchman, like East Brooklyn again, minus the teal uniform and gun. Of course, he always had the cane now—if push came to shove he could always *whack* some innocent bystander to death. She would have been in her late twenties now, he thought, almost that, just starting out. If drugs, or a jealous boyfriend, or a hit-and-run driver, or just plain despair hadn't gotten her first. But then, *he'd* gotten her first, William, the fastest gun in the East, and just maybe the least accurate. It was an accident, sure, but maybe the kind of accident that was just waiting to happen. It was the kind of accident, anyway, where sorry doesn't cut it. Where you have to do penance. His sentence was twenty years of house arrest—self-imposed maybe, but still . . . *Go directly to your*

room and do not pass Go. And he'd gone—not even a
murmur of dissent. And he'd stayed quite a while too,
hadn't he, *quite* a while. But now he was out, in front of
a town house searching for signs of life. The doctor's,
and his own.

His own was doing fine: pulse *there* if a little unsteady,
ribs mending, arthritis bearable, shoulder remarkably
numb. The doctor's was another matter. The town house
was like the house in the Night Before Christmas. The
not-a-creature-was-stirring-not-even-a-mouse house.

Okay, maybe a creature was stirring after all. A cat was
stirring. Gray, mangy, and battle-scarred, it slithered past
his cane and trudged up to the doorway like a hungover
night prowler looking for a bed. One weak meow at the
foot of the door, and the door answered, swinging open
to let him in. Then it shut again, pronto.

The doctor was up. And so was William, up the front
walk to the stoop where he knocked twice and waited.

The cat had gotten much quicker service, he thought
after a minute or so, wondering if a good meow wasn't
in order. Then, the door swung open and Dr. Morten, a
large man in a blue bathrobe, peered out at him and said
he already *had* a subscription to *The Watchtower.* Not that
he was a Jehovah's Witness or anything, just that he had
a lot of trouble saying no to people.

Which turned out to be right on the money. After all,
when he realized William wasn't a Jehovah's Witness, or
a political canvasser, or an encyclopedia salesman, or the
man from the Water Department, he *still* let him in.

"The hospital sent you, you said?"
Dr. Morten had led him to the kitchen. At least, it

looked like the kitchen. Underneath the food-encrusted dishes, the coffee-stained cups, and glutinous-looking silverware, he thought there was a kitchen there. Although it didn't exactly smell like a kitchen; it smelled like a cross between a lavatory and a gym.

"Yes," William said, sitting down at the kitchen table. "They told me you worked there for years."

Dr. Morten was filling up yellow bowls, one with water, one with milk, one with food, then another one with water and another one with milk and another one with food. And so on.

"Oh yes," Dr. Morten said, "years."

Now cats began to appear. Lots of cats. From under the table, from behind the refrigerator, from inside the cupboards, from underneath the radiators, it was suddenly raining cats. William, who was in the general vicinity of their food, had a sudden appreciation for what a wildebeest must go through right before the lions snap the life out of him. Or what Mr. Brickman must feel like every moment he spent outside. It wasn't fun being the prey; given a choice you'd rather be the lion.

"So," Dr. Morten said, "what can I do for you?" He sat down on the other side of the table; a black cat started playing with the belt of his robe.

William explained. Dead person, concerned parties, investigating, etc.

"Fascinating story," Dr. Morten said. "Why are you talking to *me*?"

"The deceased was registered in a program for Holocaust survivors after the war. Were you around for that?"

"For that and all the rest of them. World War II, Korea, Vietnam. The lot. And you know what I learned—war's war. Just the casualty figures change. And *everyone's* a casualty. Were you in the war?"

"No." He'd been drafted at the very end and sent to Army Supply in Fort Dix. While Jean had been smuggling Jews to Argentina, he'd been smuggling Scotch to corporals. So while he'd been in the service, he hadn't been in the war.

"What was his name?" Dr. Morten said, then, "Stop it, Clarence," to the cat, who was tugging on his bathrobe like a wife who didn't like being ignored.

"Jean," William said. "Jean Goldblum."

Something happened. A cat leapt across the table, throwing a shadow across Dr. Morten's face. A yellow bowl was knocked over, throwing its milk against the bottom of his bathrobe where it clung like paste.

"Cats . . ." Dr. Morten said, a little sadly. "Cats. I moved most of my files downstairs—I was going to write a few case studies when I had the chance. I'll take a look. *Goldblum?* I don't remember that name, but then there were so many of them. If he was in the program, he'll be there."

He left William in the kitchen; two cats began fighting, hissing like snakes, spraying each other with spit. Something *had* happened. A cat had leapt across the table; milk had been spilt; Dr. Morten had said *I'll take a look.* William rubbed his forehead, eyes closed, trying to figure it out. A cat had leapt, like a shadow . . .

Dr. Morten returned.

"It took a while, but I found him. He *was* in the program. Briefly. Jean Goldblum—that's the name, right? Nothing much there. His wife and children were exterminated in Mauthausen. That's it. If he had any other relatives, it doesn't say so. Sorry."

Me too.

"Anything else in the file?"

"Else?"

"I don't know. Anything that caught your attention maybe. Anything I could use."

"No."

"It's just that you become curious about a person. You start out just doing a job, but then you become curious."

"About *what?*"

"Things. Did you know he was some sort of resistance hero in the war—sure you do, it's probably all in the file. He got a lot of other Jews *out.*"

"Yes—it mentioned that."

"I always wondered why he couldn't do the same for them."

"Them?"

"His wife and children. I mean while he was smuggling everyone else out of there, why didn't he get around to them?"

"Who knows? Maybe they didn't want to leave him behind."

"Sure. There's other things though."

"What things?"

"Well, you've got an honest-to-God hero here. Everyone else was trying to save their skin—but *him,* he's risking his neck to save strangers. Mother Teresa and Jean Goldblum. See—you can utter them in the same breath."

"So?"

"The thing is," William continued, "after the war, Jean wasn't so heroic anymore. From what I can tell—from

people who knew him. He didn't help old ladies across
the street anymore. He ran them over. He became a *de-tective*, and he got a reputation . . ."

"What *kind* of reputation?"

"The kind that gets you clients who pay in cash."

"What's your point?"

"I'm curious why that happens."

"*Why?*"

"Yeah. I'm curious why someone turns. I'm interested
in the process."

"Are you asking hypothetically? Because that's the only
way I can answer you. Mr. Goldblum was a client of the
hospital. There are laws about that."

"Sure. Hypothetically. Hypothetically why someone
who's up for the Nobel Prize ends up blackmailing
queers."

"Hypothetically, you've got someone who grew up by
the Golden Rules. Someone who, hypothetically, believed
in them. Someone who was confronted with a horrible
situation. Someone who *still* believed in them. Someone
who acted on them. Someone who got sent to Mauthausen for acting on them. And the worst part—someone who lost everything he loved for acting on them.
Hypothetically, you've got someone who isn't so fond of
the Golden Rules anymore. Someone who, hypothetically
speaking, can't wait to get *rid* of them."

"Okay, that makes sense."

"And this kind of person wouldn't exactly be enam-
ored with *himself* either."

"Why?" William said, remembering those pictures shot
from boot high.

"He survived. They didn't."

They being one wife and two little tow-headed children.

"We coined a phrase," Dr. Morten said. "Survivor's guilt. We couldn't do much about it—but we gave it a name."

"*Why* couldn't you do much about it?"

"Why? Imagine yourself strapped in an airplane with your whole family. I mean everyone. Cousins, grand-mothers, uncles and aunts, your wife and children. And then you crash. You don't *just* crash—you know you're crashing for a good ten or fifteen minutes. You feel the ground rushing up to meet you. You have to listen to everyone's cries and prayers and whimpers. You have to look into your children's eyes and see the future that'll never happen. And then, when the moment finally comes, when you finally crash, after you've said your goodbyes and wrapped your arms around your wife and children for the last time—*surprise*. You don't die. They do—all of them, while you watch them go one by one unable to stop it. But you—you're still there. Now," Dr. Morten said, "what do I tell you to make you feel better? What do I tell you to make you stop wishing you'd joined them?"

Yeah, William thought, remembering that little girl, okay, not quite the same thing. But still . . .

"We started our survivors program armed with good intentions. But they spoke a different language. *We* spoke a different language. They'd witnessed the inconceivable. Everything we said to them sounded like gibberish. We didn't have a prayer. And neither did they. The program was an unqualified failure. We cut it in thirds, then gave it up completely."

"And Jean. He was a failure too?"

"Sounds like it, doesn't it. Then again, he didn't shoot himself or throw himself off a bridge, so maybe not."

Maybe not. Only maybe he *did* throw himself off a bridge, only maybe it took him fifty-five years to hit the water. But at the very end of his swan dive, *this* close to oblivion, someone had reached out a hand and said *salvation.* But who?

"What will you do now?" Dr. Morten asked him. *Other than leave my house*—which he didn't say but which he didn't have to.

"Poke around a little more. You never know."

They both sat up, one just a little ahead of the other, though it was hard to say who was first and who was second. Call it a photo finish. Dr. Morten showed him halfway out, pointing the rest of the way like a waiter indicating the direction of the lavatory. William nimbly dodged cats, as nimbly as he could with a cane and arthritis-ravaged legs, which means he stepped on only two or three of them. Dr. Morten wasn't happy about that, and the screaming cats weren't exactly thrilled about it either. All the residents of the town house were pretty happy when he made it out the door.

Then this is what happened.

He walked, okay, limped a block or two. He passed two hot dog vendors who were just setting up.

He passed a black transvestite who asked him if he wanted a date.

A Lexus honked at him as he trudged across a crosswalk, then gunned the engine as he passed, belching out a cloud of rotten egg exhaust. William coughed, limped, coughed, limped.

An acorn dropped on his head.

A homeless man defecated in front of him.

This is what happened.

A news truck heaved a bundle of papers to the sidewalk, missing him by inches.

Another vagrant yelled at him, cursing him with unbearable rage.

A girl with tall bare legs walked right past him without seeing him.

He figured out what had happened in Dr. Morten's house.

He passed a stray German shepherd, then his limp slowed, became a shuffle, turned into a slight bobbing, eased into stillness.

The shepherd barked.

This is what happened.

What was his name? Dr. Morten had asked him.

Jean. Jean Goldblum.

And then a cat had leapt across the table, throwing a shadow across Dr. Morten's face.

And that was the problem—right there—that shadow. That was the problem.

For he could picture it now: the leaping cat, the yellow bowl hurling milk, that shadow—like a still-life now, but one where everything's just off, the perspectives forced, the spatial relationships askew. The problem here was which had come first—the cat's shadow or the cat—and every time he looked at the picture it seemed to be the *shadow* when it should have been the *cat*. That was a problem all right, you couldn't account for it, or rather, you could account for it, but in only one way. And that way wasn't the way he was going, he was *not* going that way. For the only way you could account for that was this: that the shadow didn't belong to the cat at all, but belonged instead to Dr. Morten. That he may have gone to the file, but that he hadn't needed to. That the minute he'd heard that name, he'd known right off who it belonged to, known it so strongly and so immediately that darkness had touched his face like grief.

William had been looking the wrong way. But no longer. The way was *that* way, the way back.

Santini said *every case Jean took was the same case and that the case was his own.*

And *that* case was down in the files.

Now all he had to do was get a look at them.

TWENTY-TWO

Black bag jobs, hit-and-runs, in-and-outs. Santini had been the acknowledged master, Jean the unacknowledged one, and William the class virgin. After all, you didn't have to *break* in on adulterers when you could *peek* in on them. Which was just as well, since William, of course, played by the rules, and the rules said private investigators had no more rights than a private citizen and therefore couldn't go breaking into other people's houses. Santini and Jean treated this rule like they treated other people's houses, that is, they broke it, then broke into other people's houses. Santini even had enough time left over to break into other people's wives as well, which means he may have been the real master of the surreptitious entry after all.

William, then, was at a disadvantage. He'd picked up a flashlight at a local hardware store, as well as some black electrical tape, though he would have been at a loss to tell anyone *why.*

I don't know, Officer, he'd have to say, and unlike the other twenty thousand would-be burglars they'd pick up this week, he'd really *mean* it.

He whiled away the hours at a Burger King, a streetside flea market, and finally at a movie which starred Jean-Claude Van Damme, and which only one hour later he couldn't remember a single word from. Okay, he remembered a few words—the part where they explained native Alabamian Jean-Claude's accent as a residue from his attending summer camp in Switzerland. *Drawp your weepon*—he said, and this bunch of rednecks refused to, but only because they didn't understand what he'd said. That was William's guess, although they might have been just getting him mad so that Jean-Claude could do his stuff and litter their junkyard with their thoroughly beaten up bodies. William left the theater wishing he knew the martial arts, so he could simply drop-kick his way into Dr. Morten's rose-brick town house.

Which was now precisely one half block from him, and growing increasingly redder as the day faded into evening. Which suddenly reminded him of a certain white dress, that day in East Brooklyn again, *her* dress, which had turned scarlet before his eyes as he did nothing but watch. Just like that other night outside the Par Central Motel, when he did nothing but watch either. Which meant that when you toted things up, he'd spent a lot of time watching—unlike Jean-Claude, say, who was nothing if not a man of action.

The light was failing quickly and taking whole sections of the street with it. The rose brick turned to brown, then gray, and staining darker by the minute reached a sort of poor man's indigo. If it had been winter, it would have been *time,* but being summer, the street was still throbbing with urban congestion. People stood around—against cars, on stoops, and on street curbs as if waiting for something to happen. And nothing did, so they sat around some more waiting for something else. Which didn't happen either. In fact, the only thing that actually happened was that William's leg began to ache something fierce, and everyone, but *everyone,* began to notice him. It might have been his occasional groans of pain that did it—yes, he would say that definitely got people's attention—or it could have been the fact that he was leaning on a cane for hours on end without either sitting down or falling over. Maybe it wasn't *hours*—but to any casual observer, it would appear that way. Think about it. When they asked—*Did anyone notice anyone unusual*—*everyone* would have. It'd be unanimous.

Then, suddenly, deliverance. An ice cream truck rounded the corner a block away, belching out this monotonous jingle which seemed to hypnotize half the crowd into going after it. The other half—the woman in rollers, the two men playing chess across a lopsided bridge table, the man with three dogs—seemed perplexed by this sudden loss of community, and rather than wait for it to reappear, decided to forgo the night air altogether and withdraw en masse. And in the rose-brick town house—now as black and indistinct as rain clouds in a fog, the single light that had been shining brightly from an upstairs window went out abruptly as if snuffed.

Okay, Jean-Claude would definitely take this as the moment to act.

There were two basement windows set beneath the front steps. William had noticed them before; a large tabby had been licking its paws in one of them, staring out with a lazy indifference.

He shuffled over there now. Reaching the bottom of the town house steps, he turned left and stealthily slipped behind them. Translation: He made it there without tripping over his cane. It was cooler here than on the street, danker too, and he could feel moss in the spaces between the bricks. Suddenly, a large grotesque shape appeared in the window. He was this close to scramming, *this* close, when he realized the large grotesque shape was actually small grotesque *him*. Or rather, his reflection, staring him down like someone intent on doing him harm. And maybe he was—intent on doing him harm.

Now the reflection wasn't exactly grotesque anymore; more like pathetic. What was he *doing?* Even his state-of-the-art flashlight couldn't brighten his chances of success. He was out of his element, he was out of his mind. *Seventy-year-old man kills self while breaking and entering*—another headline for Mr. Brickman's collection. Old men enter houses the old-fashioned way—they wait to be asked in. He went back up the front stoop and knocked.

Dr. Morten didn't look particularly surprised. He didn't look particularly happy either. What he looked like was particularly resigned.

"You knew him," William said. "When I said his name, you *knew* him."

And Dr. Morten said yes. Yes. Oh yes. Yes he had.

*   *   *

Fair was fair. Dr. Morten had a point. They'd both told stories to each other. Now it was time to tell other stories to each other. True ones.

First Dr. Morten asked him if Jean was really dead.

Yeah. Dead all right.

Dr. Morten sighed, the way you sigh at the end of a movie that's moved you to tears. Hard to believe it's over, but it is.

Then Dr. Morten said *you go first. You're not here to settle the Goldblum estate, that's for sure.*

So he did. He took a deep breath and jumped right in, and after a while he found the water wasn't too uncomfortable after all.

"I used to work with him," he began, the way he'd begun with Rodriguez and the hooker. "We were the Three Eyes Detective Agency. We were moderately successful, but Jean was the star. Definitely. When it broke up, we all went our separate ways. It wasn't like we had bowling nights when we did work together. So no one kept up with no one. We got old and I started reading the obituaries. I had death on the brain. One day I saw his obituary. I went to the funeral because I thought it was the least I could do. It would've been. Except I forgot to say rest in peace. I started learning things. Like the fact that he wasn't retired. Ready to join the shuffleboard league and *he* wasn't retired. I think that pissed me off. I was actually mad at him. I found out he'd been selling runaway kids back to their parents. Picture it— fourteen-year-old Minnesota kids stepping off the bus and there's Jean fighting the pimps and Covenant House priests for them. I imagine Jean played the sympathetic grandfatherly type—*let me buy you a milk shake and you* can tell old Jean all about it. *Sure, I understand why you'd leave a home like that. Absolutely. Why don't you just give me your parents' number and I'll make it all right for you.* Some of them did give him their parents' numbers. And then he'd get on the phone and play the concerned detective. *I've found your daughter. Your son. Yes I have. Now if you just send me a money order to cover expenses I'll send them right back to . . . what, you don't want to pay expenses? Haven't hired me, you say? Low on cash?* Click. Jean would give them the old *fongul*. Beat it, kid, he'd say. By the next week, they'd be out turning tricks. That was Jean. That was the Jean I knew and loved back in the good old days. So, big deal right? Go back to your apartment and pick up the obits again. Except I learned something else. That Jean had stopped selling kids. Honest. Given it up for a *real* case. Something, anyway, that was real to him. Real big. Real important. I don't know if I believed it. I *didn't* believe it. Not at first. I don't know why I bothered to find out if I should. Maybe because I'd retired a long time ago and he hadn't. Maybe because I got spit on on the way to his funeral and it felt like just another day at the office. Maybe I had *survivor's guilt*. Who knows—you're the psychiatrist. Okay, maybe I'm lying. Maybe it was the case. Unfinished — and cases are meant to be finished. After a while, I think it was *that*, the case, all these missing people I was turning up. So I thought I'd finish it for him. Why not—do the same for me, wouldn't he? And then somebody threw me down a deep dark hole. Tried to kill me—just like that. Came close to doing it too. So I thought, okay, maybe Jean *wouldn't* do the same for me. Maybe reading the obits isn't so dull after all. Maybe I'll re-retire. No such luck. Now I had this *case* on the brain. I found out other things. That Jean had this case on the brain too. That it had relieved him of something. That it had somehow balanced the books. He went and had his Mauthausen tattoo burnt off with acid because he said he'd earned it. Now what does that mean? Eighty years old and he's undergoing cosmetic surgery. Now here's what I start to think. I was following this case and everyone was saying he went *that-a-way*. Remember the old westerns? When they said *that-a-way* it always turned out to be the other way. The smart sheriffs knew that. So maybe I finally got smart. This case is about what *was*. It goes back. I don't think a client came out of the woodwork to give Jean a case. I think Jean was his own client. I think this was his *own* case. I think Jean was spanking himself for a long time, and that he was suddenly shown a way out. *That-a-way*. I think he saved his best case for last."

There. Quite a speech. But he'd told it all, all he knew; he hadn't held a single thing back.

"Your turn," he said.

"What if I don't want a turn?"

"We had a deal."

"You can get out of the deal if you want."

"I don't want."

"Maybe you do, and you don't know it."

"Now you're losing me, Doctor. Come on, this was I'll-tell-you-mine-if-you-tell-me-yours."

"You don't want to hear mine."

"Why?"

"Because mine's worse. Go home."

"I can't."

"Go home, William."

"I can't. Why did you know him?"

"I can call you a cab."

"Fifty years later and you knew his name. Why?"

"Because I couldn't forget it. I've tried."

"It's your turn, Doctor."

"If I tell, you'll wish I hadn't."

"I wish I hadn't read the obits. One wish to a customer."

"Okay," Dr. Morten said. "Okay," his voice trailing off like a muffled prayer. And what was he praying for? For William to listen to him maybe, for William to take the next cab home, and leave what was buried, buried. But William had gone too far; he'd crossed that point where going back was longer than going forward. He was committed to the journey now, no refunds, no cancellation insurance. Like Mr. Leonati on another journey to hell, he was good and stuck.

"Okay," he repeated. "But I've got to figure out where to begin. Do I begin with him or with me? We're both important here. Take me. I was a kid, a psychiatric intern, just starting out. He wasn't much older. But he'd been through it. Like the rest of them. Bones—walking skeletons with that dead stare in their eyes. He wasn't different, just more bitter than the rest of them. *Help him,* they said. *Help him.* He was my first—you never forget your first, right?"

Clarence the cat was pirouetting crazily on the end table, like a music box ballerina gone haywire. Dr. Morten didn't seem to notice. He was back in time, a fresh-scrubbed intern about to shrink his very first head.

"He's a hero, they told me. Lost his family in the camps. Refused to eat when they liberated him. Wanted to die.

Help him, they said. Sure thing, I answered. After all, this is what I wanted, what I'd gone to school for. I was going to make him forget, make him come to terms with his loss.

"At first, he was uncommunicative. Sat in the corner and didn't say a word to me. I let him stew in it too—tried to use the silence as a tool. But it didn't work with him. He was back there sizing me up—even then I knew that. So I started to talk—telling him a little about me to see if he'd bite. Of course, before I knew it, I was doing all the talking and he was doing all the listening. See—he'd turned things on their head—reversed roles with me. He was the doctor and I was the patient. It didn't take him long to come up with a diagnosis either. Terminal tenderness—the fatal desire to help others. He had me right where he wanted me then.

"So he began to talk. And talk. Suddenly he wasn't so dead anymore. Suddenly he wasn't so pathetic and tortured. Because suddenly I was. I thought about getting up and leaving him. Just refusing him as a patient. Wishful thinking. We were stuck with each other. At least till the next session when he decided not to show up again. He didn't have to. He'd said everything he wanted to."

Dr. Morten leaned forward.

"But to tell you about Jean, I have to tell you about someone else first. Someone you may find it hard to believe was real. Except he was. Afterward, I looked up everything I could about him. There wasn't a lot. But there was enough—even today. In the absolute butchery that was World War II he was just an afterthought. Maybe he didn't have the right press agent—his numbers weren't up there with the big boys. But he was smarter than they were. Much smarter."

As Dr. Morten continued, William could sense something had changed. No, Clarence still sat on the end table licking his paws with undisturbed relish, the blinds still lay drawn and shuttered, the door still firmly shut to the world. But there was another visitor in the house now. No doubt about it. Someone had sneaked in through the cracks, drawn up a chair, and put up his feet on the kitchen table.

Had he ever heard of Marcel Petoit, Dr. Morten wanted to know. *Dr.* Petoit?

"No," William replied.

"Now you will." And as he told him what he knew, William felt like he was six years old again and listening to a fairy tale in the dark, one of those gruesome fairy tales from the Brothers Grimm. Just a fairy tale. Because when you got right down to it—it was easier that way.

TWENTY-THREE

Once upon a time in the little French town of Auxerre there lived a boy called Marcel. Marcel Petoit.

One day, when Marcel was nine years old he took his aunt's dog, Max, for a walk. *Good dog,* he whispered, as Max trotted faithfully beside him.

Good dog, as he settled down beneath an ancient ash tree, rubbing the soft fur between Max's eyes.

Very good dog, as he used some hatbox twine to tie Max to the trunk of the tree.

Great dog, as he lifted the carving knife from his coat pocket.

Excellent dog, as he slit Max's stomach from his collarbone down to his tail.

Dead dog, as he watched his intestines slide out onto the autumn leaves.

Little Marcel Petoit decided then and there to be a doctor.

*   *   *

Once upon a time Marcel joined the army.

Three months later, he joined the walking wounded in the military hospital at Seis. Just about a stone's throw from the Aisne valley where he'd gone and had his leg blown up on ordinary maneuvers.

Marcel didn't much like the military. And he liked the military hospital even less. What he particularly disliked about it was the haunting babble that surrounded him every night like crickets in the dark. His fellow soldiers, his comrades in arms. Some of whom had injuries just like his. Though, strictly speaking, that wasn't why they were there. This ward's business had nothing to do with healing injured bodies. *This* was the mental ward. This was the ward of babble. Which is where they put you when you did things like blow up your leg on purpose. Or, at least, when they caught you at it. He'd been hoping for his discharge papers. Instead, he'd been rewarded with an admission to loon land.

It quickly occurred to him that the only way out of the crazy ward was to act crazier. Too crazy for the French army. Sure, they wanted you insane enough to charge a hill with several hundred automatic weapons trained at your head. But not crazy enough to turn one on yourself. It was all right to yell *charge*. As long as you didn't do it in strange tongues.

So he added a few more symptoms to his file. He developed the *shakes*, the *trembles*, and the *faints*. He was constantly seen rubbing his hands together as if trying to start a fire. He threw in a little self-mutilation here and there as well.

There was just one problem with all this. He was starting to have a little difficulty telling the difference. The difference between the charade and the non-charade, between the mentally disturbed him and the non-mentally disturbed him, between faking it and *feeling* it. He found himself trembling when he hadn't asked himself to do it. He found himself recovering from a dead faint when he'd never actually *planned* on fainting. And his hand rubbing had gotten completely out of control.

There was a bright side though.

It worked.

Four months later he was discharged with a noticeable limp and an eye-catching diagnosis of severe paranoid psychosis.

Once upon a time in a little French village somewhere in the Dordogne, there lived a doctor called Marcel.

The doctor fell in love. With a charming local girl called Lousette. Then the doctor fell out of love with the charming local girl called Lousette. She no longer seemed so charming to him. She had, in fact, become annoying and irritating.

It was, truth be told, her complete and maddening inability to understand him. To understand his little thefts, for example. His little transgressions. His little faux pas. To comprehend, for instance, that it wasn't the things he took that excited him, but the actual act of *taking* them. To understand that there was something positively, dare he say it—*godlike*—about his astounding ability to rearrange the physical world. For example, to rearrange Madame Rouel's diamond necklace from her bedside jewelry box right into his armoir. Something godlike about his ability to get away with it too. And yet she seemed completely unable to grasp that.

She'd begun making vague noises about exposing him, to issue veiled threats about restitution, to talk about his having to own up or *else*. This was a major mistake on her part. It had, he was sad to say, *doomed* her. Too bad too. It wasn't like he wasn't just a little fond of her. Still, there was one Godlike act he hadn't yet attempted. One he'd been musing about, pondering, even planning. The one reserved *solely* for God.

And on a warm summer night when the cicadas were in full chorus, the time came to try it.

They were lying naked in bed. Not exactly in post-coital bliss either. More like postcoital tension, regret, and recrimination. So he whispered some soothing words in her ear. Words like *love* and *marriage* and *children*. In no time at all they were fast approaching bliss again. She relaxed and dug herself into the crook of his arm.

She'd been complaining all day about her woman's pains. He'd been promising all day to give her just the thing to cure them. It was time to keep that promise.

He reached into his black bag, where the syringe lay primed and waiting. *Roll over,* he told Lousette, *roll over so you won't see the shot and become scared.* Dutifully, she rolled onto her side, her small body tense and barely trembling; for a moment, for *just* a moment, Marcel had second thoughts. She was, after all, *pretty*—and not too bad a cook either. But then it was as if he was back in his *aunt's* garden, with Max the dog staring stupidly up at him. He eased the needle into her hip.

The syringe was filled with water and air, the two basic elements of life, the irony of which wasn't lost on him for a second. In fact, he kind of relished the irony—saw an almost beautiful symmetry at work here. The water, of course, was for show—it was the air that would carry the day. *And God breathed life into Adam.* But what God gives, God can take back.

He withdrew the needle from her trembling body, leaving the tiniest bubble of blood, which he wiped away with an alcohol-soaked cotton ball. *You have a soft touch,* Lousette told him, *I wish . . .* But she didn't complete her sentence, not because of the air bubble he'd injected into her body—that would take a while—but because she wished for so *many* things, and couldn't, at least for the moment, decide on one. She fell asleep.

Marcel cradled her from behind, cradled her for an hour, then two, and then into the third, when suddenly, it started. She began to twist and shake; her eyes popped open, her mouth contorted. He'd expected convulsions, absolutely, but not like this. He watched, completely bug-eyed fascinated. She fell off the bed, but like a maimed insect, she couldn't stay still. Her elbows and knees beat a weird tattoo against the floor while she writhed about like an earthworm on a hook. She saw him now—*help . . .* she mouthed the word as best she could, though even with him straining to hear her, not very loudly. He stood up to get a better look as her hands reached for his ankles, reached and almost touched them. But three quarters there they suffered one last spasm and froze, resembling, he thought, unearthed roots—so crooked and hungry were they.

Death didn't become her.

Now the hard part. The murder hadn't taken long—cleaning it up would. The white enamel bathtub was

waiting for her body; he'd have to slice it in sections and
drain the blood from it. Not exactly a walk in the park.
Then everything into the stove—nicely stoked for her
faithful heart and pretty little head. Preparation was his
strong suit, he thought. And given the relative ease with
which he'd managed so far, he was beginning to feel the
satisfaction of a job well done. And beginning to feel
something else, of course, too. The power and burdens
of God.

Once upon a time, Marcel moved to Paris.
He had a thriving practice.
He had a wife.
He had two sons.
But what he didn't have on the night of May 12, 1939,
was an excuse.
He was in the house of Aime Hausee's mother. And
Aime Hausee—the daughter—was dead. He'd overshot
her with morphine, a clumsy mistake. Of course, he'd
been a wee bit preoccupied at the time. Mainly with staring down at her teeny breasts as he got ready to pull her
wisdom tooth. The fact is, she should have gone to a
dental surgeon—impacted teeth weren't exactly his specialty.
An hour after he left, the mother, the hysterical bitch,
had called him up screaming. Her daughter wasn't re-
sponding—not to her name, not to long and repeated
prodding, not to *anything*. Caught in the middle of his
favorite dinner, veau à la crème with scalloped potatoes
and a good Cabernet, he'd had to leave it half eaten and
rush out into the night. Once he'd arrived, still hungry,

still irritated, he'd told the weeping mother to wait down-stairs.

Aime—his wife's dressmaker, and not at all a bad one—was not dead *yet*. She was in the more remote stages of coma, remote enough so that there was nothing he could do for her, nothing that is except loosen her nightgown, which he'd already done—loosened it enough so that her little breasts were now more or less exposed.

This would be his fourth. Imagine that.

And this one more or less an accident. Not like Madame Debaure for instance—who'd run a dairy cooperative, who'd entertained Marcel in her bed, but who, in the end, had refused to go along with his plans concerning her money. Not like poor Frascot either, who'd had the unfortunate luck to *know* about Madame Debaure, and worse yet, the dumb effrontery to try and profit from it. And of course, this one was nothing at all like Lousette. Four now. He had *four,* and the truth was, it was getting easier all the time.

He grasped the bottom of her powder blue nightgown and lifted it slowly up, up, up . . . underneath she wasn't wearing a thing. Look at that. He was struck dumb by the smoothness of her skin, by the color as well, pale as skimmed milk, except, of course, in her cleft where the color was rosy pink. He wondered how long the grief-stricken mother would wait downstairs before she'd be back up knocking at the door, yakking at him, *blaming* him too no doubt.

Ah well. He separated her legs, separated them in a wide welcoming V, as he moved his mouth to her nipples warm as sand.

Then he literally fucked her to death.

*   *   *

Once upon a time in the city of Paris, the good Dr.
Petoit went house hunting.

He found himself staring at 21 Rue la Soeur

Then he found 21 Rue la Soeur staring back. He was
quite sure of this, absolutely positive. The house was
looking back at him. And it was talking too. It was telling
tales out of school. Hidden, beastly, dark little tales. He
didn't know exactly what they were yet, not the details,
but he knew they were filled with blood and fury. Which
is what *most* of Paris was filled with those days.

It was July 1941, and Paris was occupied. Paris was
occupied and so was Marcel. He was occupied with this
house. Twenty-one Rue la Soeur. It had housed nobility,
no question, princesses and dukes and regents and chan-
cellors. It was four and one half stories high; it had twelve
gaunt windows. It was yakking away at him.

He stood across the street in its shadow, and though
it was the hottest part of July, in the shadow of the house
it was frigid as winter. This was a clue, he thought, a
hint. He began to understand things standing there across
the street from the house. Remarkable things. Things brutal and fierce and captivating. He understood that the
tales weren't finished for instance. They weren't *finished.*
The house needed *him* to finish them. That's why it was
talking to him. That was what it was trying to tell him.

This is what he found when he explored the house: It
had a huge kitchen in the basement, and in the huge
kitchen a huge drain that led directly into the Paris sewers. In the courtyard of the house there was an office,
and near the office a triangular room with one false door
and an aperture in the wall where you could see in with-

out anyone seeing out. He could do a lot with the place. No question. He could do just about everything with it.

The house would talk to him and he would listen.

Even on the day he bought the house he stood there again, ears cocked, stuck in its shadow again. He drew odd stares: from the passing lorries carrying German platoons to the Eastern Front, from the Jewish couple next door who'd negotiated the purchase, even from the two members of the French Gestapo who were on their way to headquarters just a few blocks down.

But he didn't move, not until he'd collected all the whispers and laid them end to end till they made sense. Then he rubbed his hands together and answered yes. *Yes*. It was just as he'd thought—the house had a place for him after all.

Once upon a time Marcel got his first customer.

He'd only put the word out several days ago, like casting a gleaming lure into the middle of a deep black pond, waiting only for something to bite hard. Now something had.

Marcel waited for him in 21 Rue la Soeur, staring through the window at the bare branches of the ash trees that lined the opposite sidewalk from corner to corner. It was a bitter night, the eighth day of Christmas according to the calendar. And why not? Wasn't Marcel about to receive a gift? Not eight geese a-cackling though; more like the golden egg.

Finally he saw him, trudging forward at the far end of the block, just a small dot beneath the trees. Gushenow the furrier. Gushenow the *Jewish* furrier, who by his own best guess had but several weeks before deportation to the East. But he didn't intend to be there when they came for him. He was going *south*. Petoit had promised to get him there—all the way to Argentina.

They'd met once to settle on the price— five hundred thousand francs, steep for sure, but then what was a life worth? Marcel hadn't needed much time to persuade him—Gushenow had said yes almost immediately. Besides, he was leaving Gushenow more of where that came from, wasn't he? Much more—over one million francs that Gushenow had carefully sewn into the lining of his coat and hidden in the handle of his suitcase. *And* all those furs—silver sable, black lynx, red fox—that Marcel promised to send after him.

All this Gushenow was carrying with him now, flitting between the tree trunks like a fat squirrel burdened with nuts. Marcel opened the latch, then walked back into the living room to wait for him.

Seconds later, the door squeaked, creaked open.

Petoit . . . Gushenow whispered, *Petoit, are you in there . . . ?*

Come in, Marcel answered.

Gushenow was flushed and sweating, animal fur enveloping animal fear. Marcel could smell it.

I have the pictures, Gushenow whispered. *I didn't forget . . .*

Pictures . . . ?

Yes. For the passport.

Oh. Of course. The passport. Marcel remembered. He offered Gushenow, fat, flushed, furrier Gushenow, a seat.

But Gushenow fumbled for the pictures and handed them over.

Will they do? he wanted to know.

They're fine, Marcel said, barely glancing at them.

Oh good . . . good. Gushenow wiped his forehead with a handkerchief. *It was very hard for me,* he told Marcel.

Hard?

Saying goodbye to my wife.

Marcel patted him on the back and said, *I understand.*

Not telling her. That was hard. Hardest thing I've ever done.

You must understand the risks, Marcel explained. *The dangers.*

I do. But all the same . . .

Do you have everything? Marcel asked. *For instance, the money?*

Yes, Gushenow whispered. *But I have a question. About the currency.*

Currency?

The currency in Argentina. What do they use there?

Shillings. They use shillings in Argentina.

Gushenow blinked. *Isn't that what they use in England? I'm sure they use that in England . . .*

And Argentina, Marcel explained. *England and Argentina both.*

Gushenow was more or less unconvinced; Marcel could plainly see that, but he also knew Gushenow was too nervous to care.

What do I do now? Gushenow asked.

Wait.

That's all.

Marcel reminded him about all the work he'd put into this, all the meticulous planning. Gushenow had to put his faith in him—after all, that's what he'd paid him for, wasn't it?

Gushenow had to agree. But all the same, he wanted to know when they'd be leaving.

It's hard to say, Marcel told him. *There are factors. For instance . . . the moon . . .*

Moon? But I don't believe there is a moon tonight.

Just my point, Marcel explained. *With so little light, the patrols will be more diligent than usual. We'll have to pick our time carefully.*

Okay, Gushenow said. *But isn't there anything for me to do?*

Well, Marcel explained, *now that you mention it, there is one thing we've forgotten.*

What is it? Gushenow asked, looking nervous, that is, more nervous than usual.

Nothing really. Just your vaccination.

Vaccination?

Against smallpox. I've got to vaccinate you against small-pox. That's the rule in Argentina.

But I've already been vaccinated against smallpox, Gushenow whined. *Why do I have to have another?*

There's typhus too, Marcel explained. *Argentina insists on both.*

Gushenow pouted. Is Marcel *sure?* Couldn't he just *say* that he was vaccinated?

Marcel frowned, a good frown too, one he'd practiced in front of mirrors from time to time. Just as he'd prac-ticed looks of concern, of passion and joy and paternal warmth, all of them acted out in front of the looking glass till he'd gotten them more or less down.

There's something called professional ethics, Marcel said. *Besides, typhus is a problem in Argentina.* Did Gushenow really want to run the risk of catching it?

Gushenow sighed, resigned. *Where do I have to get it?* he asked timidly.

There's a room in the courtyard . . .

No. Gushenow shook his head. *I meant what part of the body?* Could he have it in the backside perhaps? It hurt him when they gave it to him in the arm.

Of course, Marcel said reassuringly. *Wherever you want it.*

Gushenow stood up. *Where's this room then? I might as well get it over with.*

Marcel led him out of the drawing room toward the back of the house. They passed through the back door into the closed courtyard where a cat shrieked at them from the top of an ivy-shrouded wall.

Where are we going? Gushenow asked.

There. Marcel pointed to an outcrop of brick and mortar that was fastened to the back wall like coral. *My office.*

They entered a small doorway: several finely polished chairs, a recently waxed desk, a glass bookcase with a stuffed mongoose sitting on top of it.

Further down, Marcel said, moving off into a dimly lit hallway.

Then, suddenly, they were in a room.

What a strange place, Gushenow said, wrinkling his nose as if in the presence of bad cheese. *It's a triangle.*

Yes, Marcel said. *Three sides.*

Should I lie down? On that table?

Good idea, Marcel said, then began rummaging in the black bag that he'd left by the doorway.

You will be gentle, won't you?

Of course, Marcel said. *As gentle as a lamb.*

But isn't that needle a little large? Gushenow said now, staring at the syringe that Marcel was holding up to the ceiling.

Not at all.

Gushenow had already loosened his pants—they were lying bunched around his knees. He rolled onto his stomach and shut his eyes.

Marcel began to push the needle into Gushenow's left buttock and in fact had it halfway in when Gushenow asked him about Argentina.

Argentina?

Yes, Gushenow said. Could Marcel talk to him about it?

About it?

About Argentina. About what Argentina's like. Anything at all.

Well, Marcel said. *They have coconuts there.*

Ahh . . . coconuts . . .

Argentinians have to watch out for the coconuts. They have to remember to look up for them because the coconuts can drop on their heads and hurt them.

I'll remember that, Gushenow said. *What else?*

Beaches.

Nice beaches?

Very nice beaches. White and sandy beaches.

And the people there?

The people?

Are they nice? Are they a friendly sort of people?

Yes. Very friendly.

No Nazis? No Nazis in Argentina?

No, Marcel said, feeling Gushenow tremble. *No. No Nazis.*

They don't hate Jews in Argentina? They don't want to kill them?

No. They're friendly in Argentina.

No Nazis, Gushenow repeated, like a prayer, like a prayer he thought God might actually be listening to.

No, Marcel said, *no Nazis,* withdrawing the needle and wiping Gushenow's buttock with a swab.

Just coconuts.

Once upon a time there was a fire at 21 Rue la Soeur.

The smoke began billowing out of the house around daybreak, a thick, black, nauseating smoke that caused almost every resident on Rue la Soeur to batten down their windows, as if a violent storm was just minutes away.

In a sense, it was.

It was spring. Spring 1944, the kind of Parisian day songwriters liked to write about, the kind of day that sent people out into the Bois de Boulogne to feed the elephants and stare at the painted-on nylons. The kind of spring that renewed faith. For even though the Germans had begun their fifth year of occupation much the same as they began their fourth—it was common knowledge the tide had turned.

But on Rue la Soeur, the windows were shut tight, and the black smoke that had been coming out of 21 since morning kept coming and coming and hanging there up around the rooftops like a rain cloud come to earth.

Someone on the block, someone who could no longer stand an odor that was not exactly wood and not exactly coal and not exactly oil and not exactly anything they'd ever smelled before—finally called the police.

They arrived in minutes, faster than they would've responded to a murder, to a beating, or to a simple scream in the night. Gestapo headquarters, after all, was right down the block, and the German military police building and the office of the French Gestapo were more or less in the neighborhood. Screams could get policemen in trouble. Fires were safer.

There was a problem however.

They couldn't get in.

And the smoke became worse, drifting over them like a cloud of stinging locusts, leaving them teary-eyed and half blind. Not able to push in the door, and unwilling to smash a window—you never knew which German official owned which house—they called the fire department, which arrived within five minutes, launched a ladder up to the second-floor window, and broke in.

The shattered glass reopened several windows on the block. The crowd of police and firemen and fire trucks and passing dog walkers and gaping soldiers began to draw the residents out into the street. They held handkerchiefs of all colors up to their mouths, but within seconds each was black as widow's weeds.

Two of the firemen entered the upstairs window and began to warily make their way down. Down and down and down—following the odor like nervous bloodhounds.

It led them all the way to the furnace room, to the very bottom of the house, where two cast-iron furnaces were at full burn. And down there was Hades, like the one described in books: hot and red and searing and the odor, that peculiar odor, thick as steam.

One of the firemen used a metal stoker to pry the furnace door open. The blast of heat hit him full force: a wrenching, overpowering, blistering heat that almost toppled him like the aftershock of a bomb. But he didn't feel it, not really, couldn't feel what came out of the furnace, because he was thinking of what he saw in the furnace instead.

What he saw: a skull, two leg bones, several arms, one of which, detached from the elbow, was twisting in the flames as if waving at him. It was the wave he kept seeing, as if someone was welcoming him to hell.

The fireman threw up.

His partner, flashlight in hand, walked over to see what kind of mess he'd made. But he found a different sort of mess than the one he was expecting. It reminded him— he said this later, to the local magistrate, the chief of police, the two Gestapo officials, the three newspapers—of a butcher shop at the end of the day, reminded him of that because maybe that's what he was hoping, desperately hoping, it would turn out to be. It *was* a butcher shop of sorts, but just of sorts. It was littered with humans, with pieces of them, scattered about as if waiting to be wrapped, then priced for sale. In the basement were several torsos, some sawed-off legs stacked against the wall, four or five arms piled like firewood, and three human heads. Like mannequins before they're put together, he thought now, like *that,* his mind leaping to another allusion in a mad dash to get out. But there was no place to go. *There* were the bodies, raw and naked, and there was his partner kneeling beside them, making the sign of the cross, over and over, as if he were baptizing himself in a river of blood.

*   *   *

After they cleaned out the furnace, after they accounted for every bone on the floor, after they dredged up every skeleton from the lime pit they discovered in the court-yard, after they added up all the bodies and pieces of bodies they found in the sewers under the house, after they tagged and catalogued every piece of furniture, every fur, every bracelet and necklace and ring and hat pin they found scattered throughout the four floors of the house, after they interviewed and interrogated and in-vestigated, they came up with this figure:

Two hundred and fifteen men, women, and children.

Some found this figure too low. Some found it too high.

They never found Marcel.

TWENTY-FOUR

The ice cream truck had long ago departed, and one by one the people were drifting back, their giddy voices floating in through the closed windows like the laughter of ghosts.

And why not. The room, after all, was filled with them. With ghosts. With some of the two hundred and fifteen maybe, with some of *them*.

"So," Dr. Morten said, "now you know."

"Know?" William said, playing dumb, playing it with the desperate intensity of a poker player who's lost every chip but one. Call this chip hope, faith, or just wishful thinking; call it *gone* too. "Know *what?*"

"William . . ." Dr. Morten said, in the tone doctors use when they need to deliver a terminal diagnosis, but haven't the heart to do it.

"The thing is, I'm not following . . ."

"*No . . . ?*" Dr. Morten said.

"No."

"Let me clear it up for you then. Petoit's *escape route* lasted almost four years. At first, he handled all of it himself. Then like all successful entrepreneurs, he expanded his workforce. You understand. It wasn't easy killing all those people—he needed help. First a Croatian abortionist called Lazlo—an addict Petoit kept in dope. First him. Then he needed recruiters."

You understand.

Not yet. Not if Mr. Stupid had anything to say about it. Not if he closed his eyes tight enough, put his hands over his ears, and hummed something cheery. *See?* Understand *what?* He didn't understand at all. He didn't understand Petoits, he didn't understand monsters, he didn't understand the night Jean said *this needs your knowledge, William* and sent him packing to the Par Central Motel either. Even *then* he didn't understand. When it came to not understanding, he was a pro's pro. So he could continue to not understand about Jean, about where the tortured concentration camp survivor with the heroic résumé had suddenly gone to. Where *was* he . . . ?

"Recruiters. Four or five of them," Dr. Morten continued. "They'd go out into the streets looking for people whose lives were hanging by a string. Mostly Jews, of course. A few black marketeers, a collaborator or two. But mostly Jews. People who had to get away. Who'd do anything to get away. To Argentina, the recruiters said. The promised land."

And now, of course, even *he* was getting it. You can only play dumb so long, even when you *are* dumb; sooner or later the bad news will come seeping in like early morning chill, leaving you numb and freezing certain pictures in your brain. This was *his* picture: Jean, carefully placing that tattered photograph back into his pocket while he rolled up his sleeve to the elbow just daring you to look away.

"They were paid a commission, these recruiters, a percentage of the gross, a finder's fee. Like real estate . . ."

Jean, William whispered, *oh Jean . . . oh . . .*

"The perfect crime," Dr. Morten continued. "Because no one asked what happened to them—these Jews. The neighbors because they didn't care. The families because they *did.* Petoit had them write letters—ostensibly from Argentina, just to let everyone know they were fine. The recruiters would deliver them several weeks after each 'escape.' So no one asked questions, no one went hunting."

"Maybe the recruiters didn't know? Have you thought of that? Maybe they didn't know where Petoit was really sending them?"

"*He* knew." Dr. Morten said, somehow finding the heart to tell him after all. "The very first time Jean delivered a letter, he knew. The very first time he saw their belongings going nowhere, he knew. He was quite clear about that—he wanted to be sure I understood. He *always* knew."

Of course he knew. And William knew that he knew, knew it even before he'd asked Dr. Morten, knew it somehow all along. Jean had always known, and William had always known about Jean. Somewhere, he had.

But still . . .

"What about his guilt?" William said, trying to articulate a last best defense, trying to reach for something, *anything,* a piece of Jean that they might hold up to the

light and call almost *good*. "He was a criminal. Okay, he
was a candidate for Nuremberg maybe. One step below
the Eichmanns of the world. But Eichmann never said *I
did it*, Eichmann didn't own up. Jean did."

Dr. Morten shook his head, sighed, rubbed his tem-
ple, as if frustrated by his inability to get through to this
severely impaired man sitting in front of him. Here he
was spelling it out, *in neon*, and yet here was William
still in the dark. "You still don't understand, do you. You
don't understand *everything*."

*Okay. I'm all ears now. I've taken my hands off, and my
ears are wide open.*

"Jean was picked up by the Germans several weeks before the fire started at Rue la Soeur. The charge—smuggling Jews. That was what was put on his record—the
Germans were magnificent record keepers you know. But
even *they* sometimes got things wrong. They were tipped
off Jean was hustling Jews, so they snatched the 'Jew
saver' off the street and threw him into prison. So that's
what the record said—Jew smuggler. And that's what the
relief agencies found a year later when they liberated
Mauthausen. Jean, of course, never bothered to tell them
differently."

"But what about his *guilt?*"

"It wasn't for them. Not for Gushenow or Leibowitz
or Cohen or Samuelson or the eleven children of Chaim
Mendelssohn or *any* of them. Jean didn't care about
them—not when he was selling them a ticket on the
Petoit Express and not after either. Jean only cared about
his. Understand. You see Jean made a mistake. He never
told his wife what he was up to—of course he didn't—
but he *did* leave an address with her, a way to find him

if he should ever not be there when she needed him. When he was picked up, he wasn't allowed to notify her. Of course no one was allowed to notify anyone when the Nazis picked you up. You just disappeared, and that was that. So there was poor Mrs. Goldblum waiting at home, without a word from Jean. Days went by, and still not a word from him. So finally, she did what Jean told her to do if he suddenly dropped off the face of the earth. She went to that address. To *Dr. Petoit's* house. For help. And Dr. Petoit gave it to her—the very same type of help he gave to everyone who came to his door in need. He gave it to *her,* and her two children. All this, of course, Jean found out later. But it wasn't hard. It was *their* bodies the firemen discovered in the furnace that day. Theirs. And Jean found out something else later too. All that time, they'd had him incarcerated in Gestapo headquarters just down the street. The day of the fire Jean could smell the burning. All day and all night he could smell it. And all day long a gray soot kept coming in through the window till it covered every inch of his cell. Everything—even him. Later when he learned just whose bodies were found, he understood. He understood that the soot that covered his cell that day was the bones of his family. Of his children. He never forgot the feel of it. He never forgot that *smell.*"

William felt ill. He *was* ill. He needed to go back to the hospital and shoot himself full of morphine. He needed to go on vacation with Mr. Leonati and not come back. He needed to disappear. *Where is William?* they'd say, but William would be gone. He was almost gone already.

"Oh, he felt guilty. Sure. Guilty as sin. He'd made a

dreadful mistake, hadn't he. He'd killed his wife and two children, *murdered* them, just as if he'd placed them in the furnace himself. That's why Mauthausen became like a penance for him. A penance for *them*. That's why he rejected a rescue he never expected and never thought he deserved."

So. There it was. Everything he'd hoped was remotely good about Jean *wasn't*. Everything he'd thought was horrible about him was *worse*. Thinking now of Jean on his knees to a woman in SS black, accepting a punishment that lasted fifty years. Only it was the wrong penance; he was answering for the wrong crime. Those numbers on his arm represented more than time served; they were the mark of Cain. *There you go,* Jean might have said to him, *talking like a priest again.*

"You wanted to know why Jean changed after the war. He *didn't*. He was what he was. A moral monster. Not quite the psychotic Petoit was. Jean couldn't have killed a dog at nine years old. *He* would've been the one holding it down. He couldn't murder someone on his own. But then, he didn't have to. He could send them on to someone who really enjoyed it."

William was beginning to feel something both strange and familiar. Yes, definitely. He understood now that horror sort of sneaks up on you and smacks you in the face. First you go ouch. Then you go numb. But when the numbness finally ebbs away, it leaves something behind. Like frostbite leaving those little splinters of pain. What was this pain? Well, it felt a little like *betrayal*, that's what it felt like. It had been ages since he'd felt *that*— sure, from time to time he'd felt the vestiges of it, an amputee feeling pain in a leg that's no longer there. And now that he felt it again, he remembered why he'd worked so hard to avoid ever feeling it again. He had, after all, done a bang-up job on that score. He'd retreated from all but the most superficial human contact and he'd bolted the doors behind him just to make sure. He'd made peace. Okay, so maybe it was like Geronimo's peace, the terms dictated by the victors as he was sent packing to a barren corner of the reservation. But then, *then* he'd come out for one last turn around the carousel—and even if his motives had not been altogether altruistic, even if he'd plunged ahead as much for his sake as for Jean's, there'd been one eyes-closed belief he'd taken with him. Like the simple Christian believes in two distinct forces— good and evil—he'd believed in two distinct Jeans, a prewar and postwar. And the postwar Jean was worth *doing* for, because the prewar Jean had earned it.

"I *told* you," Dr. Morten said. "I told you to forget about it and go home. You wouldn't listen. You wanted to *know*. So, now you know. Now you have to live with it."

William was about to agree, he was about to bow out, if not gracefully, at least quietly. He was about to go away and lick his wounds—after all, it seemed to be his season for wounds. But something stopped him. What stopped him was that he'd forgotten something. He was absolutely *sure* that he'd forgotten something. Forgotten, in fact, the only real reason he'd climbed out of bed to begin with.

And he remembered what Dr. Morten had said.

I thought about getting up and leaving him. About just refusing him as a patient.

But Dr. Morten hadn't gotten up and left him. Dr. Morten hadn't refused him as a patient. Jean was a *case*.

Cases are like that. You don't have to like them. You just have to finish them. Dr. Morten and himself had both seen a Jean that *wasn't*. Fair enough, life is full of nasty surprises. But cases have a life of their own. Jean had known that. So had Santini.

But that's what William had almost forgotten, had nearly just misplaced somewhere beneath the shock and revulsion. The *case*. The case was neither Jean nor him. It just *was*.

You find what you look for, Jean had said.

So be sure you look for the right thing. And now, at last, he was. Not for self-respect, or second youth, or even justice. Just for a solution.

And if he had to do it for *someone*—for inspiration if nothing else, and he could no longer do it for Jean—he could do it for *them*.

Arthur Shankin, Doris Winters, Alma Ross.

Because he knew where they were now.

He came in, Mr. Weeks told him, *looking like a ghost. Just like a ghost.*

But Mr. Weeks, out of touch as he was with daily human lingo, had, of course, gotten the expression wrong.

TWENTY-FIVE

They were finally going to do something about the local lot—the *Garden of Weeden* as Mrs. Simpson so aptly called it. She'd gone and organized a committee, not, to be sure, a very large one, but with just enough pluck, and more importantly, enough hands, to get things done. That something *needed* to be done was obvious to one and all—even to Mr. Jeffries, who used it as a literal dumping ground for his household waste, not to mention his dog, Bumper's. Just *fertilizing,* he'd say.

And perhaps he was right. For the weeds had reached Olympian proportions this year, snaking out over the sidewalk and even pushing up through the cracks, so that the neighboring block was beginning to resemble nothing so much as a Mayan ruin—that is, civilization gone to seed. The houses that bordered the lot—including, of course, *hers*—seemed to be only awaiting their turn—just more fodder for the predatory jungle. Mrs.

Simpson was determined to fight back. They had three large cutters—*they* being the committee—plus one rather ominous-looking machete that Mr. Jeffries claimed to have wrestled off a Japanese soldier in the Philippines. Work would begin soon—she had pledges from both Mrs. Tyler and her husband, though she had a sneaking suspicion it would turn out to be mostly her out there, hacking away like a geriatric Jungle Jim.

Her husband, of course, was indifferent to it all. He'd taken to sleeping a lot lately, that is, sleeping even more than usual, and she lacked the heart to pester him. Though sometimes, in her more anxious moments, she wondered if this was the way it was going to be—him sleeping more and more till one day he just wouldn't wake up. The doctor had told her not to expect miracles—after all, to be up and about after two massive strokes was, in a way, miraculous enough. But she couldn't help hoping for a return to the way things used to be—if only for a while, if only for a moment or two at the end of a summer day.

In the meantime, she had her gardening—and she had her lot, her mission improbable.

And sometimes, when she was bent over a particularly stubborn shoot of crabgrass, or poised like a fountain with the sprinkler in her hand, she had *him*. Her little watcher. Her memories of him.

For she had never been able to completely remove him from her thoughts—perhaps had not really wanted to. In a way, they were linked together—the *lot* and *him,* though the fact that he'd stood in its shadow was the least of it. Maybe it was that both of them were projects, *her* projects, and just as the lot both frightened and frustrated her—so had he. There was something uncivilized about both of them—something *stalkish*. And now that she was about to root one of them out of her life, she couldn't help thinking of the other.

And the truth is, she felt just a little guilty. As if she was about to destroy the nest of last season's bird—who might, or might not, return. She was betting the house on might *not*, but reality, after all, didn't have much to do with it. It was more a psychic murder she was committing here, a cutting of ties, and she wasn't at all sure she wanted this particular tie cut.

She had, of course, fled from him, right back into her garden mitts, to her shears, weed cutters, and root grouters, back to more harmless pursuits. But after a while, after he'd refused to show up again, she'd begun to realize just how close harmlessness is to death. And she'd recalled what that woman had said to her frightened child the day they'd stumbled onto a convalescing Mr. Simpson in the front yard, just weeks after his stroke and still mostly drool and grimace. *He's harmless,* the woman had said. That's all. And she'd been right of course.

Life had turned sort of harmless for both of them—and she, for one, didn't like it. Most people her age wanted to be left alone, but she wasn't most people. She was—as her grandson might have put it—a bit *harmlessed out.*

Which made it all the more remarkable that on a certain Monday morning, two days before the committee was due to begin its dire work, nine and one half weeks After Noticing Him—another one showed up.

TWENTY-SIX

To begin then, begin at the beginning.

Begin with a French Hungarian named Jean Goldblum, who peddled people for profit. Who sought out men and women who were innocent of everything but poverty and sent them to the good doctor like sheep to the slaughter.

Begin there.

Then go on to the family—the smiling boy, the apple-cheeked girl, clinging to their mother like baby 'roos. The family portrait, the kind that's passed around over beer and sausages. Turn it into an archive.

Every case for Jean was the same case and the case was his own.

Picture Jean in a camp called Mauthausen, where he watched the bodies pile up like firewood while he only waited his turn. Death row Mauthausen was, and Jean the condemned man. But something went wrong; Jean

was liberated. And when the well-meaning refugee com-
mittees gawked at his record, they proclaimed him heroic
and quickly dispatched him to the land of opportunity.
Where thanks to the beneficence of Mr. Klein and certain of his own innate gifts, he became a detective. The
first eye of the Three Eyes Detective Agency, the detective who could spot guilt at fifty paces, then put a price
tag on it.

*You find yourself in a terrible situation. A situation where
you have to do everything imaginable. Understand?*

Yes, Jean. *Now* we understand.

Thirty years later, Jean was pinching children off the
streets and selling them back to their parents. Same old
Jean.

But then, something happened.

He came in, Weeks said, *looking like a ghost. Just like
a ghost.*

And he said, *I've got a case. A real case. The biggest
case of my life.*

What case is it? the woman asked him.

But Jean whispered, *I can't tell you. But it's the biggest
case . . .*

I know, she said. *Of your life.*

Every case was the same case, and the case was his own.

And after Jean began to investigate this case, after he'd
gone down to Florida and found what he was looking
for, he'd come back and paid a visit to a clinic.

What sort of clinic?

A bad sort, Weeks said. *That's what sort. They did some
job on him.*

And when Weeks asked him why he did it, why he'd
went and had his numbers burnt off, Jean said:

Because I've earned it.

Every case was the same case, and the case was his own.

And soon after that, Jean died.

And William, old friend, old dupe, saw his obituary in the newspaper and went to pay his last respects. Which led him to Rodriguez, which led him to a phone book, which led him to the woman, which led him to Weeks, which led him, at last, to the *case.*

Twelve old people who'd taken the banana boat to Florida and never reached the shore.

Strange case.

But a little, *just* a little, like another one.

The perfect crime, Dr. Morten said. *Because no one asked what happened to them—these Jews. The neighbors because they didn't care, the families because they did.*

Just another old person, Rodriguez said. *Another old person with nobody.*

Family, yeah, Raoul said. *But not to speak of.*

Twelve old people with nobody. With, that is, *almost* nobody. For the somebodies had gotten postcards.

Dear Greely—The weather's lovely and I'm doing fine.

Letters, Dr. Morten said, *ostensibly from Argentina, just to let them know that everything was fine.*

Twelve old people. Like most old people these days.

The herd, Mr. Brickman described them.

Refugees, William had thought on the plane, *running from the crime, the cold, the loneliness.*

Are there Nazis there, Mr. Gushenow asked. *Are there Nazis in Argentina?*

No . . . just coconuts.

Like in Florida. Where there are coconuts too.

Twelve old people *who'd taken a wrong turn.*

A *lot* like that other case, maybe *more* than a little like it. In fact, you could almost say that they were one and the same.

Every case was the same case, and the case was his own.

Twelve old people. Twelve refugees.

Why did she go there? William had asked Raoul, the janitor.

I think her doctor recommended it, he'd said.

The doctor thought it'd be the best thing for her, Mrs. Goldblatt said, talking about another of the twelve.

And when Weeks had asked Jean to seek medical help?

I've already been to a doctor, Jean answered. And laughed.

Begin at the beginning.

Begin there, and if you can't swallow it, spit it out. But if you *can* swallow it, you have to swallow all of it. Even the last part.

How did he die? he'd asked Rodriguez.

Heart attack, Rodriguez said. *The doctor came. But too late.*

The doctor came.

But no one had called the doctor. Weeks hadn't. Neither had Rodriguez.

But the doctor came.

Every case was the same case, and the case was his own.

His own.

He came in looking like a ghost, Weeks had said. But Weeks *had* gotten the expression wrong, he had.

People don't look like ghosts.

People look like they've *seen* one.

So Dr. Morten had been wrong too.

They never found Marcel, he said.

But someone, of course, had.

The someone who could recognize him, the someone who'd been staring at his face every night for over fifty years.

Jean.

Jean had found Marcel. One night, one day, he'd taken a stroll and bumped into a ghost. And then, before he could do something about it, the ghost had found *him*.

TWENTY-SEVEN

He wasn't like the other one. He showed with the same regularity, he stood in the same spot—he was, give or take a few years, the same age. But he *wasn't* like the other one.

Mrs. Simpson hadn't exactly figured out why she believed this. Other than a rather strong feeling in her gut—*pancreatic gas,* her husband called it—she had no particulars she could hold up as evidence. No exhibit As or Bs to lay before the jury; it was hunch pure and simple.

But then *hunch* had served her fairly well so far in life. Hunch had picked *Mr.* Simpson out of a crowded college mixer. Hunch had told her this house would be a happy one—despite its mortgage payments, which, at the time, had threatened to break them. And hunch had told her that the Watcher wouldn't be coming back. Hunch had been right; in all three cases, right.

Now it was telling her, fairly *screaming* at her, that this watcher wasn't like the other one.

Perhaps it was a matter—as dog show judges phrase it—of demeanor. Of bearing. *This* watcher wasn't quite as sure of himself as the other one was—she was certain of this. The other one had stood like the palace guard; this one stood there like the palace interloper. This watcher, despite no visible movement to speak of, was *jumpy*.

Hunch told her watching this watcher was going to be interesting.

Already her priorities had undergone a shuffle. Her interest in transforming the lot—her *Johnny Appleseed* complex as her husband called it—had suddenly paled, revealed perhaps, as the simple sublimation it was. For sometimes *watching* is real, and *doing* is chimera; that's what instinct told her. And there was something more: if last season's *bird* hadn't come back, last season's species *had*. She wasn't about to level the nest just yet.

But what was the watcher watching? This time, she was determined to find out.

She would take another stroll—another reconnaissance. Under the pretense of surveying her lot, she would survey *him* instead. She would get a reading. And *this* time, the sight of a firearm wouldn't make her turn tail.

It was important to do this, absolutely necessary. Because she had another feeling about this watcher—in fact, her hunches were working overtime on him. And they told her that if her maternal instincts had been misplaced the first time, they wouldn't be now. *This* watcher needed a friend. And she could be a good one. If he was worthy, she'd prove ready.

Now to the fore.

She waited till mid-morning of a rainy Thursday. She slipped on her rubbers; she tied on her rain hat—vinyl with little daisy decals. Then she plodded out, *plodded* out because she suddenly felt heavy, clumsy, as comically obvious as an elephant stalking a mouse.

He was back at his corner of the lot, as faithful as a crossing guard—more faithful, considering the fact that the crossing guard at the local school had been fired for drinking—or so Mrs. Tyler had recently informed her. The street was fairly soaked now; she had to pick her way between the puddles, resembling, she imagined, an uncoordinated child failing miserably at hopscotch. She actually felt herself blushing—would wonders never cease—when she reached his side of the street she found it difficult to actually look at him.

But she did, starting from the ground up, from a pair of beaten-up imitation leather slip-ons completely covered with beads of water, to a pair of cotton pants—*chinos* they used to call them—to a plain white shirt soaked clear through. And to the *cane,* aluminum, which, lined up with his right leg, had completely eluded her from the other side of the street. A cane.

In a way, it shook her more than the gun had. For in her fervid imagination, there'd been no room for *this,* no place for another appendage of creeping age. She had enough of *that* at home; she'd been expecting more lethal props. But when she took a moment to think about it— a moment she spent poised between two large and rather oily puddles—she realized that all it had done was confirm her basic hunch. Vulnerable she'd thought him—

vulnerable he *was*. Perhaps a friend was just what the doctor ordered.

But what was the watcher watching?

"Good morning," she said, in a voice that didn't actually sound like hers.

He turned to look at her; and smiled. No, she thought, this watcher was *not* like the other one at all.

"Good morning."

He had a pleasant voice, *homey,* her mother might have said, not too rough and not too soft either.

And then, before she knew it, they were engaged—virtually married—in conversation.

She told him her name. He told her his. She asked about his leg. He told her of an accident.

She told him about the lot, about her committee, about her husband, about Mrs. Tyler's niece's infidelity, about, in fact, the *moon*.

He told her where he lived, the name of his cane's manufacturer, the advanced weather forecast for the New York City area, the time of day.

And then, just about halfway through their conversation, he told her what she wanted. Not with words, but with a quick pointed look, a look that came *more* than halfway through their little talk, when plainly beginning to worry about the interruption to his vigil, and evidently too nice to be rude about it, he sneaked a glance across the street. Toward, she assumed, his target, the veritable apple of his eye.

Well. That was her first reaction. Just *well*. For if she'd expected some other target, if she'd settled on her own rather sinister candidates for the title of who the Watcher watched—and she *had*—she'd been proven to be sadly and completely off the mark.

For it was only the doctor, the good Dr. Fern. Beloved of the elderly, and caretaker of her own *Mr.* Simpson's precarious health.

TWENTY-EIGHT

It hadn't been difficult. In fact, given all that had come before it, all the wasted time and wasted travel and wasted pain, the ease with which he'd secured the name seemed almost pathetic. Like climbing the highest tree in the yard only to pluck a fruit so rotten it just about falls into your hand.

A phone call to Raoul. A phone call to Mr. Greely. A phone call to Rodriguez. That's all it took.

What was the name of Mrs. Winters's doctor, he'd asked Raoul. The one who recommended Florida?

Fern, he'd replied. *The old people love him.*

And *why* did the old people love him?

'Cause he's one of them. Not a day under eighty, Raoul said. *Imagine that.*

Mr. Greely had needed some time to jog his memory.

Palm, he said after a few minutes.

Could it be *Fern?*

I think it's Palm.

But it might be Fern? Dr. Fern? An elderly gentleman in his own right?

That's it, Greely said. *An old doctor, too old—that's why I don't go to him. Dr. Palm.*

You mean *Dr. Fern.*

Maybe.

And Rodriguez, whom William once more interrupted in the act of sunning himself, who took ten minutes of the phone company's time to make his way down from the roof where his ten-year-old cradled the phone before a too-loud TV; Rodriguez remembered it perfectly.

Fern, he said. *Like the plant.*

If the plant was a Venus flytrap maybe.

That's who came that night, he said. *Old—real old. That it, bro?*

You didn't call him?

No.

Who did?

Weeks did.

Weeks didn't.

What's the difference? Maybe Jean did. Before he went down for the count. Wasn't Jean French?

French Hungarian.

There you go then. The doctor parlay-vood too. He must have rang him up before he kicked.

I don't think so.

Okay, you don't think so. That all, José?

Fern. Like the plant. Remembering later how he'd stared so hard at the list that night, the list of the missing, trying to find a common denominator that didn't seem to be there.

But there had been. Fern.

Fern was the common denominator.

Fern, who lived on a dead-end street within walking distance of everybody. Arthur Shankin. Doris Winters. And Jean.

Jean, who on his way to bag another runaway had run into the biggest runaway of all. The murderer of two hundred and fifteen men, women, and children—most of which Jean had greedily taken part in, but *three* of which he hadn't, the *three* that carried his name.

What Jean must have felt that night.

To begin with, he was scared, Weeks said.

To begin with, yes. He must have been torturously scared, frightened out of his mind. But then, something else. A chance, a chance as clear as day. To balance the books, to erase an unholy mistake—to unburden himself of the only guilt he'd ever carried. To take the mark of Cain and burn it off with acid.

But not *too* fast. It had been over fifty years—no reason to rush now. And besides, though Jean may have had the morals of a snake, he lacked the capacity to shed his skin. He was—first, foremost, and forever—a detective. And the detective in him must have spotted some familiar clues, sniffed out a most evocative odor. Could it be that Dr. Petoit hadn't hung up his syringe just yet? Could it be that it was still *wartime,* and there were still *Jews* out there running for their lives?

Only now they were called the *elderly*—pushed into *ghettos* called retirement communities, forced into *concentration camps* called old age homes, ignored by most, forgotten by family, absolute fair game for everyone else. And just as Jean had been a Jew *then,* Jean had been old *now.* It must have made it seem all so familiar, so shaped by fate, or cosmic irony, or maybe even God. In the end, maybe Jean had even *believed.*

Jean, like all good detectives, had gone about building a case. Even started a file, just like the old days. Even taking some precautions too, setting up Weeks as his insurance policy in case a *safe dropped* on his head. And perhaps, *just* perhaps, even showing Weeks a picture from the past—*that's Santini there, and over there, that's William, William the Boy Scout, William the cuckold, William the priest.* Because, after all, priests tend to show up at funerals, don't they.

And then a safe *had* dropped on his head.

And now, *here* and now, was the priest.

Standing, after more dead ends than he cared to remember, in the only dead end that mattered, talking with a woman who seemed intent on devouring him with words.

And thinking *this*—as she prattled on and on—that he should go to the police. That of course he should. No doubt about it. There were twelve missing people here, and a mass murderer that made Ted Bundy look quaint, so he should go to the police. *Immediately* go there.

But then, maybe there *was* doubt about it. Just a little doubt. Sure, it was there somewhere—say *hello,* doubt, and take a bow. Like, for instance, maybe he'd made all of it up in his head. Maybe it sounded completely coherent to *him,* but maybe it would sound completely incoherent to someone else. For example, the desk sergeant at the 105th Precinct. Who'd be interrupted mid-donut by a geezer trying to convince him that the next best thing to Eichmann was hiding out just around the corner. Not exactly *hiding* out, either, but when he wasn't involved in nefarious doings—calmly going about the business of practicing the Hippocratic oath on a bunch of patients who swore by him. Maybe the sergeant would look up from his coconut-creme donut and see an average-variety *fruitcake.*

Besides, it wasn't like he exactly *liked* the police. He didn't. Not for anything in particular, but simply because in his old job, not liking the police had been an occupational hazard, like having to work on Christmas, or having your wife screw someone besides you. Of course, the police didn't like detectives much either—they were always getting in each other's way. Maybe they were simply too much alike—detectives and policemen—half the detectives having *been* policemen in a previous life. Detectives knowing half the police were shit and the police knowing they knew it. Here you had detectives taking money to investigate things, and the police constantly taking money *not* to. Both on a first-name basis with guys with funny monikers. The *Tuna.* The *Lip.* The *Bull.* Those guys. Police and dicks tending to use the same professional witnesses, to shake down the same professional snitches. That kind of familiarity couldn't help but breed contempt. Three Eyes hadn't been any different. There you had Jean ruining legitimate DA cases left and right, Santini hogging the off-duty money New York's finest counted on to send the kids to college, and William trailing his cheating hearts all over town and occasionally taking it on the chin for just being their associate. He'd suffered an overload of parking tickets, had twice been rousted downtown on suspicion of something or other which always turned out to be nothing or other, and had even gotten blackjacked outside a cop bar once by an off-duty patrolman just practicing his *opposite-field swing*.

So though William knew he should go to the police, knew, in fact, that he *would* go to the police, he wasn't going to the police just yet.

He was back on the job, wasn't he? He was back in the saddle. So he was going to run out the drill. And what did the drill say? It said surveillance.

Over and just to the left of the talking woman's head was a house surrounded by pink rhododendrons and weeping willows. A sign was stuck off center in the middle of a thick and handsome lawn.

Dr. Fern M.D., it said.

Healer of ills.

From a distance, he looked like any other eighty-year-old man. But any other eighty-year-old man wouldn't have caused William to avert his eyes as if they'd been seared by the sun. Any other eighty-year-old man wouldn't have caused his stomach to drop to his quivering knees and cause his body to start involuntarily turning toward home.

Dr. Fern had a shock of white hair—tousled, as if someone had just run their fingers through it. His body was wiry and thin. He wore black thick-soled shoes. That was all William could actually see. What he *felt* was terrified.

The old people love him, Raoul the janitor said.

Yes. He could see why they loved him. One of them. One of *us*. And he suddenly remembered what Mr. Leonati had once said when he'd returned from a trip to Germany—the Teutonic Tour or Holiday in Heidelberg or some such name.

Scared me, Mr. Leonati had confessed. *So beautiful, so*

familiar. There was a nice old man looked just like me,
roasting chestnuts in the bus station. I smiled at him—then
I wondered if he'd roasted Mr. Brickman's uncles during the
war. Okay.

Okay.

Dr. Fern looked jolly. From a distance, he looked like
the kind of doctor an older person would lean on. An
older person wouldn't mind taking off their clothes in
front of Dr. Fern. An older person wouldn't mind con-
fiding in him either. Dr. Fern would understand, Dr. Fern
knows what it's like.

And if Dr. Fern said *go to Florida,* an older person
would say *when?*

William, another older person, slid back further into
the weeds. He was sweating a lot—more than usual, more
than maybe was humanly possible. It was running into
his eyes and stinging them.

Dr. Fern was staring at his lawn now. Staring at it and
kicking it softly with his right shoe. Sweeping strands of
willow grazed his shoulders. He looked like a poster boy
for the joys of retirement. Just a man out on his lawn,
taking the air, surveying what's his. Only it wasn't his,
not exactly. It was everybody else's. He'd *taken* it from
them.

An old gardener limped out from behind the house,
pushing a wheelbarrow loaded with weeds. Dr. Fern
pointed to the lawn and said something; the gardener,
his face crisscrossed with lines, ignored him.

Dr. Fern stared after him, contemplating some further
directions maybe. But he gave none—instead he suddenly
looked up.

He was looking right at him. William was convinced

of it. Of course he was. Staring right at him like a hunter gauging the distance to his prey. William should run, scram, throw away his cane and crawl on all fours if he had to. Dr. Fern was death, and death was calling for him.

But Dr. Fern was only looking at the sky, shading his eyes as if searching for land. He wasn't looking at William after all.

William pressed back against the brittle weeds, relief washing over him like a sudden rain shower. He shivered; imagine, this close to death and still scared stiff. Scared stiff because he *was* this close to death, right across the street from it, within hailing distance.

The gardener was back now, gesturing at the flowers as if willing them to bloom. Dr. Fern walked over and said something else to him.

He seemed just a little bored with him; he listened to the doctor like you listen to someone else's child. Which, with William, had always been *every* child, always someone else's, not his and Rachel's. And now he wondered if she'd really had one, their child, and if she'd had it, if it really *was* theirs. That's why he'd never really tried to find out of course. Because he might've found out that their child, *wasn't,* was Santini's instead, conceived on a sweaty night in the Par Central Motel. That's why he never mailed the letters, why he picked up the phone without dialing a single number or uttering a word. Thirty-five years, and he couldn't get that picture out of his head. Just like Jean, who couldn't get a picture out of his head either, an image of pale dust settling like snow on a cell in the bowels of hell. Of a doctor who made you ill.

This doctor, the kindly Dr. Fern, whom the gardener was shrugging off like a gnat, as if he wasn't interested in what the doctor had to say because he'd heard it all before maybe, because he had more important things on his mind. The garden and the weeds.

William was still shivering, suddenly cognizant of his own rancid odor, like something dead, like something *almost* dead.

The gardener walked off, then came back with a single bag of charcoal. So Dr. Fern was having a barbecue, a quiet barbecue in the garden complete with weiners and roasted marshmallows maybe. But where was the grill?

The gardener unloaded the bag; it hit the ground with a sound like muffled thunder. The kind of thunder that's still far away but getting closer by the minute. The kind you huddle against in a quiet corner of your room.

Where *was* the grill?

Something was wrong. The gardener was upset about something, he was pointing at the ground and motioning to the good Dr. Fern. Ah, the bag had broken, that's all. A little of its charcoal had seeped out in a thin white line.

There wasn't a grill to be seen.

Dr. Fern was helping him out now, helping the hired help, smoothing the spilled charcoal into the soil now, cleaning it up.

There wasn't a grill anywhere.

Okay, fine. Because there wasn't any charcoal either.

Charcoal, after all, is black.

Other things are white. But not charcoal.

Like lime. Lime is white. And ash. Ash is white. Ash white.

So maybe Dr. Fern wasn't having a barbecue after all.

He dreamed about Rachel that night. A dream that left him tired and melancholy. It was a dream of something true, of something that had happened early in their marriage. A frigid winter's day, the morning after an ice storm had left everything coated in crystal. There's the happy couple, cozy as bugs in a rug. Home, with nothing much to do, nothing, that is, except cuddle and snuggle and whisper about the future, they go out for food—Mr. and Mrs. Squirrel foraging for nuts. It's a ten-block walk to the nearest grocery store, the ground as slippery as freshly waxed tile. They nearly skate there, pulling and propping each other up like the Protopovovs all the way to the store and back. They never quite let go of each other's arms, they never separate for more than an instant, they're one another's lifelines for as long as they're out there.

Later, propped up in bed surrounded by absolute silence, it seemed to William that they never needed each other quite as much as they did that day. They made it through an ice storm, but life had proved far more slippery. And *life* was very much on his mind right now. Life as a palpable, measureable, and ownable thing. As something that could be *lost, given up, taken, stolen, thrown away, screwed up,* or *sacrificed.* Take your pick. The doctor, for instance, had *taken.* Alma Ross, Arthur Shankin, Doris Winters had lost theirs. Jean had, of course, taken too. And then, when his own life had seemed all but lost, he'd tried to take it back. And where did William fit in? Had he thrown away his? Thrown it away somewhere in the pawpaw patch, somewhere between losing Rachel and losing hope, between a shattered heart and a shattered shoulder. Somewhere there. And when it's that far gone, can you ever find it, short of a miracle, that is?

Perhaps you start by *starting*. And though he'd started and stopped and stopped and started like the rusted engine he was, he was now at a fine hum, all pistons go, ready to roll. Today, for instance, he'd been a very busy beaver.

He'd paid a visit to Mr. Weeks. Paid him a visit, and told him everything, starting with Florida and ending with Fern. He'd left him with names, numbers, and one very simple instruction. If William failed to call him by noon tomorrow, Weeks was to call the police. They'd shook on it in the hallway, Mr. Weeks's hand as smooth and translucent as wax paper.

Back at the apartment building, where Mr. Leonati scolded him for not resting his leg and asked his opinion on which tour he should take this fall—the Sardinian Splendor or Norwegian Nights—he'd gone upstairs to find Mr. Brickman listening to a tape.

Hello Grandpa, the tape said, *this is Laurie . . .*

Mr. Brickman had taped it off the phone. *Just to listen to,* he said, *from time to time.* Then, looking a little embarrassed, he said, *If I ever want to, that is . . .*

William had just needed a minute of his time.

If he, William, should ever not return to his room—tomorrow, the next day, or *any* day, Mr. Brickman was to look in the top drawer of his dresser. There would be a will there. Also—he was to call a Mr. Weeks. That's all.

But Mr. Brickman, of course, wanted to know what all the mystery was about, all the *morbid* mystery.

My heart, William told him. *It's been giving me trouble.*

Mr. Brickman said he understood.

Then had come the hardest part.

He'd never written a will. Rachel had left him while they were still more or less young—after her, there'd been no one else, of course, to provide for. He found a piece of paper stuck between a magazine, took it over to his bed, then stared at it for over half an hour.

Then a word.

I.

He pondered that word for a long time—it seemed to stand for so very little. It seemed to point a finger at him.

So in the end, he just gave up.

TWENTY-NINE

First, a light.

A small cool oval, like a winter's sun. It didn't radiate warmth as much as dread. It turned his dream sour, curdled its mood, which had been syrupy-sweet and achingly familiar. A summer's day with Rachel transformed into a January's solitude. *That* fast.

Then, a slight pinch on his upper arm. Someone was pinching him but no one was there.

So the dream adapts. It's his father, his mother; it's *Aunty Em*. Rachel? She's not there, she's back amid the bouquets of August. Can't have her back. *Gone.*

So the dream evaporates like water held too close to the light. And he's suddenly, miserably, awake.

The light is a penlight. That's what he noticed first.

He was in the process of being examined.

"Who are you?" he said, or at least thought he said, but the remarkable thing is, he didn't hear himself say it. He could swear he said the words, but he could also swear they never left his mouth. He could swear both.

"Muscle relaxant," a voice said. "You won't be able to speak."

And then, William knew who it was. Because although he couldn't speak, he could still think. That's one thing. And although he couldn't speak, he could still see. That's the other.

"Please . . ." William said. Or tried to.

But Dr. Fern merely stared at him with a dead dispassion.

"I said you've been given a muscle relaxant. You can't speak."

He couldn't speak. And he couldn't scream either. He knew he couldn't scream because that's what he was trying to do. Nothing came out.

He tried to move himself up into a sitting position. No go. He felt heavy as lead, as inert as the bed he was lying in. He was the *immovable object,* the one only an irresistible force has a Chinaman's chance at. But maybe not. His fear was an irresistible force, yet it couldn't make him move. *He couldn't* move.

"Parking's difficult around here," Dr. Fern said with a faint accent. "It took me over an hour."

This is how it will end, William thinks. With Dr. Fern relating the petty annoyances of his day while he checked out to the hereafter. It'll end with a whimper after all.

"My handyman saw you," Dr. Fern said. "He doesn't miss very much. He caught you watching us."

William had planned to go to Dr. Fern today. To confront him, to accuse him, and if he ever managed to think of some way to do it, to *capture* him. But Dr. Fern had come for him instead. Just as he'd come for Jean. That's the way it works. You don't ask death to make a visit. It visits *you* when it's good and ready.

Then, a sudden knock on the door. No doubt about it. That was a knock, and then the door opened, throwing in a shaft of light, a sliver of hope, and a very sunburnt Mr. Brickman.

William wanted to cry. He'd forgotten that there's another unannounced visitor besides death. *One* other. Mr. Brickman—Mr. Brickman come to save him.

"What's going on?" Mr. Brickman said.

Yes, what *is* going on?

"He's had a stroke," Dr. Fern said. "He called me over an hour ago complaining of dizziness. He's completely paralyzed. I have to get him to my office immediately."

"You're not his doctor," Mr. Brickman said warily.

Yes . . . yes . . . *that's right,* Mr. Brickman . . . he's *not* my doctor, he's not . . .

"Shouldn't he go to a *hospital?*"

Yes. A hospital. Make him take me to a hospital.

"He'll die before we can reach a hospital. My office is close by—I have everything I need there." Dr. Fern smiled, the Grade-A-bedside-manner smile. "Perhaps you can help me get him to my car."

No, Mr. Brickman. Not to his car. *Speak up.* Stop the carnivores, Mr. Brickman . . . the herd's in danger . . .

Mr. Brickman walked over to his bed and leaned over.

"How are you feeling, Will . . . ?"

My eyes, William thought. *Look* at my eyes. Do you understand? *Do* you . . . ?

"Don't worry, Will. The doc will have you up and at 'em in no time. Isn't that right, Doctor?"

No . . . he won't have me up and at 'em, Mr. Brickman. He *won't. Look . . .*

"How do you want to carry him, Doctor? Should I take his legs? Maybe I should call Mr. Leonati?"

"We can use the help," the doctor said.

Yes, we can use the help. We can most certainly use the help. Sweet Jesus . . . oh sweet Jesus . . .

If I could only . . . if I only could . . . if I could just roll over, William thought now. I could show him . . . I *could.* He tried. He put every ounce of energy into it, every single one. But it felt as if he was pushing against a brick wall. The harder he tried, the more palpable his sensation of lying still. It was like those dreams of running where your legs refuse to move. Death itself after you and not a thing you can do.

Dr. Fern leaned over and spread back the lid of one eye.

"Yes, I know it feels strange," he whispered, "even a little uncomfortable. It won't be long."

He might have been consoling a patient such was his tone, consoling him the way William had once upon a time consoled his parade of lonely hearts, with a voice as soft as sleep.

But he wasn't ready to sleep. If he could only roll over, if only . . . repeating this to himself like a New Year's resolution, believing in it the same way: *If I give up smoking, if I pay more attention to Rachel, if I . . . if I . . . then you'd see.* And now he was trying again, fortified by a kind of hope, battering against that brick wall with the unshakable belief in his ability to do it. And suddenly, he was moving—not a lot, not enough to see, but enough, *barely* enough, to feel. The wall was tumbling down.

He could hear footsteps moving quickly down the hall.

"Here, Doctor." It was Mr. Brickman again. "Mr. Leonati's gonna lend a hand."

He could see Mr. Leonati out of the corner of his eye, looking like someone who'd been woken by bad news. He fluttered over to the bed, all commiseration and concern.

"Don't worry, William. Do I look scared, huh. If I looked worried, *then* you should worry. But I'm not worried, see?"

Yes, Mr. Leonati, I see. But me, as for *me*, I'm very worried. But no one could see that, could they? The muscle relaxant had rendered him helpless, as helpless as that night outside the Par Central Motel, when he'd stayed glued to the window as his wife and partner broke his heart into shards. *This one you take, William,* Jean had said. *This one needs your knowledge.* But he'd had no knowledge—not of the real world, and so that night he'd gotten an education. Helplessness, hopelessness, and then he was old.

Roll . . . he screamed at himself . . . *roll—you wasted life you . . . you quitter . . . you damn cuckold . . . ROLL . . .*

He hit the floor with a dull thud.

Mr. Leonati was the first to reach him.

"William . . . you okay, William? Jesus—that must have hurt . . . what do you say, Doctor?"

"Let's get him back on the bed."

"Sure thing, Doctor. Okeydokey—it's gonna be okay, William. You hear me?"

"How did he do that?" Mr. Brickman said.

"Grab his ankles." Fern again. "Nice and slow," as

William felt himself being lifted up, up, the way pall-bearers lift a coffin, with a motion both delicate and firm.

"I don't understand," Mr. Brickman said, still standing over by the door. "How did he *do* that?"

Yes, William thought. *Yes.* Mr. Brickman was still looking out for him; Mr. Brickman was his last, best hope.

"What?" Leonati finally said, between gasps of breath. "What did you say?"

"I don't understand how he did *that.*"

"Did *what?*"

"Rolled off the bed. You saw it. He rolled right off the bed."

"We have to get him to my car," Dr. Fern said, his voice completely calm, as if he hadn't heard, as if his only concern was the welfare of his patient—which, of course, it was—the welfare of his patient being something he was *very* concerned about right now.

"But you said he was paralyzed, Doctor." Mr. Brickman again, showing an almost canine devotion, William thought, *hoped,* like one of those little terriers that fasten their teeth on to something and refuse to let go. Man's best friend. "You said he had a stroke. He couldn't move a second ago. How did he roll off the bed?"

"Muscle contraction," Dr. Fern said, still dispassionate, still the doctor in charge.

"But he couldn't move, Doctor. A second ago, when I came in, he *couldn't move.* Maybe . . . maybe he's trying to tell us something. Did you think of *that?*"

Yes, Mr. Brickman . . . *yes . . . yes . . .* now if only Mr. Brickman could understand what it was he was trying to tell. He moved his eyes in a sort of sign language—over

to Fern and back again—over and back, over and back—
willing Mr. Brickman to read the message and save him.

Mr. Brickman looked down at him with concern—but
the wrong kind. Like . . . that freighter, the one that saw
flares exploding over the dying *Titanic* and mistook them
for fireworks. Mr. Brickman had misread the signs. All
night long that ship heard those faint cries, drifting over
the dead-still ocean, picturing hundreds of blue bloods
drowning in champagne. Only they were all just drowning. *He* was drowning. Mr. Brickman hadn't spotted the
danger.

"Don't worry, William," is all he said. "Don't worry."

The ship was sailing off into the night. There was just
a slow death left, and no one there to hold his hand.

The trip downstairs was quick and painless. The two
of them carried him down after putting on his shoes—
Leonati and Brickman—just as they'd carried him *up* the
stairs after the hospital. William made no effort to stop
them; he'd used up whatever strength he had left and
was feeling the awful impotence of the mute. The world
had turned deaf to him.

Dr. Fern held the door of his Volvo wide open as
Leonati and Brickman slid him in. Like sliding a body
into the crematorium, he thought, conjuring up the sight
of Jean's family as the firemen discovered them—like so
many bits and pieces of a photograph consigned to the
living room hearth. And now there was nothing he could
do. He'd tried, he'd tried harder than anyone could have
asked of him, harder perhaps than even Jean, who, after
all, was after the killer of his flesh. He'd tried, tried *might-
ily,* but he'd failed. Perhaps, in a day or two, Mr. Weeks
would write a better ending to the story. But Mr. Weeks

was old and Mr. Weeks was strange, and if he wasn't exactly senile, he was close, and it was anybody's guess if
anybody at all would believe him. Three people can keep
a secret, someone once said, if two of them are dead.
And one of them *was* dead—Jean—and one of them was
about to be—him—and Weeks, well, he was maybe half
dead. Petoit had outmaneuvered two police forces and
an occupation army; he wouldn't have much trouble with
Weeks. Whoever said the meek shall inherit the earth
was probably being beat up on a regular basis, and was
just doing some wishful thinking. The meek inherit whatever the strong decide to deed them. Jean knew that; so
did Santini. Leonati and Brickman patted his arm through
the open window.

"Take care, William," Mr. Brickman said. "We'll come
see you tomorrow."

*No, you won't, Mr. Brickman. And even if you do, I won't
be able to see you back.*

The car pulled away from the curb.

Dr. Fern didn't talk very much on the ride to his office.

"Do you remember the hospital?" was all he said. "I
came to see you there."

So, it wasn't a dream after all. Not a dream. Maybe
that explained why Dr. Fern seemed so spooky when he'd
seen him for the first time. Aside from the obvious reasons. Because he *hadn't* been seeing him for the first time.
Fern was the stuff of nightmares, and that's where he'd
seen him first, smack in the middle of a bad dream that
had been all too real. He'd been begging for his life, and
somehow he'd won. But not *this* time.

His head lay flush against the cold metal of the door-

knob. He could feel the hum of the engine and every
bump in the road. Fern was a meticulous driver; he
flashed his signal lights at every turn, the click . . .
click . . . click like the soundtrack to a cheap melodrama.
The End of the Road maybe. Or *Dead End.* Something that
reeks of despair, something whose very title promises an
unhappy ending. Only there wasn't an audience, not a
single soul. There should always be a witness to death,
William thought, someone to share its terror and mark
the end. There ought to be a law about it.

They were passing over Flushing Bridge now. The tires
had hit metal grating, and the vibrations were knocking
his head stacatto-like against the doorknob. He remembered the clock now, frozen stiff, finally telling the right
time. For he was winding down too, almost there, his
hands nearly still. Of course, his hands had stopped moving a long time ago—sure they had, only to be awak-
ened by an unexpected jolt, the way a dropped clock
suddenly springs to life. If there was something positive
to be said about his life, maybe it was that—that he, like
Jean, had saved the best for last. That final dizzying movement of the hands, when the parts were old and rusted
and better left alone. Maybe he could give himself a *bravo*,
maybe he could clap for himself like an audience of one,
and see the curtain go down with a smile on his face.
Maybe.

And yet, try as he might, and he was trying—*honest*—
he couldn't quite come to terms with it. With death. With
his own death. There was too much unresolved here,
there were too many bodies under the bridge.

And now the car was slowing down, the kind of slowing down that says you're almost there. And time was

too, slowing down for him, each passing second like a blood relation he was mournfully waving goodbye to. *Come and give old William another kiss.* His heart was banging against his ribs like an angry prisoner on the door of his cell; it wanted *out.* But the only thing it was out of was *luck.* The motor suddenly cut off, the car stopped dead.

Dr. Fern wrenched the emergency brake into position, then unclasped his safety belt, each sound like something you hear in death row melodramas. The sliding of bolts, the strapping in of legs.

When he opened the door by William's head, his face was framed by the moon, reminding William of a picture he'd once seen as a child—old man moon as a jolly night watchman. *Goodbye moon.*

Dr. Fern lifted him from under his arms and dragged him out of the car. His body settled onto the cool grass, and for just a moment the crickets grew silent and gave the night the sort of dignity befitting an execution.

The dew soaked through his pants and made him feel naked and ashamed, as if he'd just wet himself from fear. It was possible he *had.* He could feel tears on his cheeks, hot and salty, running slowly past his mouth.

Dr. Fern began to drag him through the grass. Feet first. He had to stop every few feet or so to catch his breath, the barest mist rising from his mouth like steam.

When Fern got him to the front door, he stopped again, hunched over, waiting for a second wind. William's clothes were completely soaked through now, his hair wet and slimy. He was cold too, a dull chill seeping slowly, slowly through his body like a nasty enema. He was forced to stare straight up at the stars, at the Dipper and the Great Bear and the Hunter, and down here us *hunted*, us terrified, all of the stars out tonight, as if he was being given one good look to remember them by. And they *were* beautiful. They *did* glitter like diamond studs, just like poets said they did. And they made him feel insignificant and awfully teeny, that too. Which might have made what was coming to him easier to take, if he wasn't so scared of what was coming to him, scared not just of going, but of going *now*, when—at the ripe old age of seventy-five—he was just getting started. Maybe if he'd spent just a few more nights stargazing, it wouldn't be so hard saying so long to them.

Goodbye stars.

Dr. Fern leaned over him like a shadow, like the Grim Reaper himself.

"Soon," he said. "Very soon."

He'd regained his wind. His grip was stronger now; he pulled William up over the welcome mat. *Welcome William.* Onto the doorstep and into the vestibule of the house. A pair of muddy rubbers lay flopped against the wall like dead fish. An umbrella hung from the doorknob of a closet. Fern opened it to hang up his coat, opened it for just an instant, long enough for William to see inside, and then to wish he hadn't. *Don't look.* It was filled with umbrellas—black, blue, red, pink, and yellow ones, retractable ones and miniature ones, men's and women's, like the Lost and Found at a train station. *Don't look.* But the trains at this station went but one way; there wasn't a return ticket to be had. They weren't *his* umbrellas, but they were his *now*.

Dr. Fern began to pull him down the stairs.

Down and down and down the stairs.

To the rec room maybe, for a little Ping-Pong when his muscle relaxant wore off. Or maybe they would sit around a Naugahyde bar and swap dirty stories. *Did I ever tell you the one about . . .*

About the doctor and the farmer's daughter. And the milkman's son. And the plumber's sister. And the janitor's friend. And the detective's partner. About them.

The muscle relaxant was wearing off.

Not enough to do anything, to get up and run, to karate-chop Dr. Fern—Petoit—to the ground, but enough to feel a distinct and jolting pain each time the back of his head met a stair. Enough to flinch when the distinct and jolting pain told him to.

The muscle relaxant was wearing off.

They went slowly, down and down and down, where the air began to stink and turn clammy. It felt like the inside of the funeral home in Flushing, it felt downright *funereal.* And why not? He'd just arrived at death's door; Fern was the gatekeeper. He slid off the last step and landed on the floor with a thud. And a groan. An *audible* groan. *His* groan—*barely* audible, but audible, yes.

Dr. Fern turned on the lights. It looked a little like a laundry—that's what it looked like. Or maybe like wash day at Fort Dix. Or maybe like a newsreel from a certain time and place. *Which one?* Pick one—he'd seen plenty. The kind they showed at Nuremberg, the ones that made all the gauleiters turn away and shrug with that *who knew* look they'd honed to perfection. You remember. Not the ones of bodies, but the ones of things that used to *belong* to the bodies. Before they *were* bodies. When they were still someone's daughter, or son, or husband, or mother. Those piles of glasses. Those mounds of hair. Those endless rows of shoes. *That's* what Fern's basement looked like.

There were piles of clothes nearly everywhere. Somber gray suits huddled in the corner. A menagerie of dresses so bright they hurt the eye. A veritable tower of underwear. Ties entangled one around the other like a nest of snakes. Socks, shirts, hats, and sweaters. Some piled neat as a linen closet, some haphazard as a rag bin. They were good clothes too: Sunday best suits were in there, the kind a person might wear on moving day to make a good impression on the new neighbors. And they were made for warm places, for summer, or places *like* summer. William remembered Collins Drive—the old people clip-clopping down the street in mules and Panama hats, the heat sending ripples across the pavement.

He was lying in a slaughterhouse, a graveyard; he was about to be interred there.

And *now* what?

Dr. Fern was pulling off his shoes, first the left one, then the right one. Of course. They were destined for a pile—the *shoe* pile, and that's where Fern promptly brought them, throwing them smack upon a pair of purple Hush Puppies. Then his socks, left, then right, Fern in a rhythm of sorts, William feeling a damp chill envelop each naked sole in turn. *Really* feeling it.

The muscle relaxant was wearing off.

But too slowly.

He was being prepared, being made ready for death. He spotted a white porcelain tub out of the corner of his eye, and that's where he tried to keep it, in the corner, where he couldn't really see it, and think about it, and mull its specific uses. It was a deep tub, squat and deep,

so that a person couldn't really bathe in it, but everything that *made* a person could fit in it. It was that kind
of porcelain tub. By its side was a table laden with gleaming metal instruments and he could smell alcohol wafting over from its general direction.

Fern was undoing the buttons of his pajama top now.
They said no one really wore pajamas now. They wore
sweatpants, or T-shirts, or just underwear. But even if
old men die easy—old habits die hard. William was about
to make a donation to the *pajama* pile.

One button, two buttons, three buttons, four.

Five buttons, six buttons, seven buttons, more.

Dr. Fern pulled off his top. The air made him shiver.
Even with the huge burner going full blast in the corner of the basement, the one Dr. Fern had just upped
the thermostat on so that it now glowed white hot. Even
with *that* he'd shivered. *Visibly* shivered.

The muscle relaxant was wearing off.

It was.

His pajama bottoms came off with a sharp tug.

Then he was naked.

Dr. Fern, Dr. Petoit, stood and stared at him—as if ad-
miring his work, or maybe just sizing up the task ahead.

Ashes to ashes. Dust to dust. William tried to remember, to remember back.

Though I walk through the valley of death . . .

*Though I walk through the valley of the shadow of
death . . .* the words coming slowly to him, the way they
do on instructional cassettes—one at a time, so there can
be no mistaking them.

I shall fear no evil . . .

I shall not fear . . .

I shall *not* . . .

Dr. Fern took him by the legs and began to drag him toward the tub, the deep white porcelain tub, the one that he'd kept at the corner of his eye for as long as he could, but no longer.

He was dragged past suede and lace and cotton and burlap, past Mrs. Winters's favorite blouse and Mr. Shankin's lucky hat, and Mrs. Joseph's new shoes and Mr. Waldron's loud tie. Past a thousand reminders of people no one remembered. Past *William's* striped pajamas and threadbare socks—William, who'd no one much remember either.

Dr. Fern lifted him up, grunting, sweat glistening in little beads on his forehead—up and then into the porcelain tub. Not exactly into, but across, so that his legs flopped over the sides.

For thou art with me . . .

Dr. Fern was pulling on brown latex gloves, the kind dishwashers use, dishwashers and morgue attendants.

He picked a small saw off the instrument table, then wiped the sweat off his forehead with his left sleeve.

Oh God . . . Oh . . .

William understood now. Completely understood. There was to be no injection for *him*. There was, after all, no need for it, no reason to try and fool him, to tell him tales of vaccinations and South American immigration laws. Fern was about to dispose of the body before disposing of *him*.

And now he was dressing for it, with the solemnity all good surgeons must have before the big operation. He pulled a smock off the back door of a closet—a smock that even bleach had failed to keep white. It seemed more blood than cloth now, as if the red itself had faded and not the other way around. It was a butcher's smock; it had a butcher's smell.

The furnace was starting to pop and crackle, like the sound of snapping twigs in a dark and lonely forest. The beast was coming for him, the bogeyman and the troll. No one could save him.

And now Fern-Petoit was hovering over him like the very Angel of Death.

I shall fear no evil . . . no evil . . . I shall not . . . I shall not . . .

Fern placed the handsaw just above his left knee. He gave one small glance toward William, then turned and dug in.

At first, it was as if he was looking at someone else's leg, not *his,* but someone else's, pale white and threaded with veins, hanging limply over the side of the tub. A leg that twitched with each motion of the saw, a leg that *bled,* slowly at first, then in hard, powerful spurts that splashed up against Fern's smock and collar. What a curious-looking thing—a leg being sawed in half, *right* in half before his eyes.

Then he remembered.

The muscle relaxant was wearing off.

Remembered it because his nerve endings began prodding him about it, kicking up a fuss even though he was trying his best not to listen to them. But they would have none of it.

So suddenly it was *his* leg again, not someone else's, but all his. It felt like an itch, okay a *bad* itch—at first that's what it felt like, an itch he couldn't scratch. But then it became worse than an itch, more like a burn, as if Petoit had lit a match against his leg and was holding it there, as William waited only for a breeze to come and blow it out. But there *was* no breeze. It was the valley of death and it was dead calm.

Oh God . . . oh my God . . . it hurts . . . oh how it hurts . . . stop it . . . oh please stop it . . .

His leg was half sawed through. Half sawed in half. Half and half.

I shall walk through the valley of the shadow of death . . . the valley . . .

Petoit paused to catch his breath; it was hard work sawing through bone, especially at his age, *why if he didn't watch out he could hurt himself . . .*

The burn was like a fire now, like a bonfire, like a raging forest fire. There was blood everywhere, it was *raining* blood. Hot blood too. Hot and salty blood. Like tears.

I shall fear no evil . . . I shall . . .

Petoit bent down again.

Put out the fire!

He screamed. And screamed. And screamed again. Petoit wouldn't stop.

Why won't he stop? Why please won't he stop? I'm asking him to stop. He won't stop. He keeps doing it. He keeps sawing. Sawing my leg off. My father can beat you up . . . he can . . . he can . . . my father can beat you . . .

Thou art with me . . . stay with me . . . with me . . .

He was going, he had his bags packed and he was going, he was going home, to Rachel. *I'm home, Rachel, I'm home.* He was going down, he was sinking, he was choking in blood. He was dying.

Then his bone snapped. Snapped with a loud crack. Snapped right in two.

And there was Petoit looking at him, looking at him with his black eyes dreamy almost, sort of dreamy and falling shut. Going to sleep, going to sleep right on top of him there in the tub. Petoit going to sleep.

And so was he, to sleep, soft sleep, with his leg still half there—even the bone—for he could *see* it now, though surely he had heard it crack in two, half his leg still there and hanging, and all that blood, and the raging furnace, but he was going to sleep, here, right here in the valley of death.

And as he went, he saw the Sandman, saw the Sandman on the stairs and smiled at him. Yes. He understood now. That's how it is in God's valley. Sooner or later, you find every mutt in the world there. Every one of them.

Even Weeks.

EPILOGUE

It wasn't until the early spring that he received permission to walk—or at least to *attempt* to walk.

The attempt lasted all of two minutes. Two minutes he spent negotiating his way toward a pillowed chair held out by Mr. Brickman on the far side of the room, while Mr. Leonati shouted invectives at his back—the carrot and the stick. No matter. The carrot was too far away, the stick too soft; he collapsed somewhere between the two.

Don't worry, the doctors said. It will take time.

Don't worry, he told Mr. Brickman and Leonati—*it won't.*

He tried again the next day, but with just about the same results. This time, Mr. Brickman caught him just before he hit the floor.

"At least *you're* improving," he said to Mr. Brickman, who didn't laugh, but instead demanded to know why he was rushing things.

"I just want to walk," William said. And that's *all* he said.

The doctors had really done a splendid job—in fact, it made all the newspapers (along with the rest of it, of course)—a triumph of microsurgery, in that tendon, muscle, gristle, and bone—*half* of the bone anyway—had been completely torn apart. It was, in the words of one of the surgeons, a *god-awful mess*. The kind of thing they sometimes saw in plane crashes or accidents involving farm machinery. But they'd stitched it and fused it and plastered it and set it, and finally—or so they'd assured him—*fixed* it.

Only it wasn't *working* yet. It felt artificial, not quite part of him, as if someone else's leg had been glued on. It felt neither strong or flexible—just stiff and useless.

He kept trying.

In between, he had a limited but steady stream of visitors.

Mrs. Simpson came every other day. She doted on him, in a sweetly maternal sort of way. *Mr.* Simpson, her nearly invalid husband, had passed away on Christmas day; she had no one else now. So she came and knitted scarves for him, baked him cookies every Sunday, and kept him up on all the local gossip.

The neighborhood, for example, had yet to calm down. Dr. Fern—a *mass murderer!* Kindly Dr. Fern. It was enough to cause several more deaths just from shock. After all, he'd been her very own Mr. Simpson's doctor. *And* next-door neighbor. People from who knows where still came to stare at the house, which, by the way, made it no easier for Fern's old handyman, who'd inherited the property through default maybe and found the crowds both threatening and inescapable. She'd gone over a few times to try and comfort him but the old man would have none of it. He was selling the house as soon as he found a buyer—then he'd be off. Mrs. Simpson couldn't blame him.

No, William said, between bites of a freshly baked oatmeal cookie. *I think I'm ready for another try.*

And Mrs. Simpson would call for Mr. Brickman and Mr. Leonati—and they'd do it all again. The carrot and the stick—and Mrs. Simpson the audience, adding to Mr. Brickman's plaintive protestations. *Why must you rush it? Why?*

I just want to walk, he said.

Mr. Weeks, of course, showed up too. Mr. Weeks, who'd been called by Mr. Brickman the minute after William left in the backseat of Fern's car—after all, it *had* looked pretty bad, and William *had* told Brickman to call Weeks if anything should happen to him. So Weeks, the recluse, had finally left home—but not without his army gun placed firmly in his pocket. Weeks, the Sandman on the steps, who'd interrupted Fern in mid-saw, and shot him squarely through the back.

Now that he was sort of a hero, and now that he'd ventured outside at least once and found it less threatening than he'd imagined, he came regularly—a small, withered man, as unlikely-looking a hero as Astoria had ever seen.

Sometimes the three of them sat around the bed talking—four, if you included Mrs. Simpson—talking about what older people generally talked about—doctors—the non-murdering kind, Social Security payments, grandchildren—and if William closed his eyes he found it easy to imagine that it hadn't happened, none of it, that they were simply four retiring people at a retiring age—and not witnesses, *participants* to a tragedy—a notion both soothing and sad.

And William thought about things while he was waiting to walk, all sorts of things, about Jean and Santini and that night at the Par Central Motel and he could see it for what it was now, which was two people who'd made a human mistake, and one human, William, who'd made an even greater one. Because when he'd gone back and looked for Jean, he'd found himself too of course, and he'd found Rachel. And if he shut his eyes he could almost imagine a woman about his own age sitting somewhere on a porch near Sacramento. And when he walked up to her and said hello they hugged each other like old friends, like more than old friends, and they talked about an ice storm long ago when they'd held on to each other for dear life. Imagine that.

Eventually, painstakingly, though with enough setbacks to try the patience of Job, if not Leonati, his leg improved.

He was able to make it across the room, haltingly, mincingly, but with enough balance and leg strength to get it done. He practiced at night—several times waking Mr. Brickman, who appeared at the door with his eyes half closed like a bad-tempered sleepwalker.

On a lovely spring Sunday on which Mrs. Simpson was faithfully due to arrive no later than two, William made his way down the steps and into the outside air.

The asphalt sparkled like sandpaper. The air was pregnant with summer—sweet, damp, and milky warm. William took his time, savoring it like a famished gourmet, walking so slowly that he hardly seemed to move at all. But he did—down the three blocks or so to Northern Boulevard, then half a block down to the bus stop.

The bus, when it finally arrived, seemed new as well, like the asphalt and air, freshly cleansed as it was of all its *Fuck your Mama* graffiti. Even the bus driver was different, his old black friend giving way to a fat surly Irishman who cursed under his breath as William made his way down the aisle like Speedy González on methadone.

But when he got off—he was hit flush with good old déjà vu. Everything was pretty much as he'd left it; the world had rotated clear around but come back. The Japanese, Korean, and Indian stores were still there, sort of—but the Chinese were still winning the war. He smelled the same too-pungent aromas, he drew the same non-stares. And when he reached the lot—that was the same too, the weeds and brambles already reaching toward summer with outstretched arms.

The Fern house, however, seemed to be in transition. No doubt about it. There were cartons spread out all over the lawn, along with several tightly wrapped bundles and a bunch of other odd bric-a-brac: wheelbarrows, globes, half a bicycle, and an old sewing machine. And when he entered the front door, the scene was pretty much the same. Everything was packed up, battened down, or discarded; it was moving day.

Fern's handyman appeared a second later, silverware in one hand, a small traveling case in the other. He seemed to be wondering whether to say hello or demand an explanation. No matter.

It was the traveling case that hit the floor first, just a

soft thud, quite different from the forks and spoons that crashed and clattered and flew about the floor like panicked silverfish. Last of all was the body, which landed sitting up and only keeled over with the second shot.

Then William put Mr. Weeks's gun back into his pocket, and left.

POSTSCRIPT

It hadn't come to him all at once, not like a clap of thunder or a burst of lightning—it never does come that way.
It had dawned—in the most literal sense of the word; an
eerie finger of light here, another there, a methodical
pulling back of shadow like a magician teasingly lifting
a veil. Then there it was—the light.

It came in dreams—dreams of Jean and Mauthausen,
of piles of clothing and ribbons of blood, of a cluttered
office in midtown where Jean had pulled out a picture
and whispered three names. Michelle, Marie, Alain.
Them.

And it came in the slowest part of the afternoon, when
with nothing to do but heal, he'd sifted through the phone
book just one more time and come across those three
names—there in the phone book, as if they were merely
a quarter away. Three names without a number—Alain,
Marie, Michelle—on the D page, where the homily read

Don't judge a book by its cover. A common American phrase—the kind mothers spout to their children and teachers to their pupils—the kind that would have made Jean shake with mirth. Maybe. Or maybe every time he read it but *once*. The day he "bequeathed" it to Weeks. That day.

And it came at the very beginning of his miraculous recovery—his miraculous recovery coming right on the heels of his miraculous deed—for wasn't it truly miraculous how a seventy-year-old man or thereabouts, a man retired and used up, was able to track down a mass murderer, a mass murderer who'd eluded the best France had to offer, track him down and with a little help from his friends—finish him off. A mass murderer who was more than a little clever—a psychopath who from the age of nine had always made sure his guilt fell on others. Others like Jean, who'd gone to Mauthausen while *he'd* gone free. And the rest of the hired help, most of whom had hanged for their part in the murders. Most, but not all. For instance, the abortionist Lazlo, who'd shot himself with dope when he wasn't shooting Petoit's refugees with air bubbles. And, who like Petoit, had never been found. One or two who'd fallen through the cracks. Who'd escaped just as Petoit had, maybe some *with* Petoit.

And when else did it come—when did the dawn *really* start breaking and throw its cold light on the scheme of things? How about when he was telling the story—to reporters and to Brickman and to Leonati and to everyone who was interested, telling about the penlight and the muscle relaxant, and Fern's first words to him. *My handyman saw you,* he'd said. *He doesn't miss very much.* His handyman.

So now the shadows were *truly* lifting—like walking backward from an Impressionist painting, where angles turn hard and you get sense from nonsense. The sun was *straining* now, the glow spreading like yellow stain, and then there it was, the last piece, the piece that by itself would have meant nothing, but with the rest, meant everything. Daybreak.

Because he'd remembered everything Dr. Morten had told him—*everything,* about the dog, and the girl, and about a valley called Aisne too, where Petoit had blown up his leg on maneuvers. Blown it up badly enough to find himself stuck in a hospital, blown it up badly enough so that when he'd left the army with a discharge for psychosis, he'd also left it with a limp. Not a huge limp, but a limp nonetheless.

And when he'd hid behind the riotous weeds of that local lot, and when finally Dr. Fern and then his handyman had come into view, it had been the *handyman* who limped, and not Dr. Fern. It had been the handyman.

Don't judge a book by its cover—Jean had said. For Alain, Marie, and Michelle—*don't.*

So finally, at last, he hadn't.

Back at home, Mrs. Simpson would be waiting for him; Mrs. Simpson, who'd give him tea and cookies and a piece of her gentle mind for being late.